SISTER

Sister … riences and k… in over eight… nursing profe…

Irene … general nursing (SRN), psychiatric nursing (RMN) and midwifery (CMB 1). While working as a sister in a casualty department and later in a surgical ward she studied for an academic diploma, specialising in surgical nursing (Dip. Nurs.). She is qualified as a nurse tutor (RNT), and taught for three years in a large psychiatric hospital. She is a frequent contributor to the nursing press and is a reviewer of professional literature. Now married with two young children, she teaches part-time.

A Star Book
Published in 1982
by the Paperback Division of
W. H. Allen & Co. Ltd
A Howard and Wyndham Company
44 Hill Street, London W1X 8LB

Reproduced, printed and bound in Great Britain by
Hazell Watson & Viney Ltd, Aylesbury, Bucks

ISBN 0 352 31046 4

To all those working in the British health system, striving to uphold the ideal of the National Health Service. And to the patients, for whom we exist.

SISTER

Irene Heywood Jones

A STAR BOOK
Published by
the Paperback Division of
W. H. ALLEN & Co. Ltd

Contents

ONE: PROMOTION

If in doubt, ask Sister, she'll know. Difficult relatives? Refer to Sister. Unpalatable news, awkward patients, unusual procedures and staff problems all belong to Sister.

It is common knowledge that Sister knows everything; learner nurses firmly believe it, patients and relatives rely on it and doctors like to think it, although they really ought to know better.

Suddenly it was all down to me and I wasn't sure I was ready for it.

I caught a glimpse of myself in the mirror and liked what I saw. Imagine, me, Helen Davies, in blue. Mixed with the feelings of pride, joy and anticipation were anxiety, apprehension, no, let's be honest, sheer terror. I was about to become one of those legendary, capable, all-embracing founts of knowledge and wisdom. My mind played a dirty trick by concentrating on all those procedures and conditions I'd never encountered.

My uniform was completed when I added the frilly cap; that most redundant article which is still strangely loved by patients and nurses alike. Nostalgic reminiscence of my general training was reassurance that such excellent tuition would stand me in good stead. Those principles had been well ingrained and provided a good foundation for my professional life.

Look good, feel good and be confident. I pulled back my shoulders. Oh, to hell with it, take the plunge or you'll be left as a Staff Nurse for ever. After all, I was hardly the first nurse to be promoted.

There was a sharp knock on the changing room door. Miss Ashton had returned to collect me.

'Ah, good, you are ready.' She gave a fleeting nod and smile of approval at my transformed appearance. I guessed this nicety was something of a rare treat from our Nursing Officer. She was a buxom middle-aged lady with a no-nonsense manner about her. The white dress did little for her and the maroon tippet emphasised her already ample bosom. I needed to move smartly to keep pace with her.

'I'll take you down to Parker and tell you about it on the way,' she offered, as we started walking.

At interview I had ascertained that Parker was a female general surgical ward.

It had twenty-eight beds, two of those in side rooms for the occasional private patient or terminally ill or infectious cases.

'There are a wide variety of cases, I think you'll find it interesting. What were you doing before you came to Gartland General?' Miss Ashton asked.

There it was. That most obvious question that was bound to be asked but the one that I dreaded. In essence I had come straight from being a student, albeit on a post-registration course, but kids were a different kettle of fish from female surgery.

'I've just completed sick children's training,' I admitted, and quickly added, 'but after SRN I staffed in my own hospital.' I wanted to let her know that I had taken responsibility with adults.

'Well if you've done paeds. I'll have to keep you clear of Miss Field, my counterpart in the children's unit. She's always on the look out to poach nurses, you RSCN's *are* rather thin on the ground.'

I still felt rather nervous that I'd relatively limited qualified experience. I'd not been near an adult patient for over a year.

While passing through the long corridors, I tried to make a mental note of the various departments; X-ray, ECG, physiotherapy, out-patients, haematology. It occurred to me what an incomprehensible maze this must present for the visitors.

'I've prepared an orientation programme,' said Miss Ashton, as if reading my thoughts. 'New staff do need to get to know the layout of a hospital but I also find they welcome a gradual introduction to their own department. I've arranged several visits for you but you will be based on Parker, supernumerary to the staff. It'll help you get your sea-legs before we throw you in the deep end.' She thrust a timetable into my hand. I hoped my nervous gulp had been imperceptible.

As we arrived at Parker, we had to steer clear of an outcoming theatre trolley. The N.O. peered to discern the tranquil, toothless face beneath the paper cap.

'Mrs Hampstead consented to surgery, then?' she enquired from the accompanying nurse.

'No blood though,' the nurse replied, and hurried along.

'Mrs Hampstead was due for repair of hiatus hernia, via a thorocotomy, a chest wall incision. She is a Jehovah's witness and only consented on the understanding that no blood transfusion would be given, under any circumstances.

'That was a difficult one for Mr Martin, our consultant. I know it's been causing him some anxiety. It's pretty major surgery whichever way you do it. Let's hope it goes smoothly. They can use dextran as a blood alternative,' Miss Ashton explained. 'And she's a private patient too.'

The Sister's office was glass on all sides. It was private yet not isolated and intimidating. It allowed for clear observation of the patients in front and communicated with the clinic room behind.

Clinic was the area where syringes, dressings, instruments, medicines and lotions were stored. It was here that injections were prepared, dressing trolleys set up and cleared and the preparations made for other clinical procedures.

'This is Dr Jeffrey. Doctor, this is the new Sister, Miss Davies. I'll just go and find Sister.' And Miss Ashton left on her search.

Dr Jeffrey casually looked up from the notes he was busy writing. 'Well, hello, so you're the new Sister we've been expecting?'

'Yes,' I fidgeted in the unfamiliar surroundings, clutching my handbag.

'Well you're *just* the kind of competition our Sister O'Connell needs,' he said sarcastically, and smiled.

'Oh really, why?' It sounded obvious and stupid but I felt

at a loss for any alternative.

'Let's put it this way. You're nearer twenty and she's nearer forty,' he clarified for me.

'Twenty-three actually!' I added pointedly, not wishing to appear too juvenile for the post.

Normally I would have been pleased by a little covert flattery but, in the circumstances, I thought it in very bad taste that he should make a hit below the belt about a senior colleague with whom I had to work and had yet to meet.

Miss Ashton returned with a short, round, greying bespectacled SEN, who just had to be a grandmother to somebody.

'Sister had to go down to theatre to see Mr Martin. Can I leave you in the capable hands of Nurse Burrows who will introduce you to the ward?' She rushed off to one of her many meetings. 'See you this afternoon for the grand tour.'

'Put your bag in this cupboard, we all do, but keep your purse on you.'

I was decidedly put at ease by the familiar and motherly touch of Mrs Burrows. She gave me a geographical tour, starting with the utility rooms: linen cupboard, supplies store, staff loo, bathrooms, sluice and toilets. In the kitchen, I was introduced to 'our Maria', the Italian domestic, who struck me as having an air of Mafia-type efficiency.

The clinic room backed onto the office, with a hatch between. This arrangement was to prove very useful for both staff and sisters. Everything was in apple-pie order in clinic; neat and tidy with clean surfaces and no odd bits lying about. I made a mental note of the whereabouts of the suction apparatus and portable oxygen, which would be needed in an emergency.

'What's the number for a crash call?' I asked, anxious to harness this vital fact early on.

'Cardiac arrest, 333,' she uttered in a monotone, and held up both her hands with her fingers tightly crossed. 'I'm horribly superstitious, Sister.'

The word 'Sister' rang in my ears and sent a shiver down my spine. I was really here, doing the job. It was a beautiful moment to treasure. I only hoped my slight blush went unnoticed.

'Let me take you down to the day room to meet the patients. They'll be having coffee soon, Maria likes to get it out early.' Mrs Burrows led me down the long Nightingale ward where beds are arranged in rows along each side. We picked our way around the obstacles of trolleys, a linen skip and patients in varying stages of mobility.

A patient beckoned to catch Mrs Burrows' eye. 'Can you give us a lift up love, I keep slipping down and I'm that sore?'

'Sister, would you mind giving me a hand with Doris?' asked Burrows.

'That's what I'm here for,' I replied and positioned myself at the other side of the bed.

'Slipped down again, Doris? I think what you need is a donkey, just hang on.' Burrows retraced her steps back down the ward.

Doris looked puzzled. 'What the bleedin' 'ell's she on about, Sis?' she asked in broad Cockney.

'She's going to wrap a pillow in a draw sheet, which we'll tuck under the mattress, in front of your feet, to give support. It will help stop you from falling down the bed. Mind you, I've no idea why it's called a donkey. What have you had done, Mrs – Mitchell?' I glanced at the name plate above her bed.

'Now you're asking! Feels like I've lost me bleedin' lot, it's agony. Ruddy great gash down me belly, colyoly something, gall bladder out, good job too.'

'Cholecystectomy?' I suggested.

'That sounds like it. Still can't be worse than I was before. Like a bleedin' Chinaman I was, yellow all over. All on account of them blasted stones. Look!' She attempted to reach for her locker but clutched her wound.

I held up her prize pot of gall stones. She'd get great talking mileage out of these for many months in the Peabody buildings, was my guess.

'Nasty,' I said, 'better out than in.'

Mrs Burrows returned. We rigged up the donkey and sat

Doris upright. I had to take special care as the T-tube and drainage bag were on my side. The T-tube acts as a safety valve as there may be obstruction to the flow of bile along the bile duct following swelling due to surgical interference or inflammation. The short arms of the letter 'T' nestle inside the lumen of the bile duct and the bile is able to drain along the long arm of the 'T' into a collecting bag.

'How's my handbag doing?' Doris joked.

'Coming along just fine,' Burrows answered. 'How's the BTM – sore at all?'

'No, love, the girls keep giving it a rub now and then. Anyway my old bum's tough as leather.'

'Now don't forget to keep flexing those calves and plenty of deep breathing, we don't want any leg clots,' Burrows insisted.

'OK, OK, my God you're a ruddy nag.' Doris gave Burrows a friendly tap on the arm. 'Thanks a lot anyway. Hey, could you take these mags to the day room? I've done them to death.'

She settled back on her pillows and looked remarkably comfortable.

'Think I'll grab a bit of shut-eye. Didn't get a wink last night with old Granny Jones driving them home. All right for her, she's as deaf as a post.'

I looked at her neighbour, a grey-haired old lady, sitting out of bed in a chair. One leg had been amputated at mid-thigh level. She caught my eye and returned a benign smile and nod, akin to a royal acknowledgement.

A lady in a white coat approached.

'Oh, blimey – it's Dracula again. No peace for the wicked,' said Doris, rolling up the sleeve of her nightdress.

The phlebotomist was used to this kind of greeting on her blood-taking rounds. Hers was not a face gladly welcomed, which was a pity because, as I later learnt, she was a very nice girl.

Burrows and I picked up the pile of magazines, mostly cheap romance stuff. The hospital ones were a busman's holiday and I expect by now she'd noticed a few discrepancies between them and the real thing!

'It must be very uncomfortable to have a T-tube as well as a line of sutures to contend with,' I suggested to Burrows.

'Certainly is. I had it done ten years ago. I was the classic textbook case for gall stones, female, fair, fat, forty and fertile.' She led me into the day room.

Here was a good cross-section of in-patients of all ages. I've always found it fascinating to see how much even a dressing-gown can tell you about a person.

Ivy Templeton was seventy years old and had been rushed in for emergency relief of intestinal obstruction. Husband, Bert, had gathered her belongings to bring into hospital and grabbed the only garment he knew; a rather moth-eaten green candlewick sample that was proving too warm for our central heating.

Our Bohemian friend, Mary, sported a flashy, thigh-length, silk bath-robe, miles too big, which I presumed had been borrowed for the occasion.

Pauline Cottrell had plenty of warning about her admission for removal of her thyroid gland. It is routine policy for thyroidectomies to be admitted beforehand for a rest and adequate preparation. It was a shame that no one advised her against the nylon set that she had purchased. Very glamorous and no doubt expensive, but she would be none too pleased if it got blood-stained after surgery. I decided to have a word with her at a suitable time later.

Maria pushed the trolley in. Mrs Cottrell, supposed to be resting, was apparently the unofficial group representative. Every ward at any one time develops its leader and spokesman. I've always found them very useful and they enjoy being quasi-staff members.

Pauline came up to organise serving of the coffees and invited me to join them.

I refused, thanking her, saying I didn't think it was very good politics on my first morning.

The first I ever saw of Kiki Sharma was her beam end. She was poring over some article in the newspaper, obviously engrossed. She suddenly became aware of my presence and looked highly embarrassed. Hurriedly, she removed Mrs Yiewsley's thermometer and tried to appear awfully efficient while taking the lady's pulse.

I gave her what I hoped was a kindly smile, empathising with her embarrassment. No one likes to start by giving a bad impression, especially when they've had no opportunity to prove themselves otherwise. Anyway, who was I to be cross? I'd so recently been a student myself and believed it was every nurse's prerogative to at least catch the headlines during a day's work.

Sister O'Connell breezed in. 'Ah, good, you found us. Burrows has been taking care of you, I see. Quite right, she runs the ward anyway. She and Doreen are my right and left arm. Let's go up to the office.'

I understood what she meant. The regular staff, the long-standing members, were the backbone of any ward, whatever their rank. I knew which nurses would help me with teething problems in this new environment.

Bridie O'Connell and I walked back down the ward, she setting the pace. She was slim, with an almost wiry frame, and sloppily applied make-up, desperately trying to whittle away the years. I saw what Dr Jeffrey meant.

Our brief journey was interspersed with commands.

'Miss Halliday, uncross those legs please – DVT.'

'Make sure Gillian drinks plenty, Staff Nurse, she's on Septrin.'

I wondered if it was put on for my benefit but, in the situation, it is probably best to get these things said while fresh in your mind, rather than risk forgetting them.

'Nurse Littleton, *please* see to that mess on Mrs Strange's locker. She's not able to do it for herself and I am *sick* of looking at that squalor,' Sister O'Connell blasted at a diminutive first year. Her voice was shrill, precise and bristling with irritation.

It was all a bit unnecessary. I considered it to be a less than appropriate demand during the chaos of bed-baths, cleaning and preparing patients for theatre. Anyway, it seemed nothing out of the ordinary, because the little nurse sprang obligingly to complete the task.

'Oh, Christ, don't say I've landed one of those nit-picking sorts,' I said to myself, feeling pretty despondent at the thought of it. That kind of approach was completely at odds with my thinking and we were bound to clash.

I had known one or two of those fanatics in my training hospital, keen on straight bed-wheels, a pristine linen cupboard, no sitting on the bed – and that means patients too. Sisters so busy ensuring the nurses were 'kept busy' that the girls were, by inference, not expected to talk to the patients. Nurses so structured that they were never allowed to think for themselves or help in decision-making. I wanted to be different. It is true that the length of a nurse's nails is important but so is the psychological support of the patient.

'Good job I didn't take up that offer of a cup of coffee!' I thought.

'Andrew Jeffrey, Senior House Officer to Mr Simpson, meet Sister Davies. Helen, isn't it?' Bridie asked me.

'Yes, that's right. Eh, I did meet doctor earlier.' I explained.

'Oh, so you'll have had your first dose of charm from Randy Andy,' she surmised, 'well just you remember, *this* girl is on *my* staff, she's not here to do your dirty work,' she blasted at him.

'Thank *you*, Sister, for that vote of confidence.' Andrew threw the completed notes onto the office table and ran his fingers through his ginger hair.

'In the notes' trolley, please! We're not here solely to tidy up after you!' Sister O'Connell purposely averted her eyes from him as she said it.

Having done it grudgingly, he opened the office door, moved to go out, turned to me and said, 'Nice to have you aboard Helen, I'm sure we'll get on fine.' His false grin was directed at Bridie's back, she was busying herself with anything rather than listening to what he had to say.

'Oh, great. Caught up in the middle of a bloody staff conflict before I start. Let's hope the patients are easier!' I thought.

'Lazy bugger. Just you watch him, or he'll have you running round in circles, doing bloods for him, writing path and X-ray forms, sticking them into the notes. It's not that we don't do these things to help the medics, well we all muck in, but he's such a cocky, arrogant so-and-so and takes the nurses for granted. Straight from St Harold's teaching hospital, thinks he's God's gift to surgery – and women. They must have kept him on because he was good at rugby. Certainly wouldn't get any medals for politeness or diplomacy,' Bridie said. It was quite obvious that there was no love lost between these two.

'I suppose he's a bit young and inexperienced,' I said, which sounded a bit peculiar coming from me. Pot calling the kettle black.

'Yes, he is, but I've come across many SHO's in my time and if they come out of med. school with nothing else, they do have some common decency. OK, don't let me influence you. You'll soon find out for yourself.' She waved out of the door to Maria. 'Two coffees please, Maria. Sugar, Helen?' she asked.

'No thanks.' I was glad coffee was on the way and took the liberty of sitting myself down.

We got generally acquainted and exchanged a few professional experiences. Bridie had trained at Gartland, done a casualty course and returned to be sister on Parker ward. She'd been there nearly ten years. When she said how keen Mr Martin was on the thoracic approach I had to admit that I'd never even taken out a pleural drain. She softened up a bit and said she'd do all to help me settle in to the routine and learn the new procedures. It was, after all, in her best interest to have a capable ally.

'Wretched phone, never stops ringing. Keeps you slim, running up and down to get the damn thing,' she said as she reached over to answer it.

I looked around the office, reading slips on the notice board. Bridie, still on the phone, hunted in a drawer and handed me a book. Putting her hand over the mouthpiece,she said, 'It's my book of ward information, I give it to all the nurses, have a scour through.'

It was a gem. Daily ward routine. Operation days. Surgeons' specific pre-operative preparations for the patients. Relevant telephone numbers and addresses; social worker, cottage hospital – scratched out and written community hospital –, convalescent home, GPs, community nursing service. I sipped my coffee and became vastly reassured by the presence of this informative little book, which was an obvious lifeline to new nurses – and Sisters.

I reached for the firelist and studied the register of patients. Appendicectomy, carcinoma oesophagus, carcinoma rectum – abdomino-perineal resection with colostomy – cholecystectomy, that's Mrs Mitchell, I'd already met her, stripping of varicose veins, haemorrhoidectomy ...

'Motley collection, isn't it?' Bridie said dryly, as she put down the phone. 'You name it, we get it. We rather pride ourselves on the variety we have to cope with. Mind you it makes the work interesting and we are always busy. The students love it here, they see and learn such a lot. And occasionally we get the odd man in the side-ward, which livens things up a bit. We've even been known to have orthopaedics when they are overflowing. They get bursting at the seams, especially in winter.'

Sister spotted Nurse Sharma in the clinic room and asked her to take me with her on the drug round. That was a particularly good way of familiarising myself with the patients of Parker.

'I'm just getting ready now, Sister,' she replied, filling the water jug to put on the medicine trolley.

Bridie undid the safety pin which held the bunch of keys onto the bodice of her uniform. She handed – or rather threw – the keys through the partition to the nurse.

'I never leave them in my dress pocket, I'm too scared of forgetting them. I did once. Took them home with me and had to come all the way back,' she explained. Hardly pausing for breath, the conversation was changed. 'And clear away those damn syringes, Nurse. I'll tear that blood-girl off a strip for leaving all her rubbish around.' Yet another lucky soul about to benefit from an O'Connell dressing down.

I wondered how things would work out between us. Our attitudes were so completely different.

Kiki Sharma was familiar with the Gartland drug sheets and able to read them quickly. In truth, she'd done the drug round so often that she knew them off by heart. Each hospital has their own drug sheet format and it takes a while to get used to new ones. I practised by reading, recording and checking the sheets, while she dispensed the drugs and helped the patients to take them.

'Oh good, Nurse Littleton, I see you are about to do a feed. Would you please wait until I give you the drugs to put down the tube?' Nurse Sharma then turned to me and said quietly as though she were divulging a secret, 'Mrs Yates has kidney cancer with secondaries in the brain. She came in for investigations and lapsed into coma. Her condition is remarkably stable, she's been like this for a week now. There is nothing we can do except full nursing care. Nurse Littleton was supervised doing naso-gastric feeding via the Ryles tube yesterday for the first time.'

I thanked Nurse Sharma for her comprehensive reporting. It was encouraging to see a senior nurse supervising a junior colleague. Nurses learn a lot from their peers, a sort of 'sitting next to Nellie' type of instruction.

Nurse Sharma checked that the junior nurse had aspirated the Ryles tube and tested it for acid content, to ensure that the tube was correctly placed in the stomach. This was a most important part of the procedure. The tube passes through the nose and into the stomach to enable us to give the patient liquid nourishment. Should the tube get dislodged and misplaced into the lungs, that fluid would enter the respiratory tract, with disastrous consequences.

I learned that Kiki Sharma had sat her state final exam in the previous month and was now in that awful period of limbo, awaiting the results. She wanted to Staff on Parker and I thought from my first impressions that she would probably be an asset to us.

All the nurses helped with giving out the lunches. I was given the auspicious role of serving, a privilege which cemented my seniority. It is strange how such a tiny and inconsequential job like the dishing up of food has such importance embodied in it. It has become a firmly established step in the nursing hierarchy, is totally understood and unquestionably accepted from the word go. It is seemingly such a trivial task to which to aspire, except that it holds great connotations of success and 'having made the grade'. It is stupid really, because getting food *into* patients is a far more exacting and nobler task than getting food *onto* a plate.

'I'll take you down to lunch, now Helen. You're in for the route march this afternoon, I see,' Bridie said, checking her copy of the timetable.

I raised my eyebrows.

'Sergeant Major Ashton,' she explained, 'army nurse, trained with the Queen Alexandra Royal Army Nursing Corps. She'll keep you on your toes.'

I had guessed that might be Miss Ashton's background at our first meeting.

My grand tour was edifying, although confusing, as I was introduced to a wide variety of staff, mostly the heads of departments.

The mass of new information buzzed around my head and I felt exhausted by the end of my first day. So much had happened for me since I stepped onto Parker Ward – was it only twelve hours ago? I had a few sherries to settle my racing brain, then an early night. I couldn't resist revising chest surgery and fell asleep over my surgical textbook.

TWO: LOCATION

Gartland General Hospital was a grand institution - in both senses of the word. It had been faithfully serving the local residents for nearly a century, and showed all the signs of continuing to do so.

The original buildings were the work of Victorian philanthropists intent on purchasing a place in heaven by an exemplary contribution to society. Their legacy was a solid monument, far superior in quality or architectural beauty to the many additions that were made over subsequent years.

Set in the green belt on the periphery of London, the hospital must have been fairly remote and inaccessible to the early patients, before the development of public transport systems. No doubt the function, organisation and designation of various parts of the hospital had been altered during its lifetime, to take account of changes in patterns of disease and society.

Parker Ward was one of the twelve original wards in the Main Block. Six up, six down, arranged as two letter Es back to back, they were now largely devoted to surgery.

Two were for general surgery, one male and one female, and another for gynaecology, treating disorders of the female reproductive system. One ward was divided to cope with the strange combination of ophthalmology, eyes, and ENT, ear, nose and throat, plus the occasional dental case.

The orthopaedic wards, dealing with surgery of the bones and joints, presented a classic picture. The male ward predominantly housed fit young men, who owed their downfall to fast cars, motorbikes or sports injuries.

The female ward was full of old women with fractured femurs sustained from falls and a lucky few admitted from the interminable waiting list for replacement of hips or removal of bunions. These patients were often heavy and frequently immobile, due to a combination of injury and age, and the nurses battled to stave off the complications which prey on inactive chests, bladders, bottoms and veins.

In no other speciality is there such a noticeable contrast in cases and ages between the sexes.

Gartland was a Regional Centre for neurosurgery. Their two wards for surgery of the nervous system received patients from the wide regional catchment area, as well as directly from their own busy accident department. They ran a post-registration course for nurses to complete the speciality of neurosurgical and neuromedical nursing of the statutory body of the JBCNS (Joint Board of Clinical Nursing Studies). The lively presence of this on-going course gave stimulation and impetus to a field where a high level of mortality and morbidity can have a depressing effect on staff and make for poor work satisfaction.

The twelve-bedded intensive care unit (ICU) was kept well occupied mopping up both in-patient and Casualty catastrophes that required concentrated nursing attention. It had a high staff/patient ratio and a brisk turnover of patients, with never a dull moment.

In contrast, the radiotherapy ward provided prolonged treatment by drugs and X-rays for patients suffering from malignant disease. Cancers in any part of the body were treated, often in conjunction with surgical procedures.

Two wards in the Main Block were designated for geriatric medicine. The aim was specifically to give acute treatment, progressing very positively to rehabilitation and discharge back into the community, either to the patients' own homes, their relatives or to sheltered accommodation. For those who were chronically ill or disabled, needing permanent residential nursing care, there was a geriatric hospital within the district and various privately-run homes.

There is always a heavy demand for geri. beds and, in consequence, many old and incapacitated patients were admitted to all wards in the hospital. Once in, it's often the devil's own job to get them back out again, so they get left on the general wards and block the smooth turnover of new patients. Parker was subject to such delay at times and it was hard not to let the old girls feel they were an encumbrance amidst the hurly-burly of surgery.

The resplendent, thoroughly modernised theatre suite, complete with anaesthetic and recovery rooms, was conveniently sited along from Main Block. A long sweeping corridor led uphill to the offices and staff quarters at the front entrance; departments and wards leading off from its spine. Its covered way was a relatively recently added refinement.

Four bungalow-style wards made up the medical block, one specialising in neurology and metabolic disorders and another with single rooms available for infectious cases. The other two covered the full range of medical conditions and they generally accommodated an elderly population.

These wards were erected as temporary buildings during the war and remained stubbornly in use ever since. They were patched up and painted, tarted up with chintz curtains around each bed, new roofs, central heating, up-graded to the hilt and still going strong.

This block, the structures that constituted a decrepit outpatients department (OPD) and physiotherapy, were ungraciously known as 'The Huts'. This kind of tenacious jargon helps to give character to a hospital, plus a sense of permanence and longevity, as it gets handed down through generations of staff and patients.

In conversation, if you knew 'The Huts', then you belonged. The familiar has a welcoming ring that breaks down many barriers. 'The Huts' had long since ceased to be a derogatory term and had become an affectionate one.

Gartland General Hospital was in an area typical of any London suburb of commuterland; a sprawling patchwork of buildings, interspersed with pockets of green fields, woods and parkland. People with homes and lifestyles aeons apart lived a stone's throw from each other.

A rich variety of properties represented a diversity of styles. In classy residential areas tall, stately Victorian houses stood proud in their own grounds. Some had managed to retain their classic grandeur, painstakingly cared for by wealthy families keen on preserving the original façade.

Others had lost much of their former elegance, having taken the toll of the more economic multi-occupancy flat-dwellers who had no long-term interest in the houses.

From the same era the artisan dwellings of back-to-back terraces, two up, two down, outside lav, no bath, had been saved from demolition by some timely modernisation and loving attention. The trendy *nouveau riche* gentrified their property by adding a bath and central heating and enclosing the sparse front patch with a gleaming white wooden fence. Add the pretentious title of 'cottage' and an erstwhile slum earns respectability and gains in stature.

The neighbouring towns had been subject to the usual ravages of modern urban life and the less desirable properties had become high-density accommodation for a considerable immigrant population.

From behind these many doors came all manner of persons, with an even sprinkling from all age groups, economic ranges, races and creeds to contribute to the cosmopolitan population of 'The Stable' - Gee-Gee - Gartland Gen.

Young folk in bedsits. Old folk in hovels or bungalows with wisteria gracing the walls. Families living on council estates, in flats or old tenement buildings. Families from one of the repetitious and uniform semi-detached houses of between-wars ribbon development in tree-lined roads bearing names like Acacia Avenue and Hawthorn Drive.

Here mock Tudor, there pseudo-Georgian, town houses, country houses, 'des. res.' of every style and price; the homes from which every Englishman makes his castle - and any one could come to Gartland.

Sickness is one of the greatest levellers and hospitals must provide an egalitarian haven, where each and every one there feels accepted, on his own terms, and of equal importance.

I first came to work at Gartland in the spring and my lasting associations are of that season. My mind was filled with indelible memories of lush, fresh new foliage in a multitude of blending green hues. The countryside looked and smelled strikingly beautiful, even when it rained, or more particularly, when it *did* rain. The association of new mown grass with Gartland has never left me.

Gartland had always had a fair sprinkling of foreign staff and plently of nurses from Ireland did their training there. It had also done well for recruiting staff from the local residents; married women in particular find hospital work convenient.

Doreen Walker lived not far from the back gate and knew the hospital probably better than any person around. And it was everything to her, she lived and breathed GGH.

Doreen had had a very strict and protected upbringing, by a mother who believed that the best way to avoid the pitfalls of life was never to encounter them. As a naïve seventeen-year-old, she was pushed into a marriage with a man twice her age, to guarantee her continuing security – and restriction. She was saved from a lifetime of servitude and social isolation by his early death.

Untrained, unwordly and completely lacking in knowledge of life outside the home, she came to Gartland as an auxiliary nurse. It was the making of the shy, young girl and she blossomed under its auspices. She responded by devoting herself to the life.

'Didn't you ever consider taking your training?' I once asked her.

'Who me?' was her horrified reply. 'First day here, I was asked to put a patient's false teeth into her and I fainted.'

I didn't like to point out that that was twenty-five years ago and she had come on a lot since then. But the remark she made was typical of how she saw herself.

'Never. I haven't got the brains, haven't had the education.' Such was the measure of her self-denigration. She'd been kept under so much as a child that her self-confidence, beyond her established role of auxiliary on Parker, had never developed.

Doreen held great store by 'brains' and 'education', was full of respect and admiration for bright people with training and achievement. Success had never been hers only because she had never had the courage or confidence to make the attempt.

The more I watched Doreen at work, the more I began to appreciate the old-fashioned common sense and the kind of knowledge that has been gained from first hand experience on the job. There wasn't much that Doreen, despite her absent theoretical understanding, wasn't able to do on Parker. Needs as must in times of crisis. In many instances she was a lot better than the so-called brainy ones, but Doreen wouldn't accept that.

It is the patients who really decide who is any good, the consumer, the one on the receiving end of the cold hands or hot tongue. They recognised Doreen for her true worth in terms of kindness and compassion. They identified with her as the grass-roots person, the ordinary person to whom they could confide their little worries, rather than worry 'busy Sister'. I'd get a lot of feedback from Doreen about things which were niggling and troubling the patients. I called her my own private detective. Doreen had perfected the art of listening, which was something many of the younger nurses lacked.

Mrs Doreen Walker had the affectionate hallmark of calling everyone 'dear', yes, everyone from the Senior Nursing Officer, through the medical and nursing staff to every patient and visitor. Some thought it demeaning, others found it overfamiliar but all soon realised it was just part of Doreen and she was a precious asset to Parker.

She was one of my favourite people at Gartland and we became good friends both at work and off-duty. I always thought she felt that I was the child she would have liked but never had. Doreen was always in good humour, if she ever had personal worries, they were kept remarkably well hidden. She was so sincere in all her actions, untouched by bitterness, jealousy or greed. She could be relied upon to smooth out personal quarrels and was a great one for keeping the peace.

It was a great help to me that Doreen knew the innermost workings of Parker Ward and the quirks of new staff with whom I came into contact. Her valuable assistance, always offered with the utmost politeness, guided me through several new and unfamiliar routines. I realised how little my nurse's training had prepared me for the ward management role. Perhaps the Sisters who had trained me were unwilling to divulge their secrets.

Doreen knew that I was interested in the history of the

hospital and often talked affectionately about the good old days at The Stable. Living close by since childhood, she had long been familiar with it and had been intrigued about the workings of a great hospital. Even now she considers it a privilege to work there.

Doreen was born at Gartland forty-five years ago.

'Of course the Maternity Unit has altered a lot since my mum's day. And having a baby is so much safer, quite a different kettle of fish. In her day women were dying like flies of 'plupral' fever.'

Doreen had a delightful habit of making amusing blunders by mispronouncing what she called 'long' words. Even when gently corrected, she tried, but never quite succeeded in ridding her mind of the first option.

Puerperal fever is a severe infection of the genital tract following childbirth. It used to be a killer, one of the more common causes of maternal mortality, but it is hardly heard of now, since the introduction of antibiotics and improvements in maternity care.

To call it an 'Obstetric Wing', as printed on the blurb about the hospital, was a gross overstatement. The large cottage, resembling a dower house, had been the former residence of the old-style Medical Superintendent, since turned to better use for delivering babies. It was easy to imagine that the wards where pregnant women now lay had previously been oak-panelled reception rooms.

The kitchen was hardly altered, apart from a modern stove and hotplate. Very little food was ever prepared there, as meals came by trolley from the main hospital.

The vast nursery, probably the old master bedroom, housed rows of squawling infants, awaiting their turn to be changed at the massive, low stone sink.

A modern purpose-built suite was added at the back, consisting of labour and delivery rooms, an operating theatre and a special care baby unit (SCBU) for the newborn who needed intensive nursing care or observation.

The whole new addition, vital though it was, jutted out like an anachronistic sore thumb from the dignified splendour of the great house.

Any maternity cases in which complications are envisaged are automatically booked into one of the larger obstetric centres in London.

Cases needing cardio-thoracic work, that is surgery of the heart and chest, and cases of severe kidney problems needing dialysis or transplantation go to one of the special centres of excellence in that field. Facilities for major specialisations like these are centralised for maximum use and efficiency.

Plastic surgery and serious burns cases from A & E (Accident and Emergency) are sent to another hospital which has a Regional Unit.

During her lifetime, Doreen had watched the progressive enlargement of her local hospital to offer a complete service to the local inhabitants. There had been a new children's unit, a smart Emergency department, a low-level School of Nursing, several doctors' flats and a large, unsightly nurses' home.

All the buildings had recently been adorned with the new white on blue signs, much needed to indicate the geography of the place. Unfortunately they looked painfully stark on the old, gentle, care-worn parts of the original Gartland.

One other important addition proposed at Gartland is for a badly needed psychiatric unit. The present arrangement is most unsatisfactory in that all in-patient psychiatry – acute short term care and chronic long term care – has to be carried out at the large traditional mental hospital. This depressingly archaic and cheerless asylum is secluded in the back of beyond on the Heath and carries the stigma usually attached to looney-bins and their inmates. Our students had to be seconded there for their period of psychiatric experience and it wasn't surprising that most of them came back with the idea that psychiatric nursing was a pretty futile and thankless task.

Gartland already holds psyche. out-patient clinics, which at least makes it easier for patients to attend. Some psychosurgery is also carried out, in conjunction with the neuro. cases.

The GG staff are fiercely opposed to the idea of the unit. Most have the mistaken impression that the place will be at the mercy of marauding nutters, running amok and wielding machetes. To dispel such myths may even be one extra good reason to press for the unit.

Anyway it is on the plans. The administrative powers that be are insistent that it makes rational sense to provide all necessary district facilities on one central site.

The Stable does a good job, is well respected and has gained a good reputation as a happy, caring place.

It may have been fitting for Victorian medicine to have a church and cemetery strategically located beyond the back entrance to the hospital but it is the cause of many wry smiles today.

THREE: ORIENTATION

My first week at Gartland was busy and interesting. By the end I knew my way around the hospital and felt reasonably familiar with Parker Ward, its staff and patients. Working alongside Bridie, I had a gradual introduction to my new role. I made sure to pick her brains on all the admin. side, of which there is so much new to learn in a different hospital.

I took the opportunity to sit in on the staff handover each day. All the patients had a rest period after lunch, before the start of open visiting at two o'clock. Bridie was vehemently insistent that the ward was closed to all but essential personnel. Obviously theatre cases had to come and go but doctors, radiographers, physios, blood letters, casual visitors, the lot were expressly forbidden except in emergency. No doubt they went and harassed other poor patients on another ward when they failed to gain access.

Some thought her idea old-fashioned and regimented but it was one that I wholly endorsed. The patients fully appreciated one guaranteed hour of complete, uninterrupted peace, whether or not they slept. Unless so arranged, it is quite an improbable natural occurrence in the normal course of a chaotic hospital day. They benefited enormously from the chance to relax or sleep, especially as the day starts so early on the ward. Hospital is certainly never the place to go for a rest! That is common knowledge.

The nurses assembled to discuss the progress of each patient and their relevant nursing management. That hour also afforded great possibilities for teaching, such was the richness of experience on that ward.

'That's up to you, Helen, teach away if you want. I never find the time myself,' Bridie's brisk reply to my suggestion.

'Usual old excuse,' I thought to myself. 'Why doesn't she

just say she isn't interested? It isn't everybody's cup of tea, but I'd like to give it a try.'

Bridie didn't teach – not in the formal sense that is – although the nurses learnt so much from her by practical example. Still, it was good that we each had a different part to contribute.

I was involved with several procedures with which I had not been familiar. This was rather nerve-wracking in my exalted position and I was anxious not to make an ass of myself.

Burrows and Bridie made perfect teamwork taking the pleural drains out of Mrs Hampstead. Her operation and recovery had been a resounding success, despite the initial anxiety over her refusal to have any blood transfused, on religious grounds. She had a hiatus hernïa, where the stomach slips up through the oesophageal opening in the diaphragm. It had been repaired through a thorocotomy, or chest wall incision, with a lung deflated.

Bridie talked me through the procedure; she was well practised and faultless in her technique.

Mrs Hampstead had been given Omnopon 5mgs beforehand to help her relax and co-operate. She rested her head and arms on a pillow laid over the bedtable. I stood close by and touched her hand; she appeared pleased and reached for it.

'Now, when I say "breathe in", Mrs Hampstead, I'd like you to take a really big breath in, out, in again and hold it until I tell you to let go. You'll feel the tubes come out but don't, whatever you do, let that breath out.' Bridie's instructions were clear and commanding, stressing the importance of eliciting the patient's help.

Two large drainage catheters stuck out of her chest from two neat but slightly red and swollen incisions. Internally they were wedged between two ribs – and so called 'intercostal' tubes – placed inside the pleural cavity which lines the lung. Although made of plastic the tubes looked rigid and uncomfortable, being slightly thicker than a pencil in diameter.

The lower, basal, tube drained fluid from the chest wound

into the attached under-water seal bottle on the floor. It contained the original sterile water, made murky by the additional blood and exudate which had been collected. The upper, apical, tube was to allow the escape of air and to permit the expansion of the lung that had been collapsed at operation.

Bridie was the clean nurse, the dresser. Burrows as the clean assistant removed the light dressing from around the drain and revealed the end of the tube pouting from her skin. It was held in place by one black, silk stitch. Another 'purse-string suture' had been inserted in readiness to close the hole left when the drain was removed.

Bridie freed the two ends of the purse-string suture, wrapped them in a gauze swab and handed it to Burrows.

'You must make sure you cut the holding stitch and not the purse-string stitch,' she emphasised to me as she snipped and pulled.

'The whole secret of this is expert co-ordination, so that as we remove the tube, the hole is immediately tied off and no air is allowed to get in. The patient must inhale to fill the lungs to capacity and create a pressure inside the chest.

'Mrs Hampstead, are you ready?' she asked.

I felt the patient grip my hand tightly and utter a muffled 'Yes' from the sanctuary of her pillow.

'It'll be all over in a jiff,' I reassured her, 'hang on tight.'

Burrows had prepared a loose knot and held the two ends ready to tighten.

'Breathe in, breathe out, breathe in – and hold it.' Bridie's order took effect.

'One, two, three.' She pulled smartly on the tube and it made a squelching sound on its messy exit. Simultaneously, Burrows tied her knot, while Bridie held a swab over the former hole.

The smooth, tidy procedure was repeated for the apical drain in the upper part of the chest. Mrs Hampstead was thankful for the removal of the incumbent tubes and now, able to get up and about, felt she was well on the road to recovery.

Burrows assisted me with the removal of my first tubes and I sweated on that, but subsequent ones were plain sailing.

Every success built my confidence and I began to feel ready to take charge.

It takes a special kind of self-assurance to confess that you can't be an expert on all things – firstly to admit it to yourself and then to others. There is so much that the nurses and patients expect of a Sister, it is quite unrealistic. Oh that wretched blue uniform! But it managed to conceal a few secrets. I became artful when caught out and got resourceful at latching on to people or aids that would guide me through a hazy patch.

Bridie had asked me to do the stump bandage on Granny Jones and to show the new nurse how it should be done. My orthopaedic experience was in the dim, distant past and the details of the special bandage eluded me. I found an orthopaedic textbook in the ward shelf-library and asked Nurse Cathcart to read it out as we did it. I turned it into a teaching session, not knowing whether she appreciated that it was as much a lesson for me as for her.

It was years since I'd dealt with an amputation, although I was reminded of the grisly occasion in my theatre allocation when, as the lowly student, I had been the one detailed to hold the lower part of the leg. My stomach turned over as the surgeon sawed away through the bone, a sickening, grating sound that I'll never forget.

I was supporting the black, gangrenous limb. At the moment it was separated from its owner, it assumed an unprecedented heaviness and I was shocked by the sudden weight of the isolated portion. The theatre porter was standing by at the ready with an open disposal bag. I dropped the cast-off flesh in, putting the cut, raw, bloody end in first. But the bag was too small and the blackened foot stuck over the top, peeping out on its final journey to the incinerator.

Back in Parker, I introduced myself to the patient and made a point of calling her '*Mrs* Jones' – loudly, as I remembered Doris had told me she was deaf.

During my training, one of our tutors had been very insistent that we never use degrading or depersonalising names when addressing patients, like 'dad', 'pop', 'ma', 'grandad'. It had been drummed into me and I thought to demonstrate this excellent advice to the student. But it backfired on me.

'My! Grand today, aren't we. "*Mrs* Jones," I ask you! You must be new here.' The old lady scotched my introduction.

I nodded.

She drew herself upright on the bed, supported by two intently straight arms and stared straight at me. '*Granny* Jones I've been for thirty years and no upstart smartipants is going to change that now.'

I felt a bloody fool in front of the nurse, who was no doubt fully acquainted with this old lady's forceful personality. My good nursing point had fallen completely flat on this occasion. I suppose it was the exception that proves the rule.

As I unravelled the crêpe bandage to expose the amputation, I spied Nurse Cathcart wince at the unfamiliar and uncanny sight. A short stump was left where the leg had once been, curtailed above the knee. It looked weird lying next to the long good leg. The rounded end of the protuberance was slim and firmly moulded by good supportive bandaging.

I held my hand above the deficient limb and pointed out to my student the cleanly healed scar line. Taking me quite unawares, Granny Jones suddenly made the stump jerk up at me and I felt the softness of the amputated end against my palm, like warm pastry. I withdrew my hand rapidly and recoiled from the unexpected texture.

My cheeks burned red at my stupid response. She chuckled in amusement.

'Wicked old devil!' I thought to myself angrily, as I nursed my embarrassment together with the disagreeable feeling of the fleshy stump.

She quite obviously saw me for the greenhorn that I was and enjoyed a joke at my expense.

Granny was no respecter of the inexperienced, the inadequate, the weak or squeamish. In her ancient world of struggle and hardship, those creatures followed the law of the jungle and faded into an obscurity which she no doubt felt they rightly deserved. According to her personal philosophy, hospital was a necessary evil and she took pleasure in getting one over on anyone mug enough to let themselves be got over. For the newcomers on Parker, it was a hard lesson to be learnt, but from then on they were armed against further taunts.

My reaction was understandably hostile, but it was only momentary. I had to admire her spunk in challenging the accepted subordinate role that we have come to expect of the 'good' patient. Granny had made a remarkable and courageous readjustment to a disability coming so late in her life. She was making her own stand to retain her individuality in any way she could.

'Thought that'd give you a little turn,' she teased me further, 'it usually does.' It was patently a well-used trick.

Nurse Cathcart was the soul of discretion, thumbing through the book to find the chapter on stump bandaging, probably thankful that she hadn't been on the end of the jibe.

I wasn't prepared to go to pieces, either with this simple task or at the hands of this menacing old lady. Having composed myself, I enlisted Granny's assistance with the bandaging and she knew full well what to do by now. Wide crêpe bandages in layers covered the length of the stump, from the groin, firmly up and over the end, down the back to the crease of her bottom. She held on to the two ends by her body while I completed the turns to produce a neat finish.

The stump felt so light in comparison with her good leg and it was easy to lift up and manoeuvre. Now used to it, I felt no revulsion at handling the amputated limb.

'Jolly good. Lovely neat job.' Her praise for me was an unexpected delight and all at once my anger and anxiety were dispelled. I'd survived her test well and this final result cancelled out our poor start.

My task was completed to my satisfaction and I'd found my footing with another Parker patient and nurse.

Whenever possible my orientation to a department matched a need on the ward. Bridie was very disparaging about the fact that Miss Ashton had said I was supernumerary, extra to requirements.

'We never have enough staff but they get used to us

managing and then it becomes the norm,' she complained bitterly.

So I was very glad to be able to help out.

I went to the X-ray department to watch the cholangiogram test on Doris. During surgery to remove the gall bladder and explore for more gall stones, a T-tube had been inserted to drain bile from the operation site. Now, just over a week later, she was having a radio-opaque dye injected into the tube, to ensure that the biliary tract leading to the gut was patent – clear and open to resume the normal passage of bile. The X-rays were fine, all was well and the tubes could come out.

'Not before bleedin' time,' the delightful Doris replied.

Later in the week I visited theatre as an observer. It had me on my toes, brushing up on the special rules of conduct in these surroundings. Generally I kept my hands held behind my back, lest I touched and contaminated any sterile equipment or sterile-gowned member of staff. To be aware of having done so is like having an electric shock stop you in your tracks at the realisation of the mistake.

I accompanied old Mrs Strange, stayed to watch her operation then brought her back to the ward. It was very satisfying to see a patient the whole way through from preparation to recovery and she herself appeared reassured to see a familiar face as she woke from the anaesthetic.

The theatre staff were exceedingly helpful to me. I felt I was an intruder in their orderly, organised department. I changed my weight from one foot to the other, trying to see but not wanting to be a nuisance and get in the way. Theatre Sister offered me a footstool and positioned me next to Mr Martin, introducing me as the new Sister on Parker.

'Hello there, come to see where all the damage is done?' he joked. He was the sort of man used to putting people at their ease with his casual manner.

The face mask was irritating me beyond belief. I balanced on the stool, watching his skilful surgery and taking care not to touch his 'greens' – the sterile green theatre garb.

Mr Martin delved into the gaping abdomen, held wide apart by massive metal retractors.

'Checking the old liver.' He thrust his gloved hand up towards the right side of her ribcage.

'Fine. While I'm in, I'm giving her a thorough going over. She's no spring chicken, you never know what may be lurking about,' he explained as he searched and poked with complete familiarity with the human torso.

At this stage the surgical field wasn't very bloody. The initial incision through skin, fat and muscle had produced its fair share of bleeders – cut blood vessels. All had been sealed off, either with catgut or with diathermy, coagulation by heat. The smell of burnt tissue had hung in the air for a while.

The two doctors made a good team; speedy, efficient and thorough; burning and sealing the leaking vessels as they gave a short spurt of blood. A smooth slice through the peritoneum had revealed the slithery, glistening intestines.

After the consultant had had a rummage around the abdominal cavity, he prepared to enter the gut.

'Bowel towel and tools, please Sister.' Mr Martin called for the special items needed when the intestines are opened. There is a real danger of contamination of the sterile contents of the cavity and peritoneal lining by infection from micro-organisms spilled out when the lower bowel is opened.

He lifted the colon onto the towel, a large red ruched tube held together by a network of friable tissue and vessels, called mesentery. His big fingers palpated and examined the organ deftly.

'Just as I thought from the barium – diverticuli.' He demonstrated small swellings on the gut wall.

From the inside these act as little pouches in which faeces collect and set up pockets of infection and inflammation, called diverticulitis.

I had looked at Mrs Strange's barium enema X-rays on the ward but had to agree that it takes a trained eye to spot these small anomalies.

Mr Martin did a bowel resection and anastomosis. He cut away and removed the affected part and stitched the two ends of bowel back together. The repaired bowel was packed back into the abdomen. It was like trying to get a snake into a handbag. There didn't appear to be quite the same amount of room when putting it back as there had been when taking it out.

'No wonder they get abdominal pain and wind afterwards,' I couldn't help remark. It was useful for me to be reminded of what the patients go through on the operating table. The ward staff are inclined to lose sight of this when they have a conscious patient with a tidy line of stitches.

'Yes, but it all settles itself eventually,' Mr Martin replied, as he started to sew up the layers of flesh.

I met him again in mufti – out of uniform – when he came to do a ward round. No one would have taken him for a surgeon, let alone one with a penchant for delicate chest work.

Taking great strides down the ward, with hands thrust firmly in the pockets of the shabby tweed jacket with leather patches that he always wore, he looked more like a gentleman farmer than a surgeon. He paid little attention to his dress and usually presented a dishevelled and unkempt appearance. He had red rosy cheeks, like two shiny apples, and a narrow moustache that was badly in need of trimming, set on his kindly, open face.

Mr Martin was calm, unruffled and down to earth, comforting to the patients with his natural stance of leaning on the bed-rail as he chatted away.

Rob Martin and Bridie were on the same wavelength. Rumour had it that she was sweet on him and I certainly noticed that she made a point of disappearing to freshen up her make-up if she knew he was coming. She flirted discreetly but was a little too frivolous in his presence. Bridie was very jealous about her close understanding with Mr Martin and gave indication that I should keep my distance.

I later learnt from Doreen that Bridie and he had a romantic interlude in the past but since his wife's illness all that had ceased. Rob Martin's invalid wife had advanced multiple sclerosis, was incontinent, paralysed and confined to a wheelchair. I stifled a smile as Doreen, in earnestly confiding this to me, made one of her most memorable bloomers of all time.

'She's in a bad way – got a severe case of M & S.'

Perhaps Bridie had secret hopes for the future. Whatever

their private longings, their work together was like magic, the one always able to anticipate the other's needs. If Bridie guessed he'd be asking for a convalescent bed, she'd put the wheels in motion to arrange it and present him with a *fait accompli.* She knew his views on antibiotic sprays and preference for wound irrigating solutions – and how many sugars for his coffee. The end result was that the patients benefited from this harmonious duet and patient care went like clockwork. I was hoping I would soon learn the whims and fancies of the men in charge.

The other surgical firm was led by the consultant Mr Simpson. Poles apart from Rob Martin, Peter Simpson was Harley Street personified, with a dapper grey suit and button-hole.

He was an excellent surgeon with a marvellous reputation and never without a queue of private patients. It was unfortunate that his fine veneer of sophistication set him apart from the staff and patients. I'm sure he didn't mean to be stand-offish, but he had an air of command and superiority that made him difficult to approach.

I always felt I should touch my forelock, click my heels together and say 'Sir'. It became apparent that the patients felt the same, only it must have been harder for them.

After I had left the entourage of his ward round, Pauline Cottrell called me over for a translation. I wasn't surprised. I later found it useful to follow on with an explanatory round each time after he left. Patients were often nervous to ask questions of what they perceived as the lofty, distant great man. So awesome were the rounds that the patient found difficulty in perceiving and understanding what had been said.

I had been watching Pauline's eyes glaze over as she stared at him, trying so very hard to comprehend what he was saying to her, but obstructed by her own high level of anxiety.

'Clips – yes.' She nodded obediently, knuckles white as she fiddled nervously with the ribbon of her bed-jacket.

'Drain off the area.' Her shoulder muscles trembled as she held them contracted so tightly, playing the part of the attentive, acquiescent patient in bed.

'Yes Mr Simpson, yes, thank you, doctor.' She mouthed

her gratitude parrot fashion and I guessed she hadn't an inkling of what he had said.

I sat beside her and virtually repeated everything that he had told her. But I gave more explanation, used more common terminology and allowed time for discussion. Feeling at ease and not intimidated, Pauline was able to grasp the details pertaining to her forthcoming operation to remove the thyroid gland.

'Michel clips are used instead of stitches where a good cosmetic result is required. You mustn't be alarmed when you first see them, they look large and ferocious. But when they are removed there will be no tell-tale holes left, merely a neat, faint scar line, following the natural crease around your neck,' I clarified for her.

'And what did he mean, "draining the area"? Sounds like a gravel pit,' she asked, screwing up her face.

'I'm afraid nurses and doctors are always talking loosely about drips and drains – it's all very basic. After many types of operation a tube is left in to, literally, drain the area of excess blood and exudates, all discharging liquid waste matter. If left at the wound site it collects and clots, causing what is known as a haematoma. This can then act as a nice soggy, inviting site for bacteria, resulting in infection and delayed healing of the wound. As far as a thyroidectomy is concerned, the haematoma could press on the windpipe and cause breathing difficulties.' I hoped that was sufficient explanation without being alarmist. I purposely avoided emotive words like 'choking' and 'suffocation'.

'Don't worry, we'll be keeping a close check on you after surgery. Anyway the tube usually comes out after forty-eight hours, along with the first half of the clips. Anything else worrying you?' I enquired, wanting to put her at ease prior to surgery.

My confidence had been given a good boost when she asked for my help. This, and other small instances on Parker, made me feel completely accepted as a working member of the ward staff. Almost without consciously realising it, I had slipped into my new role effortlessly with the help of all the people around me.

FOUR: ACTION

My initiation test on Parker came in the form of a crisis on the Sunday night of my first weekend in charge.

Nurse Littleton was beavering away in her usual earnest, quiet way. A likeable first year student, madly keen to do the job to her utmost ability, she was a salutary reminder to me of how little a new nurse actually did know. Young-looking, fresh-faced and wide-eyed with deference to her experienced senior colleagues, she made me feel so horribly old.

I admired her enthusiasm and hoped like hell that it would last. There were so many obstacles that could mar the way; gory sights, sour relationships, unhappiness and disappointment by the bucketful and hopeless cases that could cripple even the most dedicated nurse. All set against the guts, determination and optimism, which we all start off with. I had seen so many good nurses undone by the realities of nursing, regretting to leave their chosen profession but unable to take any more.

Anne Littleton showed great potential, with a lively interest in her work and a special kindness to the patients, shown in a genuine willingness to help with little extras, like getting bits of shopping or posting letters. My fear was that her idealism didn't prepare for all eventualities.

As a willing nurse, she tried very hard but, in accordance with her inexperience, she was apt to be cack-handed with the execution of new and unfamiliar tasks.

Four new patients had been admitted that day and the two for surgery on Monday had been prepared. Mrs Green, a frail old lady with defective eyesight was due for a haemorroidectomy, repair of painful, swollen veins at the anus. I had asked Nurse Littleton to accompany her to the bath. It wasn't worth taking any chances where accidents were liable to occur, I was being most careful in my new responsibility.

After visiting was over, I joined the patients in the day room and snatched a quick tea from the drinks trolley. I liked the opportunity to have an informal chat amongst the patients in a relaxed group, when it was often possible to detect undercurrent anxieties not officially voiced.

Bridie preferred to keep her distance, in the emotional sense; she thought it was more professional that way. Surgical nursing could be made to be like that – a clean slice to excise the part and the problem. I knew there was more to people than chopping and sewing. We get so used to ops. on a daily basis, but for each patient, for them personally, it is a new and frightening experience. I liked the patients to know there was an approachable human being who could come out of that small glass cage of an office.

Mrs Hampstead had also ventured to the day room, clutching at her side, trying bravely to walk erect. She was in good form, regaling the group with a mother-in-law story. I faintly heard Nurse Littleton call from the ward. I made a slow but definite response by edging backwards to the door, keeping my ear cocked to catch the punch-line.

I was taken by surprise as I bumped into Ruth Abbott, one of the other new patients, coming in through the door.

'Sister, quick! Nurse needs you over there.' She pointed over to where Anne Littleton was holding onto Mrs Green, grasping her under the arms, half slumped over the bed.

'Oh *my* God!' was all I could manage as I raced towards them.

Fainting after a hot bath? Sixty-six years old – stroke? History of heart problems? Epilepsy? I quickly thought through the options.

Anne was doing her best to support the limp dead weight of the patient. Obviously her first thought had been to get Mrs Green into the sanctuary of her bed. I pulled back the patient's shoulders.

The bluey-mauve lips stood out vividly against her grey-coloured face, wet with clammy perspiration. Her eyes rolled skywards and mostly the whites were showing.

'She just collapsed on me, Sister,' Nurse Littleton

hurriedly tried to explain, 'her chest seemed to be hurting her, then she was down.'

'O.K. get her onto the floor,' I said, dragging her down myself and fumbling to elicit a carotid pulse in the neck.

Nothing. Bloody nothing.

My hands were shaking but my mind was amazingly crystal clear. I didn't want this junior to botch the crash call and waste valuable time.

'Dial 333. Say "cardiac arrest, Parker".'

She ran to the office and within seconds those very words reverberated back to me over the tannoy system.

I was straddled on the floor beside Mrs Green and my hands were shaking visibly as I felt for her breastbone. I formed my hand into a fist and gave a hard thump to the end of her sternum. Her slight body jerked from the considerable force.

Both sets of false teeth were resting loosely in her mouth, so I had to remove them before starting mouth-to-mouth resuscitation. I extended her neck until almost the crown of her head touched the floor, to ensure a patent airway to the lungs.

As I did so, Doreen appeared. Some patient had had the good sense to summon the auxiliary from the kitchen.

'Doreen! Oxygen! Sucker!' But without needing to be told, she was on her way to collect the vital emergency equipment.

I breathed into Mrs Green's throat. Holding her nose, I enveloped her wet, flacid mouth with my own and blew down hard. I glanced across at her chest. It rose. Thank the Lord, I was doing it right.

Two more puffs, then Nurse Littleton came back and I set her to work on the cardiac massage.

'Heels of both hands here and push hard – give firm jerks.' I showed her a couple and returned to the head.

My head started to swim from all the deep breathing, like the light-headiness from blowing up balloons. Kneeling on the floor, even doing this life-saving task, I was acutely aware of a ladder creeping up my tights.

'Harder girl,' I shouted across to Anne, doing ladylike

presses, 'get the full weight of your body behind it.'

It seemed that we were working on her for ages but it could only have been a minute or two before the resus. team charged into the ward. Two doctors immediately took over from us. Then the nurse saw chest thumping at its best.

The second medic took the self-reflating Ambu-bag, which Doreen handed him from our feeble selection of ward emergency equipment. It at least made easier work of the breathing part by handpumping to inflate the lungs.

I realised I was bursting to go for a pee but that would have to wait.

A loud rattling noise heralded the arrival of the 'Red Devil', as it clattered along the stone corridor, then changed tone on the parquet wooden flooring of the ward. The porter swung in with the resuscitation trolley, a large metal cabinet on wheels, painted pillar-box red, packed with all the life-saving equipment and drugs that we might need. He smartly lifted the head end of the bed off and I guessed he'd been involved with cardiac arrests before.

The anaesthetist ran in, his emergency bleep still buzzing away. He wanted to get the patient onto the bed.

'Get a board!' he yelled impatiently.

The porter put the resus. board on the bed and Mrs Green was lifted, almost thrown, by all hands onto the firm surface that allowed for effective cardiac massage to continue.

The bedclothes and pillows were shoved out of the way onto the floor and I was aware of kicking them under the curtain, which some mystery person had pulled.

I collected the tray for intubation to help the anaesthetist get respiration organised. Intubation is the vital and immediately necessary process of passing a plastic tube into the patient's trachea to give access to the respiratiory tract to enable us to maintain a clear airway.

'Will someone get this effing sucker working!' the anaesthetist bellowed.

Oh, Christ! It was all intact, ready for use, but being an old ward, Parker had a shortage of electric sockets in the wall and the sucker wouldn't reach the nearest one. I'd seen a plug board somewhere on the ward, in some nook or cranny, but where? I couldn't think straight. I called Doreen to bring it. What a blessing to have at least one person who knew their way around the ward.

I was missing the brand new equipment that we'd always taken so much for granted in my training hospital, piped oxygen and piped suction above each bed, ready at the touch of a switch.

At last it was working and the machinery hummed to life, making vigorous noises as the suffocating saliva was cleared out.

Laryngoscope. Lights, battery. Working? Miracle, they are.

The anaesthetist stretched the neck and passed the large, cold steel instrument down her throat, followed through with the hollow plastic endotracheal (E.T.) tube. Even from the outside, I could see the tube tracking its way to its destination of the windpipe.

The anaesthetist had his hand laid open ready for the next piece of equipment. He snapped his fingers crossly. It was obvious that he was used to having a competent and experienced theatre sister working by his side, who could anticipate and provide for his every need.

It was a long time since I'd been involved in this procedure and wasn't too familiar with the hardware.

'Connection. Tubing.' He gave me the cues.

I fumbled for the correct pieces, praying they were the right size. Any delay in restoring oxygenation to the brain longer than three or four minutes could result in permanent brain damage.

He got her connected up to oxygen and was bag-squeezing the life-giving gas into the unresponsive patient. Luckily I remembered to hand him a syringe and forceps to blow up the cuff on the E.T. tube to keep it safely in place.

Tape to secure the tube to her neck, then we'd be through here.

'Shit, I haven't got my scissors. Never got my bloody scissors when I damn well need them.'

I stretched over to Nurse Littleton who was looking redundant and bewildered. She cut the tape, obviously glad to be involved in the action.

Respiration under control.

One doctor was busy trying to fix the electro-cardiograph, E.C.G. leads to each limb. He cursed, finding it difficult to get them to stay on as the patient had sweated so profusely and her skin was soaked.

The other doctor was frantically searching for a suitable vein to get a drip established before the circulation collapsed. Anne's help had been enlisted to squeeze and steady the arm.

I turned to prepare a giving set and had just run it through with normal saline when he managed to force the stilette into a vein.

'We have lift off,' he said with relief, as the infusion and needle were connected. Lovely Doreen was at hand with the drip stand, so I wasn't left holding the bag in midair as had happened to me often on previous occasions.

The drips fell in healthy abundance and the flow was established.

Circulation under control. We had a direct route into the body.

'Get this damn nightie out of the way, Nurse.' The doctor addressed his remark to Nurse Littleton, as the one with the scissors. She didn't understand.

I reached for her scissors and slashed up both the sleeves, pulling the nightie down to reveal the slender, mottled frame.

'100 mls. Soda Bic., Sister.' The doctor ordered the infusion fluid to be changed to sodium bicarbonate, a solution which would neutralise the acid contents built up in the blood due to the absence of respiration.

'Nurse, make a note of the drugs given, name, dose and time,' I directed my order to Nurse Littleton who was hovering around, engrossed at the organised chaos. I understood so well how she was feeling, desperate to get involved and anxious to help but with not a clue of what to do unless guided.

'I've got it here, Sister,' I looked up to see Miss Ashton waving a notepad with all the progress details. She had slipped in unnoticed by me. Quiet, efficient, unruffled.

So different from me, getting very red in the face, choking

on my tight collar and smelling the nervous perspiration that was leaking through my uniform at the armpits.

I was all thumbs with the plaster – sodding stuff – and made a pretty messy job of securing the I.V. cannula to her arm. Still it would have to do in the circumstances.

Circulation under control.

'Nurse! Nu-urse! I want a bedpan.' Would you credit it? Granny Jones taken short right in the middle of this emergency. Anyway, I doubt if she realised the importance of all the commotion, so far from her at the other end of the ward. It probably wouldn't make the slightest impression on the thick-skinned old dear.

'I'll get it, don't worry.' I recognised the voice of Ruth, who had virtually stationed herself in the ward as surrogate staff to help out. Doreen was half keeping an eye on the other patients but we kept calling her away from the main ward.

'We've got something,' said the doctor reading the E.C.G. monitor, which gave the precise information on the working of the heart. The two doctors from the medical team conferred. Dr Jeffrey had just arrived in reply to his bleep and peered in to read with them.

'She's fibrillating. We'll have to shock her. Is the defib. ready?' he asked as he started to put on the protective rubber gloves.

It was. The defibrillator machine gives a high-voltage electric shock to stop a heart that is trembling like jelly and beating ineffectively. The idea is that once it has stopped trembling, it will restart with a good, strong, regular heartbeat, vital to maintain the circulation of blood. One doctor grasped the two large electrodes by the handles and the other smeared them with conducting jelly, to prevent electric burns to Mrs Green's skin.

He slapped them on her chest, one at the midline, the other on the left, below her tiny, flat breast.

'Paddles in position. Everyone stand clear of the bed,' he ordered. I put my arm in front of Anne and eased her back from the bed. Any contact with the patient or bed as the electric current is released and the charge passes through anything or anyone in the way, giving them a mighty shock.

'Right. Ready?' This was his final warning. Doctor looked around to check it was all clear and held himself free of the bed.

All the staff stood back, momentarily looking at the small, flacid body of Mrs Green, rigged up to the wires and tubes, with the frayed nightie lying pathetically around her hips. Mercifully, she was unconscious and unaware of all that was being done to her. At present she was at the mercy of these two cold electrodes hovering on her chest.

'Shoot!' He pressed the button which released the massive electric charge. It passed through her chest, her heart and in fact stimulated all her muscles, causing her entire body to arch and jerk violently.

Both doctors hurriedly checked the ECG. There was no change.

'Give her another shock. Bigger dose.' He adjusted the machine and repeated the defibrillation, then continued cardiac massage by hand.

The other doctor from the team drew up a syringe of adrenaline and attached a needle, some four or five inches long. Anne Littleton's eyes widened in horror as he plunged it into the patient's chest, in order to get the drug directly into the heart.

'Intra-cardiac adrenaline.' I saw Miss Ashton write it down and check her watch.

I glanced at the ward clock. Twenty minutes since we started, is that all?

Both doctors were busy drawing up drugs to give shots into the established I.V. drip; calcium chloride, isoprenaline and a drug to raise the blood pressure, the name of which I was unfamiliar with. Better get up to date on this.

It was a blessing to have been able to establish a patent intravenous line before the circulation shut down in physiological shock. Much preferable to fiddling about doing a cut-down, a mini-operation to find and use a suitable vein. Thank God we'd been spared that complication.

'OK. She's in sinus rhythm now,' doctor said with relief. The heart was beating again with a regular rhythm. 'Let's get her along to ICU.'

Miss Ashton had already rung to prepare ICU for a new admission.

'Could you also bleep the radiographer, we'll need a portable chest X-ray as soon as we get down there. And tell the staff I'll want to pass a catheter to monitor urinary function,' he called to Miss Ashton.

'Can we wait till we get to ICU to take blood gases?' he checked with the anaesthetist.

He got a nod from the grumpy gasman.

It was tidy-up time. All systems were stable and in control; heartbeat, respiration and circulation. I removed the remnants of her nightie and called for a 'cuddly', a flannelette sheet, to cover and make her respectable in transit. Miss Ashton applied a splint and bandage to support the arm holding the drip.

I asked Nurse Littleton to check and record the pulse and blood pressure, while I gathered together the notes and old X-rays in readiness for her transfer.

Kate Ashton accompanied the prostrate lady and her trappings down the corridor. It was preferable to wheel Mrs Green down on the bed for the short journey, rather than move her on and off of a trolley. The anaesthetist scooted along with one knee on the bed, continuing to bag-squeeze as they went. Kate held the drip high, while the doctors and porters pushed for all their worth. The worst possible thing would be to have a repeat arrest between wards.

'I'll drop the Kardex and wash things into ICU later,' I called as the troupe left the ward, - much later,' I added under my breath.

Our first priority was to get the ward straight, it looked like the demolition squad had been in. The resus. trolley had to be tidied and returned to the neuro. ward, where it was stored. Their staff had the responsibility of checking the equipment and replenishing the stock.

Doreen had cleared away the bedclothes. Anne Littleton picked up the nightie and took a long, reflective look at the garment before putting it into the locker. I went over to collect the towel and sponge-bag, plus Mrs Green's loose dentures, which I wrapped in a tissue.

I could see that Anne was winding down from the tense excitement and the full emotional impact was imminent. The nerve-shattering reality of what she had witnessed was about to hit her - hard.

'Go to the kitchen,' I told her, 'let's have tea for all hands, I expect the patients are feeling a bit jumpy too.' She'd need the time and space to recover.

In situations like this the patients co-operate as best they can. Invariably they are sensible enough to organise themselves away from the action and give it a wide berth. The ambulant ones had congregated in the day room but I wonder what kind of conversation you can have if, less than twenty yards away, a battle is ensuing to snatch some poor wretch from the jaws of death. Several kindly patients had stayed in the ward to sit with those who were bed-bound and naturally upset by the emergency.

The patients had gelled together as a group as never before. The screen had been drawn so there had been little evidence of the actual person, but the trolley and all the paraphernalia were on show. Urgent activity was apparent, as were the unnerving noises from the gurgling of the suction apparatus, the clatter of instruments and machinery and the commentary by commanding and assertive voices.

No one enjoyed such a crisis. It brought to the surface everyone's underlying fear that they might be the next one in line. At that level they felt personally involved. It was traumatic to be a participant in a cardiac arrest but almost worse to be a helpless, inactive observer.

The atmosphere was electric with tension as I entered the day room. No one dared ask the direct question, so great would be the disappointment of a wrong answer.

Pairs of eyes rested on my face, hoping for an inkling of encouragement.

'She's OK at the moment ladies, you'll be pleased to hear,' I had a job to make my announcement, my throat was choked with joyful emotion. 'She's been transferred to Intensive Care.' I wanted to allay any fear they might have when seeing the empty bed space.

It was as if I had released some communal shutter from

their vocal cords, as they broke into unbridled, tension-relieving chatter amongst themselves. Their faces beamed, visibly relaxed. They were jubilant for the success, just as they would have been mortified by the failure. They had felt intrinsic concern for the outcome.

'Tea will be coming shortly. If you still feel a bit aereated and lively, it's quite normal, ask the night nurse for a sleeper.' I wished them all a good night. I'd still got a lot of clearing up to do before the night staff came on. Not least of all Anne Littleton.

Predictably, I found her shedding a few tears over the tea trolley. She smartened up as I came into the kitchen, wiping her wet face and apologising.

I asked Doreen to pour two teas for us before she took the big pot down to the patients.

'Sit over there.' I indicated to the chair behind the fridge door, which I knew all the staff used now and then for a surreptitious cup of tea or coffee. 'Let it all out, it won't do you any good to hold your feelings in. You've just experienced a whole set of stirring and violent emotions. It's bound to take it out of you. Don't fight it.'

She sobbed softly and freely. 'But I felt fine at the time. It was all so exciting watching the team at work. Now I'm cold and shivery. I feel really sick. I don't know why I'm like this, I feel *so* silly.' She was very cross at what she saw as letting herself down after putting on such a brave show.

'I shouldn't worry. I threw up after being in at my first arrest,' I confided to her, 'it's nature's way, no one can help it. Your body lets you cope supremely at the time by pumping out adrenaline to keep you going. Then when the action stops and you aren't needed anymore, the adrenaline gets turned off and you are left as a quivering heap. You feel exhausted, achey and absolutely drained. The let-down reaction is to be expected and is necessary for recovery. It must be allowed to run its course. You did really well, Nurse, you were a great help. As you saw, there is so much needing to be packed into a short but vital time.' I wanted her to understand that her response was natural and inescapable.

She held tightly to the cup and sipped her tea, shivering

with nervous cold, but I knew it would pass. I was prepared to bet money that within half-an-hour she'd be repeating the episode with graphic details to her contemporary junior students. Such an exhilarating experience would need to be shared.

Miss Ashton returned with the latest report when the patient had been settled in ICU. It was up to me to inform the next of kin.

Husband. Same address. No phone. Neighbour's number. Poor Mr Green. I had met him earlier in the afternoon when he brought his wife into hospital and had left her safely and happily in our hands. He was probably settled in front of the tele, supping his usual nightcap and feeling strangely alone without his partner, who he imagined was tucked up in her hospital bed. What a ghastly shock to be summoned next door with 'an urgent message from the hospital'.

I did my best to soften the blow by starting with the good news, 'She's fine now but had a turn for the worse and has been transferred to Intensive Care.' Simple, truthful, easy to grasp. No point talking in unintelligible terms of cardiac arrest, ventilation, shocks and drips, which he couldn't assimilate at that moment. He didn't inquire further, so I left it for the doctor to explain to his face, which is much better than the phone.

I made sure he'd written down 'ICU'. He was going to get transport, he wanted to come and see her straight away.

After a late handover to the night staff, I stopped off at ICU with the belongings. Mrs Green still had the endotracheal tube down her throat but she was breathing unaided and her pinky colour had returned. Both were good signs indicating her recovery. The ECG machine bipped and bopped a healthy heart sound. I thought her chest would probably ache a lot when she recovered consciousness completely and the pain-relieving drugs wore off.

Mr Green was there holding his wife's hand in profound silence. He looked more pale than she did now. I didn't disturb his contemplation.

I didn't see Mrs Green again. She was automatically taken over by the medical team and was no longer fit to undergo surgery in the immediate future. For the present, haemorroids were the least of her problems. It was, I suppose, quite providential that she had her heart attack in the right place, she may not have survived an arrest at home, where medical attention could have been nowhere near as quick or efficient.

Kate Ashton had been kind enough to congratulate me on the initial handling of the arrest. Each person's contribution, however small, is vital to the cumulative effort. We all shared in the praise and pride of the successful outcome, it had been tremendously rewarding to see Mrs Green respond to our diligent efforts.

What a pity it can't always be the way. Resuscitation is a formidable process to watch, which is why many a nurse and doctor swear they will get tattoed on their sternum, 'Do not resuscitate.'

FIVE: MUTILATION

'Recovered from the action?' Bridie greeted me as I reported for the afternoon shift the next day.

The ward was back to its gentle throb of activity. A solitary, cleanly-made bed filled the space that last night had been so crammed with people and instruments. After the chaos that had reigned, the cubicle looked decidedly calm and clinical.

I'd had difficulty settling to sleep after the arrest. I was overstimulated and alert, dog tired but unable to rest peacefully, as I felt the need to exorcise myself of the experience. I tossed around, going over every detail of the event, wondering how it could be improved upon; resolving how much better I would do next time. Finally I drifted off to sleep in the early hours, dead to the world, and woke later that morning, feeling heavy but refreshed.

'Lucky for some,' piped up Dr Jeffrey, 'I've just had a bitch of a weekend.' He looked like death warmed up and could have done with two matchsticks to help keep his red eyes open.

Mrs Green hadn't been one of Andrew's patients but, being the duty surgical SHO, he had been called in on the case. It transpired that she was the beginning of the end for him.

Having handed her over to the medical team, he was called to A & E (Accident & Emergency Department). They gave him a punctured gut to stitch up, resulting from a knife attack after the pubs had turned out.

Then the prostatectomy from upstairs, who'd been troublesome all weekend, finally developed clot retention in the middle of the night.

'I was up there doing a bladder washout at four this morning. I'm knackered. Martin's team are the lucky ones, they've got one less for their theatre list.' That was one way, I suppose, of giving an optimistic view of Mrs Green's arrest.

'I'd give my eye teeth to crash out,' Andrew added wearily.

'Never mind,' Bridie said sarcastically. 'Soon you'll be a Registrar, then you'll have your own underling to do all the dirty work.'

I thought she was being unduly unfair and I felt sorry for Andrew. There was no doubting that the junior doctors had it hard. They were required to put in inordinately long hours, that no other group of workers would tolerate, for financial rewards that were minimal. And, they were hours of life-threatening responsibility where, above all, they needed to be alert and attentive in order to be safe practitioners.

Andrew had been in the operating theatre on Friday, then on call all over the weekend, representing both surgical teams. On call could mean an easy, quiet time in the doctors' residence for studying. Or equally it could mean constantly being bleeped, down to casualty, along to theatre, male ward, female ward, admitting new patients, seeing relatives, briefing sisters, consulting with colleagues.

Doreen brought him a welcome cup of coffee and said with a motherly tone, as she stirred his drink, 'There you are, dear.' Her tenderness towards him counteracted Bridie's constant acidity.

'I'll see the new patient, Mrs Abbott, I didn't get a chance last night. Then I'm hoping to get my head down,' he took the cup and stifled a yawn.

Bridie gave me a quick handover report and went off to lunch. I went around to speak to all the patients before they settled for their rest. The day room set were able to report that Mrs Green was making good progress. News had filtered through via Margo, the physiotherapist, whose workload was spread between male and female surgical and overspill in ICU.

I started getting organised for tomorrow's proposed discharges; out-patient appointment, prescription sheet, GP letter and envelope, all set out for the other SHO to fill in. Mr Martin's young doctor was a resourceful chap from Sri Lanka but he needed quite a prod to remind him of our services liaison. Bridie prefered to push the forms under his nose for signing, rather than risk an omission in communication, which would reflect badly on us.

We did as much as possible to complete all the necessary data to take the load from the doctors. Each patient had a sheet of identity labels containing their basic details. These were made out in medical records and were useful to affix to all forms and letters relating to the patient, as well as on pathology samples of blood, urine, sputum or wound swabs. We were badly in need of a ward clerk to do all this routine administrative work and, although the idea was in the pipeline, financial constraints were likely to scotch the plan. It did seem a waste of a nurse's training to spend so much time in form filling, day in, day out.

Mrs Abbott knocked on the office door.

'Ah good, Dr Jeffrey has finished with you,' I said.

'Well I'm afraid not yet, well not exactly. He's still with me in a manner of speaking,' she answered and left me puzzled as I looked towards her screened bed.

Andrew had been sitting on the bed to take the details of her medical history. His writing had slowed down to a halt, his head bowed forward and he had keeled languidly onto the bed in a deep, natural sleep.

'I've brought his bleep so he wouldn't be disturbed,' she said, dangling it in front of her, 'he looked all in, I think the rest will do him good. After last night, I'm hardly surprised he's exhausted.'

She'd got all the gen from the night staff. Ruth was an SRN herself and fully understood the position of doctors stretched to the limits of their endurance.

Whilst on the subject, I thanked her for her valuable assistance during last night's affray.

Ruth was to become one of Parker's special patients.

Mr Simpson rang through to say that he had a girl in OPD, the Out-Patients Department, with a lump in her breast, and wanted to admit her straight away.

Every surgeon has at least one favourite hobby-horse which triggers them off. Peter Simpson was adamant about breasts. Early treatment, as with any cancer, gives the most reliable chance for a cure. Any lump was seen stat –

immediately – on that score there was no argy-bargy with waiting lists – straight in for examination and the knife. He believed, quite rightly, that any delay should not be allowed and precious days not lost.

The patient wondered what had hit her. To her query about a suspect lump there had been an urgent response from her usually unhurried GP. And now Mr Simpson had told her expressly to return home for her night things, then back for admission and onto the next operating list. It was too much for her to absorb. He mentioned the possible necessity for mastectomy, removal of the breast, but I don't think it registered amid all the other immediate arrangements she was making in her head. She had asked to delay admission until next week, as she had an important function planned for the weekend. That made him see red. He'd insisted that she come in immediately, that there was nothing at all more important than seeing to this lump and her good health. He was fanatical about breasts.

Josephine Woodman was an extremely nervous person by nature and all this speedy and insistent service had put the fear of God into her.

If only she could realise the advantage of such prompt and early treatment. It was all too often the case that fear at the first symptom actually inhibits people from seeking advice, particularly if they fear the worst. It is as if they can't bear to find out the truth on an emotional level, even though at a rational, intellectual level they know they need help. Consequently, too many cancers are not seen until they are at a relatively late stage, when the chances of complete cure are diminished and treatment is prolonged and uncomfortable.

It is unfortunate that pain is not a feature of an early cancer. Only later on when it starts to get invasive, to encroach on other tissues and nerves, or cause obstruction, is there the kind of pain that would spur a patient to seek help.

By then it may already be too late. All we may then offer is kind nursing, pain relief and a gentle end.

My classic and memorable example had been of an old lag, who had been living alone like a hermit in a near slum and had developed a rodent ulcer on the face. This is one of the cancers most amenable to treatment for a complete cure, if caught in time. He had left it too long and by the time he was found, the tumour had completely eaten away the flesh on one side of his face. The eye had been eroded away and the socket had filled with fibrous replacement tissue. We had to irrigate and dress a wide open wound, soggy with yellow pus, that was an offence to the human appearance.

Andrew skulked back to the office after waking from his forty winks on Ruth's bed. He looked around sheepishly to see who was on the ward.

'Here's your bleep. I covered for you, no one else knows.' Apart from that, neither of us made reference to his cat nap. Andrew wasn't one to laugh at his own inadequacies. He was very sensitive about being caught out even in a minor misdemeanour. I think he was relieved that Bridie hadn't been let in on the secret. Even I realised that would have given her below-the-belt ammunition for ever more.

He looked despondent when I told him of yet another patient to see before he could get off duty. I'd helped as much as I could by preparing the X-ray and blood forms and I had the consent form all ready for both him and the patient to sign. I also offered to take the blood for cross-matching when he'd finished with her, as the blood-letters only do the routine morning bloods.

'She's awfully scared,' I told him, preparing him to meet a nervous patient, but he was in mid-yawn as I spoke. 'One of Mr Simpson's rush-in jobs and he had to twist her arm at that. You know how keen he is on breasts.'

By slipping into the colloquial, I left myself wide open for his next remark.

'Aren't we all,' he smiled, 'given half a chance.'

Nevertheless, his comment was indicative of people's attitudes.

Boobs are news. Tits are trade. The message is clear for all to see when passing a paper shop, news stand or hoarding.

Breasts shape fashion and fashion shapes breasts, with garments designed to accentuate those which are an asset or to camouflage those which are less than adequate in the eye of the beholder.

Two handfuls of sexual attraction, these undulations delineate the girls from the boys. The textbooks would have us believe that the mammary glands are for suckling the young. Fleetingly, if at all, the 2.4 babies of a typical British family get a chance to suck and feed from their birthright. This fundamental use of the breast has been far outweighed by their function as secondary sex organs. Breasts make a woman. Knockers are necessary.

So does loss of a breast make you less of a woman? Intellectually the answer is no but emotionally perhaps the answer will be yes. No other operation carries such deep, personal emotional connotations as a mastectomy, the removal of a breast by surgery. A hysterectomy, removal of the womb, can have powerful traumatic impact because it means the absolute termination of childbearing abilities. But at least there is no glaring outward evidence that the uterus has gone, a visible absence to remind the patient every time she gets undressed.

The loss of the breast is disfiguring and apparent for all to see by the asymmetry of the chest wall. It affects the woman's appearance and reflects on her self-confidence and awareness, which can lead to a severe depression. Any missing part disturbs the body-image, that inner psychological impression that we have of ourselves, built up over the years we have had to get used to our distinctive features, shape and size.

Attraction, womanliness, desirability, sexuality and breasts are all inextricably linked. The presence of breasts is commonplace and to be expected, so their absence is noticeable.

Following mastectomy, the outward appearance can be rectified by the use of a false breast to match the remaining partner. A prosthesis which fits into a bra feels soft, smooth and spongy, so lifelike that no one would know the difference.

Not until you are in close personal contact that is. Will the sight of scars at the site where once there had been a full and inviting breast be repugnant to a husband or lover? Intense personal relations are at stake when she wonders how she will fare as 'half a woman'.

So may questions are thrown up by such brutal and

devastating surgery that will profoundly alter a person's whole life – or at least they think it will. Was sex possible? Will it be any different? What about swimming, tennis, sports, sunbathing? Swimsuits and evening clothes, low necks and cut-away sleeves? Pain, stiffness, rejection, depression, lifting, working, feeding babies, telling the children.

As hard as nurses could try, as an outsider with the plain facts, it was difficult to fully understand the effects of this mutilating operation and all its implications at a personal level. Our answers were the best we could give as uninvolved onlookers but they had a ring of cant platitude and I was never surprised when a patient replied, 'Well, how would you know?' Our help to specific individuals was often stopped short, because our role was so diversified.

I had come to believe in the tremendous work provided by self-help groups that provided first hand experience of their conditions in order to help others. All the questions posed were best answered by someone who had had the operation, a mastectomee, someone who had once asked all the questions themselves, passed through the devastating emotions – and was now glad to be alive.

It was the policy on Parker to contact a member of the Mastectomy Association to visit the patients either before or after the surgery, usually both. That person would also offer empathic support when the patient was discharged home. This in fact was often the time when they needed it most, sitting around with no nurse to call upon, no patients to chat to, plenty of idle time for getting worried.

In the early days of the association, it had been the social worker who got in touch with the local branch to arrange for a visitor. They sent a mastectomee, matched to the patient with similar age, and lifestyle, to give maximum comparison to their problems. Now the ward staff had a list of willing contacts, many of whom had been operated on at Gartland, previous patients in Parker ward, providing a good starting point for conversation.

'It's too late to get hold of anyone now,' Bridie said when she heard about the unexpected new admission. 'Anyway, there is no certainty that she'll lose the breast, at her age it's unlikely. As long as she's prepared, we can leave it until after the operation.'

Josie was a carefully-groomed, vivacious young woman of twenty-eight, recently married, with a promising job with the B.B.C. I can see her now, short, dark hair, prematurely peppered with grey, and slightly buck teeth that she licked constantly. She wore a jersey dress with vivid radial stripes, one of those figure-hugging styles which only the slenderest of females can wear with complete confidence.

Her nervousness was manifest by an irrepressible urge to chatter constantly. Nattering was her way of relieving tension, her little release valve. Pauline Cottrell was making steady recovery from her thyroidectomy. She was not over keen to talk a lot with a sore neck, so Josie made an entertaining and light-hearted companion – too light-hearted under the circumstances, I thought.

Josie was organising her bits and pieces into her locker when I went to take the bloods. I would need quite a lot, because we would need to get a few pints cross-matched in case of extensive surgery.

'Ugh, not the needle already.' She spotted the charged syringe in the receiver.

Despite her jokey protestations about my taking blood, she managed to maintain deliberate conversation throughout. I didn't mind if it helped her through the procedure but thought it could become wearing after a while.

To take blood isn't painful. After the initial sting as the needle pierces the skin, there is nothing more to feel. However, patients can often be alarmed at the sight of the blood in the barrel of the syringe and feel faint and queezy at the thought of losing blood. I thought she might well be this type.

I applied a venesection tourniquet to her upper arm. The veins below began to stand out; bluey-mauve, stringy vessels became clear to see. As I cleansed the skin with a spirit swab, I suggested she look away.

'Does this business take long, the operation, I mean? I've got a christening lined up for next weekend with my new in-laws. I'll be meeting a lot of his family. I've really been looking forward to going. I've spent a fortune on a new outfit. I'd hate to miss it now. Your surgeon fellow wasn't much of a sport. Gave me a real dressing down and dragged me here. It's a wonder he didn't put me in a strait jacket! Honestly I can't see what difference a week would make.' Her pressurised conversation, flitting from point to point, made it hard to decipher the original query.

She flinched as I pierced the skin and was momentarily silent. The dark blood filled the syringe.

'How long do you think I'll have to be in?' Now her question was direct. It was unnerving to be put on the spot during a procedure demanding precision and concentration.

I released the tourniquet, withdrew the syringe, pressed a swab to the pin prick and bent her elbow up.

'It all depends on the result of the biopsy,' I said and indicated that she should hold her arm in the bent position. Without hesitating, I had to fill the path. bottles; immediate transfer was crucial, delay would allow the blood to clot in the syringe and it also had to be added to the reagent in the bottles or the result might have been affected.

As I did so, Josie carried on, 'Well, it's only a little lump; it surely can't be much of an op. to remove it?'

I was by now wondering what idea she had about her condition and how much she had actually assimilated about her whistle-stop admission to Parker.

'What did doctor tell you about the operation when you signed the consent form?' I enquired.

'I signed something to say I agree to the anaesthetic and operation. I didn't bother to read it. I'm in now, so they might as well get on with it.' She was quite resigned to surgery but not to the nature of it.

And I suppose Andrew hadn't bothered to explain. Tired, hurried, anxious to get away, he probably made a cursory examination suffice.

There was no way she could be allowed to go to theatre without being prepared for the eventuality that she might need a mastectomy. Nothing could be so traumatic as waking up to find a breast removed, drains in and blood up, if you think you are going down to have a pea shelled out.

'I'll take these bloods and come back.' I promised to return.

Bridie was livid. 'Typical! No consideration for the patient – or the nurses, who have to clear up the mess. He gives no thought to the psychological aspect of people at all, they are just a body under his knife! I've a good mind to bleep him and get him back over this.'

'No, don't, he's off-duty now and I think he deserves to be after this weekend. It was naughty but probably an oversight.' I guessed he'd banked on the fact that Mr Simpson had spoken to her earlier in OPD.

'Oversight!' Bridie didn't like my defending Andrew and glared.

'Read that.' She pounced and pointed to the consent form clipped to the top of the notes. 'The operation . . . the nature and purpose which have been explained to me by Dr . . . It is a legal responsibility.'

'I'll discuss it with her,' I said, taking up the notes.

'Well it's no good getting the other houseman. We have to translate everything he says as it is,' she added icily.

'I'll do it,' I repeated, getting a bit het up myself now, 'just tell me, what are the chances of malignancy?' I wanted to know whether to sound optimistic or pitch in heavily.

'It's remote but always a possibility, which is why they are so keen not to ignore it.' She calmed down, seeing that I was in command of the situation. 'She's young, so it's more likely to be a benign lump, which they'll excise rather than take the chance that it will turn malignant.'

Josie was shocked when I gave her the form to read – operation of 'Biopsy of left breast ? proceed to left mastectomy.'

I elaborated on the technique. 'To rule out any serious complications,' – I meant cancer, – 'the surgeon will take a small sample of the lump tissue – a biopsy – and send it for an instant analysis while you are under anaesthetic – called a frozen section. If all is well, he will remove the lump and you will be left with a tiny scar to heal. If the lump is dangerous – and let me say at your age it is less likely – he would have to proceed to take away the whole breast, necessary in order to excise a wide area of tissue to prevent any spread.'

I felt certain that Mr Simpson would have already given a similar explanation and she nodded in recognition of my words.

'We get you to sign consent to the further procedure only *in case* it proves necessary at the time. It is by no means a certainty that it will take place, they just like to be covered for all eventualities. It is improbable that it will come to that but, as you see by his actions so far, Mr Simpson takes no chances.'

She quietly crossed her arms, as if to feel the presence of her breasts as she did so.

'I hadn't banked on that. Christ, what would I do with one missing?' The full portent of the situation had hit her. Then she bounced back. 'They're not very big but I would miss one – they *are* a matching pair.'

I admired her courage in making a joke and it enabled us to talk further.

'There is no denying that it is a tremendous loss but I'm sure you would agree that it is a worthwhile sacrifice to curb the spread of a serious disease.' Again, I purposely didn't mention cancer. Nor did she. 'You can get a false, matching breast to insert into your bra, so no one would be any the wiser. It takes some period of adjustment but sex is no problem, neither is feeding a baby.' I tried my best to be optimistic.

Josie was obviously turning it over in her mind. 'He'd only get half rations though.'

'That's right. Well, no it isn't strictly true, the body is very good at compensating for the lost organ from a pair. Listen, don't start worrying until you have to. Let's cross each bridge as we come to them, there is plenty of help we can offer if it comes to the crunch.' I nearly said, 'comes to the worst' but didn't think that sounded very encouraging. 'We want you to go down for surgery prepared for whatever proves to be necessary in your best interests. Forewarned is forearmed.'

'Thanks.' As an afterthought from her flitting train of thought, she asked, 'By the way, why is the top man called plain "Mister", instead of "Doctor"?'

I smiled and clarified this strange anomaly in British medicine. 'All doctors complete a broad-based course in training, equipping them with a general knowledge in all branches of medicine and surgery. These are the junior doctors, the housemen, the SHOs, that you meet on the ward.

'A doctor who continues to specialise and get higher qualifications in surgery is then called "Mister". This occurs in general surgery or for any of the specialist surgical fields, such as gynaecology, orthopaedics, ophthalmic surgery and others.

'It's a tradition which stems back to the days when surgical work, crude at that, was done by barbers. The physicians, those who used non-surgical methods to heal, deprived the surgeons of the estimable title of "doctor". And so they have always been known as "Mister".

'As it has happened, in the medical world, the title is something of a professional accolade, a career achievement to become a "Mister". Of course lay people are puzzled and, like yourself, think he has somehow failed to make the grade, when in reality, quite the opposite is true!'

It wasn't long before she was back in the ward telling all the patients about her case. It was not in her nature to keep her problems to herself. I didn't know if she did tell her husband but he never came to talk to any of the nurses.

Josie's plight was the gossip of the day room. All the patients were swapping mastectomy stories, sticking only to the happy ones. Everyone knew someone who'd lost a breast; an auntie, a workmate or a neighbour. The patients were buzzing and her news spread along the line, 'Have you heard about that poor girl?' Sympathy was flowing for Josie, especially for the uncertainty of her fate.

Josie was a bubbly type of person, who bubbled even more under pressure. And it was catching, everyone thrilled to the vicarious anxiety and the ward was bound up with her problem. For anyone the waiting period before op. is stressful, but in her case, even more so.

Josie woke from the aneasthetic and immediately asked about her breast. It was intact. No malignancy had been found. She was a lucky young woman to have had a benign – that is non-cancerous – lump.

I overheard two of my junior nurses talking about the outcome. They had been untouched by the hysteria involving

Josie, feeling that she had a lot less to worry about than many other patients on the ward. There were plenty having massive surgery and with decidedly life-threatening tumours, all she might lose was a piece of decoration.

I hesitated, wanting so much for them to understand a patient's concern for such a brutal mutilation. But they were young and used only to seeing patients on the ward, where comparisons were easy but useless as a measure of personal reaction. Perhaps I had been the same as them at the same level of training. Kept busy by the continuous pressing activities of the ward, it was hard to comprehend those emotions. A mastering of the routine work wouldn't leave much mental space for those long-term implications to filter through.

The finer, deeper aspects of mastectomy were something I could deal with in a tutorial. Words, education, facts would feed the mind but I knew that experience and maturity were necessary for the more complete understanding of human reactions and fears.

SIX: RECREATION

I shared a flat with Susy French, also a nurse from Cottingham. She had been in training two years my senior, when we met during a spell of night duty on male orthopaedics. We found we had a lot in common and had remained friends ever since.

Susy had enjoyed the experience of her nurse's training but didn't see herself climbing to the top of any part of the nursing structure. Not for her the frilly cap of the ward sister or weekend work. She had been disenchanted with the hospital and nursing hierachy and wanted out. After further training, she had become a social worker and was now located in the community around Gartland.

My going to GGH was a lucky coincidence for us both. Her previous flat-mate walked out and I walked in, thus solving each of our problems simultaneously.

The flat was reasonably spacious but utilitarian to say the least. It was damp, cold and decidedly musty. The grace-saving features were an incredibly low rent and each having a room of our own. It was the second floor of a tall, old converted Victorian house, one of those promised to be redeveloped sometime by someone, persons unknown. Meanwhile we got away with cheap and cheerless accomodation, which suited our needs fine. Neither of us was particularly interested in home-making, especially not in investing our hard-earned cash into up-grading our temporary residence, so an eye-sore it stayed.

Susy and I were single, young career girls, intent on getting the best that life could offer. Our interests were varied and often dissimilar but then we often met on common ground. We had both recently got disentangled from love affairs so it was probably a good thing that our taste in men was diametrically opposed. We valued each other's opinions and desire for privacy. In general we found the company supportive, yet not claustrophobic. Whenever neither of us had a man around, we would join forces for entertainment, if our off-duty coincided.

The flat's running expenses were shared between us, so were the cleaning tasks. Visitors were always totally amazed at the regular shambles of our flat, expecting that we, as nurses, should be pristine tidiers and organisers. That was one habit that I left at the hospital gate but I was always criticised by people who would say, 'And you being a nurse, too!'

With our varied working times, Susy and I decided early on to cook for ourselves, it was too complicated to arrange otherwise. Cooking wasn't something that thrilled either of us, so, in practice, the chicken and chip shop down the road got a lot of our custom. We both fared pretty well when we were taken out by our respective male companions, who had the mistaken impression that nurses were too poor or too tired to eat well. Who were we to disillusion them! I ate regularly at the hospital, stocking up on adequate, subsidised meals from the canteen.

On one occasion I was able to invite Susy for a Chinese meal, courtesy of the family Lee. Mrs Lee was the venerable grandmother of an immense family of obscure oriental origin, all contributing to the successful restaurant business.

She had been admitted to Parker for investigations of swallowing difficulties and loss of weight. A thin person naturally, with this extra emaciation her petite frame was emphasised. The facial bones were sticking prominently from her face, her cheeks sunken and her almond eyes pronounced.

Our biggest headache had been with language. Her knowledge of English was limited to the numbers relating to the menu card, 'Yes please', 'No please', and 'tea'. The staff were stretched to use their imaginations to get information across to her.

The family were simply marvellous and offered to come at any time we needed their help. I thought we would probably have her relatives in constant attendance after surgery to translate our instructions.

Where possible we tried to anticipate her needs and get relatives to explain during the previous visiting time. I had the job of describing the operation and necessary preparation and aftercare. I tried to visualise every eventuality she should be prepared for and her son translated it all.

She appeared to understand, but it was difficult to tell. With her own kin she was so vibrant and chatty, she was like a different person. Without them the communication barrier was up and she retained a fixed pose in her bed or chair, giving the occasional gratuitous smile, but obviously bewildered by the alien surroundings and voices. The other patients did their level best to make her feel included in the ward, as did the staff, but there is a limit to the scope of a one-sided conversation.

Mrs Lee was limited to fluids only and even these she was finding difficult to get down.

'So what are they going to do for her?' Susy asked in rather a loud voice.

I filled her in on the details of the case, quietly so none of the restaurant staff would know I was discussing their relative.

She had had a barium swallow, an investigation where the patient swallows radio-opaque dye in a drink and X-rays are taken. This had shown a marked and definite obstruction in the oesophagus, the tube leading from the throat to the stomach. A biopsy examination of a piece of tissue was taken via an oesophagoscope, a long unpleasant tube passed into the oesophagus. This confirmed the provisional diagnosis of a cancer which was the cause of the problem.

'She's booked for an oesophago-gastrectomy. They excise the lower part of the oesophagus and the upper part of the stomach and join the two ends together. We are building her up for surgery now, giving her blood IV and nourishing fluids by mouth, as much as she can tolerate. She's such a poor little thing and it's all made that much harder by our inability to communicate. It's a hell of an op. but I suppose it's a chance. I don't think the prognosis is very good in Ca. oesophagus. There isn't any evidence of metastases but secondary deposits from the tumour are always a possibility.'

Susy liked to hear about my work and keep abreast with new developments and I found it relaxing talking to someone who knew the jargon.

'Hey, do you remember that girl at Cottingham, the psyche case who swallowed bleach?' Susy would often lapse into memories of her training. Nurses tend to do this and can't help but keep a clear and vivid picture of patients who make an impression upon them, for whatever reason it may be.

The unusual, the fascinating, the bizarre, the horrific they captivate the imagination of the nurse. For our own interest we would pore over the details of any interesting case given third-hand.

'Yes, I never saw her, she was on Intensive Care,' I struggled to recall the circumstances. 'They said she was a schizophrenic, she heard voices which told her to drink bleach to cleanse her of impurities. The whole of her oesophagus was sclerosed, absolutely ruined.'

She was the faceless patient who had become the conversation piece for the dining-room on that day. Ironically, neither of us knew her name but remembered the details very clearly. Another of those cases immortalised by a generation of nurses, who, on the periphery, could gasp at the startling facts and marvel at the peculiarities of human nature. Those closer to the bedside could appreciate the deeper significance of the personal tragedy and the feelings of the loved ones involved.

'I remember she had the oesophagus removed and a piece of large bowel was dissected out and sewn in its place,' I added, now realising the connection with Mrs Lee.

'Charming! With chop suey, Helen,' Susy said, more as a statement of fact than as a reflection of her emotions.

Nurses very quickly adjusted to discussing even the most distasteful of bodily functions over meals. It is only when in the company of non-medicals that you get pulled up short by others who are unfamiliar with human sewerage as a matter of fact in their daily life.

'Then there was that one on gynae. Born without a vagina. Her bowel was used to fashion a vagina, wasn't it?' Susy rambled on. I could see there was no stopping her going down medical memory lane.

'Seems like you miss it a bit, Sue? Am I right?' I asked her.

'Well, I enjoyed it at the time. The experience has been of great benefit to me in social work. And I like the close contact with the patients and a bit of drama now and then. But the nursing hierachy would really cheese me off.'

She bucked against the constraints of an institutional set-up, whereas I thrived on, what was for me, support from an organised system.

She went on, 'It's tolerable as a student, being treated like a kid – or a moron. All that fussing about the length of hair and keep taking your nail varnish off after a night out. It's not just that, but I feel I get more respect and responsibility as a social worker and am allowed much more freedom as an individual with decision-making for clients.'

Oh yes, of course, the 'clients'. Not the 'patients', plonked in bed and allowed to regress – but clients, supported and 'therapised' through their 'problems' – that deep pit of never-ending problems.

I suppose she was right in one way. Even as a Sister, I wasn't officially allowed to give a Panadol or a Senokot unless it was on prescription, ordered by the doctor. However, I liked working alongside other professionals and valued the team approach. I wasn't envious of some of the decisions Susy had to make. Whether battered children should remain with their parents or be taken into care. If old people should live alone or had to be removed from their life-long homes or if people were mad enough to be taken to the psychiatric hospital.

Susy liked the autonomy of social work and its glamorous aura, she felt it sounded slightly more upper crust than being a plain ordinary basic nurse. Never-the-less, many a time I knew she was exasperated and frustrated by the pressure of her job, by a family clamouring for more and more help, obviously never going to survive without that crutch.

I had to admit to prefering the tidiness of hospital care; in, out, better, worse, diagnosis, treatment, and a wave bye-bye.

'Hey, but what about that guy after the circumcision,' she said with a throaty chuckle. Susy was really well into her reminiscences of the pelvic region.

Still, that did have to be our stock hospital anecdote, the 'what's the funniest thing that ever happened to you as a nurse' party line.

The poor patient didn't find it in the least bit funny – well not at the time – he was madly embarrassed and bloody scared, no doubt. It was panic stations when it happened, but telling it afterwards, it certainly had an amusing ring. I often wondered if he recounted his story with as much hilarity as us giggly student nurses, I sincerely hoped he could see the funny side of it after the calm had settled.

This young chap, in his twenties, came in for a circumcision, the removal of the foreskin over the penis, which was tight when it retracted and was causing him pain during intercourse. He was naturally shy about the whole business, having his sex life exposed so ungraciously.

The operation went fine and he had a neat ring of stitches around his penis. On the following day he called for help when he found the penile dressing soaked in blood. He had an unexpected haemorrhage from a blood vessel, which occasionally happens after surgery, once the blood pressure has returned to normal and its force loosens a weak stitch.

The nurse, doing as she has always been instructed to cope with external haemorrhage, applied pressure to the bleeding part. She grabbed his John Thomas and held it all the way as he was wheeled back to theatre, where the vessel was tied securely, once and for all.

'Poor sod, I hope he wasn't left with any ghastly complexes after that. Fancy going through the mill, then finding out you weren't able to use it after all!' Susy said bluntly. 'Men generally get away lightly where all that is concerned. Think of all the hassle we have with periods and babies, menopause and gynae. problems.'

'Anyway, how are you getting on with your old battle-axe of a Sister?' she asked, returning the conversation to Parker Ward. 'Is she like those old crones we had at Cottingham?'

'No, not at all.' I surprised myself by springing to Bridie's defence. 'She's a very experienced ward Sister, great at administration and nursing procedures. Somewhat brusque and short with the patients, she falls down a little on communications and relationships. Everyone is kept at an emotional arm's length. It's difficult to put your finger on it. She lacks warmth and diplomacy about finer feelings. Not a one for hand-holding and TLC (tender loving care) but the patients know where they stand with her and admire her smart efficiency. And there is no faulting her on techniques. On the whole, I think we'll make a good team. I'm interested in teaching the nurses and being with the patients, so we have our own territories. It's probably better that way. We can't all be good at everything. I'm only too happy for her to rattle her brains with doing the off-duty plan and ordering the drip-sets and toilet rolls.'

'But do you feel like a Sister or are you her understudy?' Susy was going onto her autonomy tack now.

'Maybe I am just a glorified Staff Nurse, with the uniform, pay and title of Sister. That's the way promotion goes, creeping up the ladder. I don't mind working under her, I'm learning a lot from her. There is so much to assimilate about the running of a ward, that our basic training can't possible equip us for. The very fact that I am in blue puts different situations before me that I never encountered as a student; relatives, phone-calls, patients' questions, other departments asking advice,' I told her.

'It's unlikely that I'll contribute many changes to Parker but that's because it is so well run, they don't need any. Perhaps later I might try to institute a ward training programme for the students we have.'

Being a junior Sister, or second Sister, is a difficult position. The senior person could easily feel threatened by an intruder and if Bridie were to take it out on me, then I'd be the loser in the long run. I felt I was walking a tightrope where personalities were concerned and was content to keep a low profile at present.

'Oh well, it's a start, and it will give you a good grounding. Anyway it will look impressive on paper when you apply for another job,' she answered, very matter of fact.

'Hold on! I've only just got this one,' I retorted.

Philip Lee, the grandson, came over. He welcomed us to the restaurant and wished us an enjoyable meal. Very tactfully, neither of us mentioned his mother in report form, he merely said how grateful he was for all that the staff had done for her. He assured me that she was quite happy in the hospital, although not able to express it directly.

Looking at Philip, I realised how attractive he was. Susy

cued in on the vibes and the conversation turned to men.

'Changing you affiliation? He's hardly like "our Tony",' she said facetiously.

Tony was the recent and long drawn out affair from which I was escaping.

One of my main reasons for applying to Gartland in the first place was simply to get to the other side of London – and free from him.

We had met when we were both in training at the Cottingham, a provincial teaching hospital.

He was a doctor intent on specialising in children's surgery, so I followed when he moved to his new appointment. It had been no secret that my prime motive for doing paediatric nursing had been to stay near my beloved Tony. It was done partly out of love and loyalty but also partly in the hope that our relationship might develop along the lines of marriage. On reflection it was stupid to expect a young man on the verge of a promising and demanding career to think of getting tied down. Still, slavishly I followed *my* ambition – him. Not the first, or the last, nurse to fall for the first good-looking medic.

Kids had never been one of my favourite specialities but I had hoped his enthusiasm would rub off on me. With his help, I learned a great deal and sailed through all my exams, but was never dedicated to the field of paediatrics. An interesting and useful experience and an extra qualification, that was all it was for me.

No way could I ever become besotted like Sister Rudgely. Thirty years of unrelenting devotion to her 'littlies', as she so irritatingly called them. Over the years, she'd seen them through diphtheria, scarlet fever, polio epidemics, but was showing the strain of keeping up-to-date with modern technology. Sister Rudgely had demonstrated to me that if you stick around long enough a disease that had been eradicated will return to take a nasty hold and you will be needed again.

Her work was her life. Off-duty was an anathema to her. Even when she went on holiday, she would ring up to enquire after her littlies. Staff took make-believe bets on when she'd ring. It was cruel but irresistible.

At the time, some of us 'biggies' found it all slightly nauseating, possibly fearful that our own lives might end up revolving solely around twenty-five beds and their tiny occupants, who belonged to someone else. Later, I began to respect her dedicated contribution and saw that the profession lost something as these old-time Sisters retired. They offered a comforting stability to the ward, particularly in paediatric work, as the parents found her irreplaceable for compassion and interest in their children. Despite her irksome little traits, Sister Rudgely deserved much credit for her splendid career. It was painful to think how she would ever manage the day she lost her work and was asked to retire in favour of a new-comer.

After I had completed my training period of just over a year, I was disenchanted with paediatrics and decided to move on and look for promotion. Most of all I had decided to make a clean break from Tony. It had been a traumatic, although necessary, decision on my part to extricate myself from our fruitless relationship. I suffered plenty of heart-searching aggravation and tears before I finally resolved my dilemma and could walk happily into a new part of my life.

My final spell on paediatric night duty came at the crescendo of my indecision and despair. I needed time and clarity of thought to work through my feelings and that usually meant having a good cry. I always tried to get to feed a tiny, emaciated Cypriot girl, who was dying of a congenitally malformed gut. It would legitimately take an age to feed her and I could sit in her cubicle cuddling her as she slowly sucked her bottle. Many times she had felt my tears fall on her little head, as I talked her through my problem. The pathetic brown eyes in her sweet bronzed face followed every word as I argued with myself. Her life dragged on, as did my dilemma. Tony and I parted amicably but I decided to ensure a clean break, so moved across London, still within reach of the bright lights.

I'd had a taste of the life as a doctor's partner and decided that I wasn't sure that it was right for me. They work such devilish long hours. Even their off-duty has to be devoted largely to studying for the exams, which are vitally important to secure promotion prospects in their chosen field.

Our relationship had gone on for too long and had drifted into a sexual convenience. Tony became more and more involved in his job and less and less interested in me. He stood to lose most by our break-up. I was the kind of back-up he needed to help in his studies.

I firmly resolved to give medics a wide berth from now on. I'd enjoy playing the field, look around and avoid getting involved again. Susy and I were keen to widen our interests and meet men with jobs different to our own.

In their view , men generally fall into one of two categories. Those under forty see all nurses as a good screw, game for anything and anyone. Men beyond the age of forty tend to view us all through rose-coloured glasses as ministering angels, clones of Florence Nightingale, pure in thought, word and deed.

The plain truth is that nurses represent a cross-section of the female population and come in all shapes, sizes, shades and temperaments. The mere fact that the vast majority enter training at eighteen makes them likely to be male-orientated adolescents, raunchy or otherwise, equivalent to any other teenage student group.

It is also true to say that nurses work hard and are equally likely to want to play hard. There's nothing so hellish as dropping into bed at 3 a.m. after a Saturday night out, only to be woken by the alarm at 7 a.m. Going to work on a still, peaceful Sunday morning, when the traffic is scarce and the pigeons are plentiful, can be the one time when you wish for the normality of a nine to five job.

SEVEN: OBSTRUCTION

Ruth Abbott was a most attractive person, both in her looks and her manner. A tall, handsome woman, with long hair swept up in an elegant style, she exuded a warmth and confidence that you couldn't fail to admire. She was possessed of the kind of wit and charm that is bestowed on but a few, which made everyone comfortable in her presence.

I could predict from the outset that she was going to become one of those popular patients.

It would be crass naïvety to pretend that all patients were *liked* equally. Some were more obviously engaging personalities, more welcome to the weary nurse struggling towards the end of a shift.

Professionals aim to give equal and impartial care to all the people whom they are given to serve. We try to curb favouritism but, with the best will in the world, even nurses fall prey to those human weaknesses that make us veer towards patients who make our lives more manageable and help us over the humps of the day. Ruth would be the one they would chat to in the lull of those last ten minutes before the night nurses took over the ward. Nurses would get revived by a dose of Ruth after being harassed by a dose of Granny Jones. She was plainly therapeutic in that sense and, for her, latching onto other people's problems probably made her own more bearable.

Hospitals weren't alien territory for Ruth and the jargon was within her grasp, which was another attraction in talking freely to her. As a health visitor, she had taken the SRN training, plus an extra qualification, to enable her to work in the community in the preventative side of health care.

Health visitors were commonly thought of as on a par with drain inspectors or nitty Nora nurses, keeping the community germ free. In fact her work was with pregnant mums, pre-school children, the old and the handicapped and a variety of clinic sessions. She loved her work and had been pleased to return to useful and interesting employment when her own daughter had left school. I thought she was a charismatic person, ideally suited for the role of health visitor.

Being a nurse at heart, she felt terribly at ease with hospitals and familiar with the routine. She had no compunction about being admitted, although she wondered how her husband would cope alone, never having been one of the best house husbands. Ruth was always so willing to help out in the ward wherever she could; doing flowers, giving a hand with bedmaking, helping with the teas. With Pauline Cottrell laid up after surgery, Ruth naturally fell into the patient-leader slot. Her practical assistance on the night of Mrs Green's arrest had impressed me and she continued to involve herself, without being interfering or critical.

Ruth didn't take kindly to being incapacitated and useless, which was probably why she'd managed to struggle along for so long with her pressing symptoms. She took an interest in all the people and the activity around her and was generally teeming with plans and ambitions. Even despite not feeling her fittest, it was apparent that she was up to her elbows in life. Many of us identified with this vibrant lady.

Ruth had lots of visitors, from work especially I noticed, and hardly a post round went by without her getting a letter. But Ruth deserved her popularity. She worked hard at being thoughtful to others and caring about *their* needs. The nurses responded to Ruth's delightful ease in communication. She was like a human sponge whom everyone felt, quite naturally, that they could off-load onto – and she loved to be on the receiving end, in with the minutiae of hospital life. I could see how the younger nurses went to her and confided their secrets, but Ruth was so discreet that the information went no further. Not so young, in her late forties, she had mature, yet modern attitudes. She was enough like a mother to give reassurance but enough of a stranger not to cause embarrassment. Her own daughter was on the verge of making her a grandmother and we all shared in the excited anticipation.

All the nurses were drawn to her, myself included. Many snippets of personal news were passed on to Ruth, who acted like a magnet. She made people feel she was interested in them. Amidst a sea of giving, giving, we couldn't resist one line of genuine caring for us.

Staff Nurse Witherden talked about her children and even I found myself discussing work. Ruth Abbott was just like that. She had the capacity to unlock people, to allow them to feel free to talk about themselves. Ruth had been with us for a week, having a battery of investigations, during which time we had all become fond of her. Her poise and demeanour belied the constant nagging symptoms that she was suffering.

Facially, Ruth resembled my own mother and was of a similar age. None of which made it easy when Mr Simpson told us there was nothing he could do for her.

Ruth had developed a marked and persistent jaundice, a yellowing of the skin, which caused an intense irritation. She was also experiencing a nausea, like the morning sickness of pregnancy, except that it wasn't confined to the morning. Lately she had noticed that her faeces were light coloured and greasy-looking, rather than the normal rich brown. She was a textbook case of obstruction somewhere in the biliary system, although it was difficult to pin-point the precise cause. It was possible that something sinister was lurking but she hoped, as did we, that it would turn out to be simple gall-stones, as with Doris. They were comparing notes, Doris being tickled pink to find someone else who looked, as she said, 'like a bleedin' Chinaman'.

The day had come when Ruth was to go to theatre for a laparotomy, an abdominal incision, to positively identify the cause of the trouble. She had been taking the opportunity to rest and, although she never let on, I think she was now feeling pretty rough; tired, sickly, some pain and certainly a marked reduction in her appetite.

That morning coincided with the results of Nurse Sharma's final exams. We all knew they were due but somehow we all maintained a silence along with her. To build up to an event that may not occur would impose a nasty embarrassment on the girl. Kiki kept herself exceptionally busy that morning but did ask to go to first coffee to collect her post.

She came back from coffee clutching a long brown envelope. Her speedy return to the ward said it all. Words weren't necessary. The triumphant glow of success surrounded her. She was fit to burst with excitement.

I had to relieve her of this pent-up jubilation. 'Well?' I inquired, knowing full well by now the answer and also knowing how difficult it is to pronounce those words for the very first time.

'I passed!' She divulged her news with an air of complete and utter amazement.

Then she burst into tears of overwhelming joy and relief. I gave her a hug and a congratulatory pat on the back, which also helped to suppress my choked feeling.

'Of course you did,' I croaked, and patted her again.

We could be seen through the glass surrounding the office. With this signal that all was well, the nurses appeared from every corner of the ward to come and add their good wishes. It was a merciful deliverance for us all. Nothing is worse than the misery of seeing a student suffering after failing her state exam. All her colleagues shoulder some of the burden of her agony and disappointment and the circumstances are embarrassing for everyone. Her sad presence affects the whole ward for a time. Life goes on and the exam comes around again – as does the traumatic waiting period. It isn't the end of the world to fail but it seems so when that awful resit form arrives instead of the pass chit.

The ward routine came to a standstill while the buzz of excitement centred on Kiki Sharma. Doreen posted herself in the ward, as she tended to on any occasion where the nurses gather together: 'You go and enjoy yourself, dear, I'll keep an eye out here.'

Kiki was saying how she had requested to stay on Parker. So here was our new Staff Nurse, who would soon be sporting a stripe on her cap and a black belt, the insignia of her new office.

Normality returned when the theatre sister rang through to ask us to give the pre-med to Mrs Abbott. I thought I'd best do it with one of the juniors, our Kiki would need a while to calm down to boring things like injections.

I noticed Ruth walking up the ward.

'I'm on my way with the pre-med, Ruth. Could you do a last visit to the loo and pop into your gown,' I called.

She signalled an aye-aye captain in acknowledgement.

I prepared the drug in the clinic room, then saw Ruth hovering outside the office door. She knocked quietly and walked in.

'You passed then did you?' she asked Kiki.

After receiving the happy affirmative nod and a huge grin, she grasped and squeezed one of Kiki's hands and kissed her on the cheek. Then from behind her back, Ruth produced a huge envelope and a gift-wrapped box.

We were poised in the clinic room watching this unexpected presentation. A small group of ambulant patients had gathered outside the office and most of those confined to bed had their eyes trained on Kiki.

She was overwhelmed by the lovely congratulations card and started another little weep at the spontaneous gesture. I think she liked the card even more than the pomander, which was the gift.

'I only managed to get a few of the patients to sign in time. Pauline will get the rest while I'm down for the chop. I hope it will be a nice momento for you to look back on and remember this set of patients on the day that you got your SRN,' Ruth explained.

She and Pauline Cottrell had cooked up this winning idea, although I suspected that it was on Ruth's initiative. The patients were delighted to have been given the chance to participate in the nurse's happy and momentous day.

It was so typical of Ruth, to be concerned with someone else's pleasure, when her own fate was held in the balance. With an operation looming, she was still moved to organise a small collection amongst the patients and go down to the hospital shop to choose a suitable card and gift.

Ruth knew how much the importance of those three basic letters meant to any nurse. It was the culmination of three hard years of training and studying but it was also the beginning of a career with endless possibilities.

The meaning attached to that small token was inestimable for the nurse. It would be one special momento that Kiki would treasure with affection. The simple thought was received as warmly as it had been given.

'The day shouldn't be allowed to pass unnoticed. It's such a tremendous occasion, one that every nurse remembers clearly,' Ruth said, dismissing her action lightly, when I asked her about it during her final preparation for theatre.

'Oh, but she was truly thrilled, Ruth. It was the nicest thing that could happen to her today. She hasn't any family here with whom to share her success. And you feel like shouting the result from the roof tops.'

'I know. They are all in Guyana. That was why it was so important that we did something for her,' Ruth continued.

Of course, I should have known. Ruth would have made it her business to find out all about Kiki and this was the very satisfying result of her endeavours.

I gave her the pre-med. and tucked her in to sleep. I had an overwhelming urge to kiss her on the forehead, to let her know that her generosity and kindliness were recognised and appreciated. Still, I resisted, we are not supposed to give vent to our emotions so freely. I squeezed her hand and she replied by squeezing mine. Our touch said it all. I felt involved with Ruth as a person, not as a medical case to be sorted out, but as a real, tangible, lovely individual. She was really somebody and the world could do with more like her. After an hour Kiki took her down to theatre and I watched as the lady went by peacefully on the trolley, cocooned in a pack of blue theatre blankets.

I had a busy morning ahead. In addition to the routine ward work, one of the clinical nurse teachers was bringing a group of introductory students to Parker. They wanted a guided tour around a typical Gartland ward and to help in a basic procedure.

The new nurses were always given an early introduction to the wards and the patients. Their theoretical tuition was given a realistic reinforcement by putting it into practice in a ward situation. There was always a temptation to show them the fascinating, high-powered or unusual aspects of the work and they in turn would always want to run before they could crawl. But at their stage of training, blood pressure recording was a nightmare, bandages a mystery and how to operate the bedpan washer was one of life's major technical difficulties. Washing and feeding patients were as hard for them as removing pleural drains had been for me. I stuck to the simple and informative but omitted the gory and detailed parts; plenty of time for that once they'd grasped the elementary procedures.

I allocated them for a bed bath on Mrs Strange, to be demonstrated by the teacher. Mrs Strange was more than willing to be a guinea-pig and I felt certain she'd keep them entertained with her lively chatter. They would appreciate a sprightly and responsive victim! It would have been unfair, both for the nurses and the patient, to subject an immediately post-op patient to a long-winded discussion surrounding the bed bath procedure.

Mrs Strange was well recovered from her gut operation. Nicely healed, stitches out, then, out of the blue, she developed a DVT. A deep vein thrombosis is a blood clot in a large vein which causes obstruction and pain in the leg. If left untreated, the great danger is that it may become dislodged, travel upwards and through the heart, to settle in one of the vessels which supply blood to the lungs. This is known as a pulmonary embolism and, depending on the size and site of the obstruction, can create anything from minor lung problems to sudden death.

Mrs Strange was crippled by arthritis, which impeded her mobility and this was undoubtedly a contributory factor leading to the stasis of blood in the vein. To watch the dear lady trying to hobble around the ward was agonising. Even using a Zimmer frame to lean on, her progress was slow and deliberating, so stiff and painful were her hips. The joints in her hands were similarly affected, with swollen, shiny, deformed joints, also limiting her fine movements.

Mr Martin liked his DVT's to be on anticoagulant drugs to disperse the clot and insisted on bedrest, to minimise the chances of stray clot fragments travelling in the circulatory system. Ideas differed on this management but we had to follow the instructions of each particular surgeon's regime.

The clinical teacher arrived with her small group of fresh, keen, new students. I remarked that we never saw them so smart and tidy by the time they started full-time on the wards. They giggled obligingly.

'Mrs Strange. Age seventy-five. Laparotomy with resection and anastomosis of colon for diverticuli. Healed. Sutures out. Lately developed a DVT – leg bandage, anti-clogs. – Heparin in I/V bolts every six hours, started oral Warfarin this morning. Bed rest. Needs a bath. Thought she'd be a nice one for you to do. She's quite looking forward to it, a dear old girl, she'll enjoy the audience.' I put the teacher in the picture with a brief resumé of the patient's case details.

'Oh, and she has some *lovely* arthritic joints of the hands. Don't forget to point those out to the girls.' I knew the girls would be agog for any abnormalities to tick off in their books and Mrs Strange could provide a good assortment of lumps and bumps and scars. 'She's badly incapacitated by her stiff hips but very resilient and cheerful with it.'

I took them to meet their patient, who had prepared her wash things at the ready on her bed. I estimated that I had a good hour before I'd be needed to show them around. They followed behind their mentor as she collected all the items needed for the bed bath. What a major task it must seem to them now, yet in two months they'll be doing three a day and thinking nothing of it.

I had to smile to myself when I saw Nurse Littleton pass the small entourage of fledgelings. She pulled her shoulders well back and increased her step along the ward, looking very serious as if to let them know she was on some urgent business. It was an important sight for her, a new set of nurses in the school. This meant she wasn't the most junior nurse in the hospital any more. Oh, happy day.

Opposite Mrs Strange lay Mrs Yates, still in a coma, her condition unchanging day in, day out. Hers was routine care and I thought she may be a patient that I could point out to the visiting group.

From behind her screens came the unmistakably coarse voice of Sandra Dix.

'Oh, hell, she's shit the bed, *again*.'

I shot behind the curtains, feeling ashamed that the junior group opposite might have been witness to this most unprofessional remark.

'Sorry, Sister, I didn't know you were there.'

Precisely. All sweetness and light, to be seen to be doing the right thing in front of Sister. Then all effing and blinding when Sister's back is turned. I despaired of this silly girl.

'But she's got the trots, we cleaned her up last time we turned her.' I raised my eyebrows at the vernacular turn of phrase, which tended to be Sandra's hallmark.

She tried again but it wasn't easy for dozy Sandra. So summoning all her wits, 'Mrs Yates has diarrhoea for the second time this morning. She had it yesterday too. It must be the Complan she's having down the tube.'

No one objected to expletives, we all lapsed now and again, but only between ourselves or jokingly. Never as a derogatory gesture to any patient and certainly not concerning functions over which they had no control. We'd tried all ways to get Sandra to curb her tongue but she was unable to discern these different instances. Sandra, it was true to say, had no concept of professionalism.

I asked them to clean her up again and I'd look into the problem later. It wasn't one that I wanted to embark on with the young students at this juncture. I suspected that the patient might in fact be extremely constipated. Complan is more likely to cause constipation than looseness, as the patient isn't receiving the roughage of a normal diet.

Mrs Strange was left in her bed looking positively cherubic; flushed cheeks and freshly combed, fluffy hair, surrounded by plumped up pillows, *all* covered with clean, white pillow cases. Probably my whole day's supply taken up in that one demonstration. So much for understanding the reality of the constant bane of our life – shortage of linen.

'Good luck, girls,' she waved them on their way and they replied in unison.

The nurses were eager to absorb the atmosphere of the

ward in their short excursion from the false world of the classroom. The more I told them, the more they asked, hanging intently on my words, utterly polite and with their hands clasped regally behind their backs.

Pauline was pleased to demonstrate the beautiful thin scar line around her neck left by her operation. Granny Jones was on her bed having physio. Her stump had been recently bandaged, so I pointed out her amputation, which caused great interest. I kept the girls well away at the end of the bed, not wanting any of them scared silly by our resident comedienne.

'Brand new nurses,' I bellowed down to her, 'still in school, introductory block.' I think even she could appreciate their vulnerability.

I discussed the case of Mrs Yates briefly, making certain I was not at her bedside. This, I explained, was because, although she was unconscious, there was no way of telling exactly what she was able to hear or understand. A fact that I would need to remind Nurse Dix of in a quieter moment.

Mrs Yates was a perfect example of total nursing care. Absolutely everything had to be done for her; washing, feeding, turning, pressure area care, mouth care, eye care, a catheter in her bladder to drain the urine and her bowels opened at will in the bed. Predictably, they loved 'the tubes' and were eagerly awaiting the time when it would be their turn to pass a naso-gastric tube. I used that enthusiasm to return their attention back to the more mundane, although no less important, task of fluid balance charts, showing them the various columns to fill in.

Once they had left the ward, I took Doreen and a suppository tray to get Mrs Yates' bowels sorted out.

'I think she may have constipation with faecal overflow, so I'll try a couple of these to open her bowels,' I told Doreen.

When constipated stools accumulate in the rectum, the bowel behind increases its peristaltic action, waves of muscular contraction, in an effort to shift the obstruction. Liquid faeces behind the mass are able to squeeze around the side of it and dribble out, as what appears to be diarrhoea.

Mrs Yates had been left turned on her side, lying on a

disposable incontinence pad, which was soiled again by liquid faecal matter. I wore a glove, wiped her anus and prepared to insert the glycerin suppositories, which would lubricate the stools.

'Just hold her top leg clear, please, Doreen,' I said while I parted the cheeks of her bottom.

The suppository glided through the outer sphincter, then came to a halt. I couldn't push it any further and it fell out.

I felt inside her back passage. The rectum was chock-a-block full and the internal sphincter distended and poised open, allowing easy entry of my fingers. As I had expected, I encountered a mass of dry, hardened faeces, causing the liquid incontinence.

'Solid as a rock. Looks like she's impacted. I'll have to do a manual removal,' I said to Doreen. She was used to these, having done a few in her time on Parker.

It was as if Mrs Yates' rectum were packed with an immovable piece of lumpy concrete, hard to break up, it was so solidly formed over a period of time. I was hooking and poking with two fingers, shifting a little at a time. Still, every little helps towards relieving the blockage. My wrist was straining from working in such a small area and I was relying on tactile sensation as feedback for my progress. I picked at the mass to clear out as much as I could reach. Before me lay a collection of faecal marbles like stones from the beach.

'I can feel there's more to come but I can't reach it. Plenty up there. With the dried up blockage removed, I can get the suppositories in and now they'll be able to work.'

Then I removed the inco. pad and replaced it with another, in readiness for the deluge of faeces which eventually passed with ease.

'A good job well done.' Doreen praised my efforts.

By no means was it a pleasant job but it was somehow satisfying to see such good results from a small effort. Had she been conscious, her glow of utter relief would have been praise enough.

Ironically, lunches were next on the Parker itinerary. After a good tidy away and a scrub up, I was serving meals; the patients none the wiser to my previous task.

'In one end and out the other,' I smiled at Doreen.

'That's right. That's what it's all about.'

Burrows had collected Ruth back from theatre and I moved the lunch trolley to let them pass. I glanced at the ward clock. She hadn't been in theatre very long.

I left Doreen to start going round with the puddings, when I saw Burrows going into the office, after having settled Ruth.

'Well, what did she have?' I asked as Burrows reached for the Kardex.

'Open and close.'

'Oh, hell, no!'

It was a possibility but no one was seriously prepared to think the worst. Open and close was our surgical expression for a hopeless case.

'Massive tumour of the head of pancreas, riddled with cancer. He did a by-pass to relieve the obstruction. No hope. She's terminal.' Burrows gave a run-down of the explorative operation.

I was shattered. I couldn't believe it of Ruth. Her days were numbered. Ruth was dying.

'Oh damn! Damn! Bloody damn it!'

EIGHT: INITIATION

Wednesday was always a hell of a day. And I loved it. We were so busy with admissions and discharges and a long list for Mr Simpson, many of whom were increasingly being done as day cases. Quantity, as well as quality, of care meant a mass of extra work all round; changing beds, cleaning equipment and a pile of paper work. Each patient, even when a day case, still had notes, observation charts and drug sheets to keep up. Each one still had to be watched carefully, as they had the same chances of post-operative problems. Under any circumstances these are rare but it's that odd abnormality that we have to be alert to; concealed haemorrhage, trapped nerve, the inhalation of vomit. I've always thought it very unfortunate that these rare cases are the ones that hit the headlines and there is never a mention of the thousands of successful operations performed each year.

Bridie and I usually managed to work together. I took the eight to four-thirty shift, to fit in yoga in the evening, and she had the late span. Bridie preferred to do the office work, which was considerable, and I supervised and helped with the ward work. Sleeves rolled up, get stuck in, just like the old days. I enjoyed this opportunity to work with the nurses and to get really close to the patients.

I went down to collect Marjorie Mansfield from theatre. I thought at the time she'd been there for an inordinately long while. She'd had a routine decompression of the median nerve, a release of the nerve which supplies the hand. Her hand was bandaged and elevated on two pillows.

'Was she a day case?' asked the anaesthetist, a slight Indian lady.

I didn't like the sound of 'was'. I nodded.

'Well she isn't any more. She reacted badly to the

anaesthetic and took a long time to wake up. Her colour was poor and blood pressure pretty low. She's all right now but I'll want to keep her in overnight for observation.' She scribbled on the notes and handed them to me.

That little administrative hiccough was handed on to Bridie.

'Great! It's just fine for them, deciding who comes and goes, picking and choosing, it's us poor buggers who do the juggling at this end. Like ruddy musical beds here on a Wednesday,' she said abrasively, and did one of her usual efficiency rattles of papers on the office desk. But I knew she'd get it sorted out – with a scream and a shout.

'You get going now, Helen, it's almost time. Take the others with you.'

I collected my bag and called to the other early duty nurses.

Doris waved a newspaper. 'Do you want the paper, Sister? I'm done with it.'

It was most definitely a night for the bus. My feet were aching and I felt done in. I looked forward to a long hot bath – I'd hoped Susy had turned the immersion on. Yoga would be especially welcome tonight.

That bus stop had a glorious seat, well any seat would have been glorious. It felt heavenly to take the weight off my feet.

'Bloody strikes again!' I said to myself as I opened the paper. 'Why doesn't someone come up with a newspaper designed for happy news?'

I got stuck into a juicy court case, and kept half an eye open for the bus.

A nauseating feeling welled from my stomach. Old Spice. Yuk, Old Spice, the guy sitting next to me reeked of the stuff. It wasn't his fault it made me retch, not the manufacturer's. I was trapped on that seat and thought back to another hectic day in the Cottingham.

George Dennis was a nice patient. But was he big? Sixteen stone in his underpants and with a corporation hanging over them. He was just the image I pictured of the policeman in the song 'The Laughing Policeman'. Ruddy complexion, broken veins on his cheeks, a strawberry nose, tubby on short legs. His hair was sparse, he was fifty, had cancer of the bladder and was a heavy smoker. All things considered he was a poor surgical risk.

I met him during my spell as a first year on '5 surgical'. After that ward, it was surprising that I had got where I was today. That was the nearest I ever came to leaving nursing altogether.

Mr Dennis had a big operation and I looked it up in the surgical tome that lived in the ward office.

Remove bladder and tie off the urethra, which leads to the penis. OK. Transplant the ureters, the two tubes carrying urine from the kidneys, into the bowel. So urine would be passed out of the anus along with faeces.

Dr Sharpe looked over my shoulder. 'Reading up about Mr Dennis, Nurse?'

As a first year, I was still somewhat scared of actually speaking to a doctor. I suppose I still held them in the same kind of awe that lay people do. Mind you I soon learnt that a doctor could be a valuable asset in giving a detailed and precise synopsis in a flash, whereas I could be left picking through a book for ages.

'Does that mean that he will have persistent diarrhoea or faecal incontinence?' I asked, taking advantage of this golden opportunity.

'No, it all settles down in time. He'll experience a bowel motion more frequently and it will be looser than normal.

'It's a difficult one this. With transplant of ureters into the bowel, it has a nice cosmetic result but carries a constant risk of infection travelling up from the bowel to the kidneys,' he continued.

'The alternative is to put the ureters into a loop of cleansed bowel and bring it out onto the skin, like an ileostomy. It's as broad as it's long and not everyone likes the idea of a permanent stoma. He is such a size, I think it would be difficult to manage anyway. He is a surgeon's nightmare!' I really appreciated that succinct explanation from Dr Sharpe.

Mr Dennis was never right after surgery, even though the operation went well. There was too much against him. It's like saying that the sewing was good but the material was rotten. He'd had the routine bowel prep. and was on antibiotic cover but the abdominal wound was poor in healing.

I watched when sister removed the dressing for the first time. The skin was red, inflammed and soggy. It was only the presence of the deep tension sutures that prevented the whole thing from bursting open. The regular skin stitches sat ineffectively trying to appose the two sides of the incision. His lower abdomen was peppered with holes and these wretched sinuses oozed yellowy-green pus, which spilled over the large stomach.

I looked at Sister. Her face gave no hint of emotion. I admired her strength. Mr Dennis was in a poor shape but I realised that he too was searching her face for information. She never once caught my eye, knowing full well how telling such glances can be to the perceptive patient. I admired her tact and discretion and her thoughtful consideration of the patient.

However, even she couldn't pretend that all in the garden was lovely. Mr Dennis felt grim, he had all the symptoms of a generalised infection and was in considerable pain and discomfort.

'Little bit pusy here, Mr Dennis. I'll have to get doctor to have a look,' she told him calmly and smiled as she redressed the wound with a wad of gamgee. This is a thick absorbent pad of wool and gauze, used to dress large, discharging wounds.

'Christ, was that the understatement of the year!' I said to myself. Situation well handled though. I wondered if, deep down, she was feeling as shocked by the sight as I was. Hardly, she's a Sister. End of subject.

Mr Dennis was heavy to nurse and needed a lot of care as he wasn't able to do much for himself. He was getting progressively weaker and his bottom was getting sore from the continual leakage from his bowels. He wasn't able to manage his motions and unless we kept him clean and dry there was every chance that a bed sore would develop. My back ached from turning and helping this heavy patient to sit up. My heart ached to see this cheerful man deteriorate before my eyes.

His chest was ropey. When he did manage to cough, up came viscid, green, infected sputum. Mostly he was too weak to expectorate.

The wound went from bad to worse. It broke down completely and became a gaping hole, smelling more dreadful each day. The nurse splashed after-shave around liberally to try and counteract the foul odour. Poor Mr Dennis, reduced to a delerious mind and a wrecked body, captive in a hospital bed, soaking and drowning in his own discharges.

Mr Dennis wasn't the only patient needing a lot of care on '5 Surg', which specialised in GU, genito-urinary, surgery. Come to think of it, there weren't many who weren't in a bad way.

I'd hit a hot spot. I found out subsequently that all wards tend to go in good and bad phases. All the patients were in a sorry state and the nurses were rushed off their feet. Some were terminal, others had severe infections, several had had strokes, others were incurable. A few tragic cases – or were they the lucky ones? – had been subjected to extensive heroic surgery, with the best intentions aimed at saving life but thereby leaving a mutilated body with the massive task of healing and repair – with varied success.

Added to that were the occasional ones who went dolally after surgery or due to uraemia, where the blood was poisoned by retained waste products. I probably did and saw much more than would usually be experienced by a nurse at that stage of training. It was frightening. I had a lot of responsibility and limited supervision, because all the other nurses were equally harassed and busy.

There wasn't even one patient who could take round the tea-trolley, that stalwart of in-patient assistance. It was all such damned hard work. But worst of all it was depressing, disheartening and soul-destroying. I was too junior to take this bad patch in my stride. I hadn't come into nursing to help people into a tin box and despatch them to the mortuary.

Where were the smiling faces; the grateful thanks; the happy family reunions as relatives collect their loved ones, saved from the jaws of death by yours truly. The destruction was too much too soon, I was near to cracking and jacking the whole thing in.

I used to return to the nurses' home shattered with exhaustion, both mental and physical. It was impossible to unwind, such was the tension of the day. I desperately wanted deep, refreshing sleep but my mind buzzed with the anxieties of the ward. My nights were disturbed and I'd often wake, alert, miming some procedure. Every professional has to come to terms with the realisation that even their best is sometimes not enough. The secret is not to feel defeated by the losses, that is professional suicide.

Men's wards are generally notorious for their absence of flowers and other homely, personal nick-nacks that are always in abundance in their cheery female counterparts. But '5 Surg' was ridiculous, not a pleasant sight on the horizon. Just drips and drains, catheter bags and urine collection bottles. The droning noise of fans and suction pumps, whirring away to collect exudates and discharges. Old men coughing and spitting. Old men groaning. Young men crying.

And the smells! These were all pervading and the worst of all to tolerate.

The ward atmosphere hung heavy with the smell of Hycolin. To my knowledge, '5 Surg.' was the only ward to use it and to this day I've never been able to touch Crème de Menthe, which it closely resembles. It was thick, green, viscid fluid with a characteristic disinfectant smell that got trapped at the back of your throat and clung to your clothes and body. I'd change and bath, yet still my hair carried the hospital message. My boyfriend said I smelt of bedpans. I could taste them too!

Mr Dennis was transferred to the side-room. The end was within sight. We wore masks to do his dressings. The stench was indescribable. I stifled a retch as it reached the back of my throat and mingled with the Hycolin. How much worse it must have for Mr Dennis, surrounded by this atmosphere constantly; at least we could get out. Poor Mr Dennis. The dressings took ages to do and we used masses of gamgee to pack the crater.

I gave him a bed bath and shaved his face. His body was losing weight noticeably and his skin hung in a flabby mess. His eyes were red and dull. I looked at him and tried to make cheerful conversation on general matters. I splashed on the Old Spice in profusion, on his face and chest and arms, and a quick shake into the air. It had been used so much that it too was beginning to get associated with the vile odours.

Mr Dennis grasped my arm and pulled me towards him, whispering in earnest, 'There are bodies under this bed.'

I screamed and screamed inside myself. The collection of hideous experiences and emotions on this ward were summed up in the prophetic words of this dying, delirious man.

As I cleared away the debris from his treatment, in the sluice, I suddenly became a bundle of hysterical laughing and crying all mixed up. It felt lovely. The tension was relieved.

George was dead the next time I went in. He was the first dead person whom I had seen. I was so glad that it was him, we'd become good friends over the weeks and I was pleased for him that his misery and suffering were over. It was a blessing.

At first I thought he was just asleep until I realised that his wheezy, laboured breathing had ceased. For the first time, I had seen him serene, rather than wracked with pain or troubled by delusions. I had expected to feel overwhelmingly sad at my first death but for George I felt relief that his torment was over. I also realised how unrealistically death is depicted in the cinema, especially the horror movies. Corpses don't stare or look frightening, quite the opposite in fact.

I laid him out and was pleased to be involved in this final duty for George. A relief nurse came to help out, a girl whom I knew quite well in the nurses' home. She was more senior but even she was shocked by the state of his body.

We packed masses of cotton wool into his rectum to prevent oozing in transit. The abdominal wound also required extensive packing and securing with sticky plaster.

We helped the porters to lift the corpse into the tin

mortuary trolley, the large shrouded form, wrapped in a sheet labelled for despatch. The lid was shut and a blanket draped over. This was an affectation for the benefit of passing visitors; all hospital personnel knew what was hidden under the blanket.

The porters struggled to get the trolley out of the side-ward, banging into the door, disrespectful of their sombre cargo.

Goodbye George Dennis, I will never forget you. Your life – and your death – didn't pass unnoticed.

The bus came at last and I could get clear of the malodorous Old Spice addict.

The experience with Mr Dennis had been harrowing for me at the time. Having come through it, I found it hard to imagine that I could ever meet with anything quite so distressing. Bearing that in mind, gave me the strength to carry on. It had been my own professional Rubicon.

NINE: ABORTION

One of our additional duties was to provide trained staff cover at evenings and weekends to the ward opposite. If a student were left in charge of Harvey, I had to be on call for emergencies and to check drugs and any blood for transfusion. In similar circumstances, they would reciprocate the favour.

Harvey dealt with the speciality of gynaecology, the treatment of the female reproductive organs. I always welcomed the chance to slip over to renew my acquaintance with the unique, slightly euphoric world of women's disorders. The atmosphere on gynae. wards is universally predictable. A light-hearted jocular feeling of cameraderie, smattered with plenty of references to legitimate sex.

Everyone knows what everyone else is in for; there can be no secret or dispute about the area in need of attention. There are many veiled references attributed to disorders of 'that region' and troubles 'down below'. Gynae. is the arch speciality legion with euphemisms understood by all. The 'front passage' is the polite term for the vagina, with 'I'm losing' referring to vaginal bleeding. Hysterectomy is the removal of the uterus and is generally dismissed with 'I've had it *all* taken away.' Menstrual periods are 'visitors', 'auntie', 'the curse', or just plain 'I'm on'.

Obstetrics is the productive counterpart of gynae. where everyone is in the process of delivering babies. In both obs. and gynae. patients are tremendously supportive of each other by the nature of a very basic, shared suffering. Gaggles of gynae. patients drift easily in reminiscences of their baby days. They manage to retain the most vivid of memories of 'when I had my first' or 'now, the time I had my boy'. Confinements are florid accounts of the pains, the waters, excrutiating enemas, heartless midwives and tails too sore to sit upon.

Gynae. presents total strangers to each other in close proximity, where discussion of their intimate parts is the point of contact. There are no holds barred, absolute freedom of expression and a flow of emotions because you know it will be received by an understanding and sympathetic body of companions who are similarly placed.

Middle-aged and elderly ladies, who one assumes are normally quite reserved about their private life, share in frivolous geniality by alluding to their proposed sexual activity, after hysterectomy or repair. Now 'it's safe', 'there's nothing to worry about', as their uterus falls into the bucket, taking with it the last chances of reproduction and eliminating the need for artificial contraception.

Our consultant used to call a hysterectomy removing the nursery but leaving the playpen. Judging by some of the devastating depressive reactions that followed the operation, the two appeared to complement one another, particularly at a deep emotional level.

Gynae. is the butt of the hospital jokes, favourite with the porters posted to the 'fanny farm'. New nurses are teasingly sent to theatre for a pack of 'fallopian tubes' which are in fact anatomical tubes linking the ovaries to the body of the uterus.

Gynae. is a place with a feel all of its very own, somewhat akin to the happy confidences shared by girls at secondary school behind the lavs discussing their puberty and physical development. For the most part it is a cheerful speciality, rarely dramatic or world-shattering. It ticks over with bread-and-butter surgery, saving a lot of women from considerable on-going chronic misery and the discomfort of heavy bleeding, smelly discharge and prolapsed organs.

Young women are admitted for problems associated with infertility or disorders of early pregnancy. Otherwise the majority of patients are older women, around the time of the menopause, or 'change', in for cold surgery, meaning they are booked in from the waiting list. Time for the ladies to get prepared to come in looking their best. Time for a perm or blue-rinse or to get the roots touched up. Time to get to

Marks and Spencer to be treated to a new dressing gown, only to find that the rest of the ward had the same idea.

Admission to gynae. brings out the best in people and most seem to get buoyed along by the general level of high spirits, which can mean they feel low when recovering at home alone. In hospital, having at last got to 'being seen to' brings relief and they settle in for a good rest, and a good laugh, with people in the same boat.

Nurses also seem to enjoy their allocation on gynae., finding the patients optimistic and responsive, and the tidy subject easy to learn about.

The air is heavy with the scent from potted plants and roses, from generous sprays of perfume and liberal use of toiletries. A vast box of chocolates lies open invitingly at the corner of each bedtable to tempt each passing nurse. There is always an on-going box in Sister's office, drawn from a pile stacked in the cupboard left by grateful patients.

Masses of floral tributes fill the personal area demarcated by the curtains. Those from the very nearest and dearest take pride of place on the locker, others adorn the window sill. Fading and wilting bunches spill out onto the public ward space.

Get-well cards are religiously arranged and re-arranged when they inevitably blow over. These are the trophies of love and affection which need to be displayed prominently. A boutique box of tissues stands by the traditional fruit bowl, with its mandatory bunch of grapes.

On Tuesday evening Janet Morrison had already stayed behind until six o'clock. They'd had a hectic day on Harvey with a long operating list. To crown it all, the last case had started bleeding heavily and had been delayed in the theatre.

Miss Ashton had warned me that a busy evening lay ahead. The Staff Nurse was off sick but she had managed to give them a twilight shift auxiliary to help out. Tuesday was Parker's day free of surgery and my staff were coping with our routine work.

'I'll have to go now, Helen. I phoned Bob to give the kids their tea but he draws the line at bathing the horrors when he's due on night shift. The last case is *still* in theatre.

Penelope Shenley is threatening to abort but the pain has been getting worse and I think it's now inevitable that she'll lose it. The houseman knows, Penny was getting in one hell of a state, so she's had pethidine.

'I've done the evening report as far as possible. It's just post-op. drugs and there are two drips up. Nurse Budhram is in charge. She's into her third year, been with us for a few weeks, so knows her way around. She's a good kid, conscientious, very able but a bit scared of being left in charge. I told her to call you for anything, so I'd be grateful if you'd keep an eye on her.' Sister Morrison gave the verbal handover as she put on her coat, 'Must fly – thanks.'

I popped into Harvey to check if Nurse Budhram needed anything and to let her see that I was willing to avail myself. While it was quiet, I suggested she went for supper, to be back in time to receive the theatre case.

When I returned from my break, I saw the Harvey patient being wheeled back to the ward. She was conscious but had blood up. Another drip to attend to. I accompanied the trolley into the ward and helped to lift and settle the patient into bed. I wrote out her charts and took the first set of observations. The woman looked pale but her pulse rate was steady and she looked relaxed, ready to sleep. That was the ideal after surgical trauma.

I checked the other post-op. patients of the day. One of the hysterectomy ladies was vomiting badly and holding her stitch site.

'I'll get you something to ease the sickness,' I touched her shoulder as a comforting gesture. 'It'll mean an injection,' I added, checking with her prescription sheet for I.M Maxalon.

'*Anything* would be better than this awful, constant retching, Sister. I'm not too good with anaesthetics. I was just the same after I had my appendix out but hoped I'd be better this time.' She rested back on the pillows.

'Shall I sit with her, Sister?' Another patient walked over and offered her services.

The lady indicated that she would be happy for some company and I went off to draw up the drug.

The work on Harvey was constant and unremitting but it was fairly routine stuff for the surgical nurse. Nurse Budhram was in control of the situation and pleased with her own capability but there was no doubting that the patients liked to know there was a Sister at hand.

As I was leaving, there was a call from A & E, a ruptured ectopic gestation was on the way.

'Don't worry, that won't be for some time yet. She'll be going straight to theatre. Your surgical team have had quite a day of it.' I told Nurse Budhram of the new case.

When a pregnancy settles in the fallopian tube, instead of the uterus, it grows for about eight weeks until the whole tube gets distended and eventually ruptures. This constitutes a surgical emergency, with internal bleeding, and needs urgent attention.

'It'll probably mean another blood drip. Still, get everything ready to hand over to the night staff!' I tried to reassure the student that she would, indeed, survive her shift.

I returned to Parker to check that my staff were managing, when the twilight auxiliary was sent back to collect me.

'The miscarriage lady is getting worse.' She automatically avoided saying 'abortion' and used the euphemism of miscarriage instead.

It is a common mistake by lay people to assume that the term 'abortion' infers criminal interference or that the woman doesn't want the child, and the word has developed unsavoury implications. By contrast 'miscarriage' is used when a wanted baby is lost by natural means. In fact 'abortion' is a standard medical word meaning the loss of the products of conception before the twenty-eighth week of pregnancy for any reason, whether by natural causes, interference or medical termination. Because of the general misunderstanding of this knowledge, nurses tend to go along with the use of miscarriage, rather than risk hurting or offending patients.

It was the usual sad story for Penny. Desperate for a baby, she took a long time to conceive, then, just as she was getting confident with the pregnancy and used to the idea of having a child, the troubles began to start.

At twelve weeks, a recognisably dangerous time when the placenta takes over as the supporting organ of the foetus, some slight brown vaginal loss was suggestive of a threatened spontaneous abortion. It was hoped that bedrest and hefty sedation would enable the pregnancy to settle down and continue to term. But she wasn't to be one of the lucky ones.

When I first saw her, Penelope was frankly distressed. Blanched in the face, tense and perspiring with the pain. She alternated between holding onto the bedrail behind, then clutching at her belly and folding up in agony. The spasmodic nature of the pains made her catch her breath and hold herself taut. Tears welled up in her eyes, as she realised the implications behind the surge of stomach ache.

'It's getting really bad now,' she said to me falteringly.

'Cramps? Spasms? Rhythmic?' I enquired.

'Like period pain but much, much worse,' she rolled about the bed, as the mini-labour pains enveloped her whole existence.

I screened the bed from prying, inquisitive eyes.

I checked the vaginal pad, which was held in place by her bikini pants. Fresh blood and plenty of it, some congealed into clots. A long stringy clot hung from her vulva, marking the outlet for the abortion. In her locker was a disposal bag overflowing with her collection of recently soaked pads, saved to give some indication as to the quantity of her blood loss. The flow was definitely increasing and rejection of her uterine contents almost certainly was established.

It seemed only fair to warn her that she would soon abort. Her anxiety would only be increased if she didn't know what was happening inside her body.

'I'm pretty certain that you're going to pass it all soon. Then it will be all over.'

I took her flannel and rinsed it under the tap to give her a cool, refreshing face wipe. From behind the screens I called Nurse Budhram to get an injection of ergometrine prepared and handed through the prescription chart to her.

Penny was in severe pain, which must have been exacerbated by her distraught emotions. I was at a loss for words. What can you possibly offer to someone to comfort them through the mental agony of losing a much-wanted child? Any attempt would be an intrusion into her personal wrestle with torment. I stayed at her side, hoping my presence would be a welcomed comfort and support.

I had sat with labouring women during my obstetric secondment. It was then that I realised it wasn't called 'labour' for nothing. My God, how they suffered. It was truly astounding to see their massive stomachs tighten and change shape with each successive contraction. But between the excrutiating pains they were relieved and happy in the knowledge that a wonderful, longed-for baby would be theirs at the end. That goal seemed to sustain them through the hell of it all. They were encouraged to work hard in anticipation of the result. Each pain was one less towards the end of nine months of waiting and wondering.

But Penny had none of that; there was nothing to look forward to but an empty void of heart-ache. She was beside herself with the agony, compounded by her misery and disappointment.

From the relative silence of the ward, I heard the rapid clip-clop of a pair of mules on the wooden floor.

'What's all the racket about?' I heard the voice of a young woman behind the curtains.

'Ssh, she's losing the baby,' the auxiliary whispered.

'Lucky thing, wish I could drop mine that easy. I've got to go to theatre to clear mine away,' she remarked.

She may have been interpreted as being a heartless bitch but, more likely, she had made that all too common mistake of believing that the screens blocked out sound as well as vision.

I heard the auxiliary shoo her away angrily. The auxiliary was an older lady who didn't come from the era of abortion on demand and the easy scraping away of mistakes. Hers was one of angry fathers over daughters who 'got themselves into trouble' and young boys who spent the rest of their lives looking their error in the eye.

I guessed the auxiliary would be disgusted and contemptuous of the girls who casually came in for planned termination of pregnancy; horribly offended by their indifference to the operation which would dispose of an unwanted foetus.

For a nurse, it wasn't always easy to hide one's own feelings on such emotive issues and this was one of the hardest things to come to terms with in retaining one's professionalism.

Penny couldn't help but overhear the casual, unthinking remark. She turned and sobbed into the pillows, her tears flowing uncontrollably. I held her hand but the damage had been done.

This small aside highlighted the cruel irony of gynae. Here girls lie side by side, the unfertile and the overfertile, one desperate to have a baby, the other desperate not to. Both suffer similar severe anguish but for totally opposite reasons.

Penny asked for a bedpan, urgently, as she clutched at the pad between her legs. She could feel the seepage of blood.

I helped her on and let her rest on my shoulders. As I removed the pad, everything came away. A gush of fresh blood and clots, like pieces of liver, slithered into the pan. Amidst this residue lay the remnants of her baby, wrenched from the safety of her womb. She was having difficulty balancing on the pan, her legs were tense and the muscles trembling. She turned away to avoid seeing the discharge in front of her.

I called out for a pack of sterile bunnies, the term for sanitary towels which seems to be used exclusively in hospitals. Nurse Budhram returned with them and I told her to give the charged syringe of ergometrine into Penny's buttock. This drug is given to help the uterus contract, so as to completely expel the products of conception; the foetus, placenta and membranes.

The bedpan was covered and gingerly removed, while I helped her pack a couple of sterile towels into some clean knickers. I whispered to nurse to leave the pan in the sluice, covered and labelled for doctor to see later.

I tucked Penny back into a reclining position and checked her pulse and blood pressure, which were fine. The blood loss looked more serious than it was.

'You'll feel better now, try to sleep.' Already she looked

more calm. Free of the distress and discomfort, both of the pain and the uncertainty of the outcome, she was able to rest.

'Doctor will be in to see you later,' I added, but refrained from telling her that she would probably need to go to theatre tomorrow for an EUA & D & C. She'd had enough for one day.

An Examination Under Anaesthetic is usually done following a spontaneous abortion, if there is any doubt that any products of the pregnancy have been retained. It is to ensure that the uterus is perfectly clean and empty, as any slight piece of tissue remaining can cause continued bleeding and also set up a site for infection. The cervix is dilated widely open to allow the entrance of an instrument called a curette, which is like a sharp-edged spoon. It scrapes around the lining of the womb, so the procedure is called a Dilatation and Curettage, or in common usage it is refered to as a 'scrape'.

I drew the curtains back sufficiently so that she could be seen by us, but left enough to signal to other patients that she wanted privacy. They tactfully kept away from her bed at this delicate time.

Nurse Budhram was busily checking the post-ops, it was a constant round of taking observations in this initial period after they had returned from surgery. She also made sure that the blood drips were maintained at the correct flow, they can be temperamental at the best of times.

The lady with nausea had settled.

At the far end of the ward, I noticed a lady in a cerise quilted dressing-gown having a quiet cry to herself sitting on the bed.

'Och, dinna mind aboot ma greetin, Sister. I canna help it,' she answered in a broad Scottish accent when I went to her.

The lady reached for a tissue. 'But ahm that affronted, Sister, ahv wet the bed again.' She was so upset at soiling the drawsheet on top of the bed and also her nightie. She was profusely apologetic for causing extra work, having seen how frantic the ward had been all day.

It was easy to understand why she was so disconcerted. She felt angry and ashamed for having wet the bed but more than that, she was disappointed with what she thought was a set back.

She had been making a good recovery after having had a vaginal hysterectomy in the previous week. She was glad not to have had an abdominal wound to contend with, as the uterus had been removed through the vaginal opening. The operation had been needed to remove the uterus which had prolapsed and was protruding out of her body, down through the vulva.

Bladder problems had been a symptom of the pre-operative condition. There had been that uncomfortable feeling of 'something slipping out' from between her legs and the pressure had made it difficult to hold her urine.

She was then naturally disheartened when the incontinence returned, after she had been doing so well. As far as I could remember from my gynae. lectures, a slight incontinence was a likely minor problem after this operation, due to irritation of the urethra or laxity of the perineal muscles. I did my best to assure her that it could be cleared up and that the operation had not been a failure. I suppose she was wondering if it had not all been a mistake to go through the surgery if she was going to be no better off afterwards. It was a natural thought in the circumstances.

'I'll get you some more bunnies, that'll save you wetting your night things. Don't be afraid to use them generously and do remember to change them as soon as they get soiled. I'll report it and doctor will see you tomorow. Maybe you have a slight urinary infection or need a bit of physio to get those tail muscles tightened. It'll clear up, I'm sure.'

'Ahm awfy sorry for the trouble,' she repeated apologetically yet again, 'the wee lassies have been on the go a' the day, such a shame.'

'Don't you worry now. They are here for your benefit too.' I know how difficult it can be for patients who are considerate to the nurses and don't want to add to the burden of pressure by mentioning their minor irritations, which appear so trivial in comparison to other seemingly more important activities.

This lady had obviously suffered in silence, then cracked.

What a pity she had brooded for so long and bottled it up, so as to get into a state. I daresay she was still feeling physically run down and emotionally delicate following the operation.

The night staff were coming on duty. They looked so fresh and tidy, compared to the exhausted day staff with grubby, crumpled dresses and hair escaping from kirby grips.

I passed on my few messages to Nurse Budhram and wrote them in the Kardex, before heading back to do my own handover on Parker.

However, I couldn't resist a peek into Penny's bedpan, as I was sure neither would any other nurse on Harvey that night.

A tiny but perceptible human form was evident amongst the now congealed debris.

For Penny it was time to start thinking of conceiving all over again and for the doctors to start making sure this time she would keep her pregnancy. She would have to mourn the loss of this little one and, in time, would become reconciled to the disappointment. I wonder if she would ever come to appreciate that this might have been nature's way of discarding a defect. Probably she could not completely believe that until the day when she held her own healthy new-born baby in her arms.

TEN: OPERATION

Less than six weeks later, I was a patient in Harvey. I'd developed a cervical erosion and vulval warts, innocuous but irritating minor gynae. complaints.

I was suffering from a persistent and offensive vaginal odour and heavy discharge. I was washing and washing, squirting and spraying, all to no avail. No manufactured product could dispel it.

I took myself to the gynae. consultant when there seemed no chance that the condition would recover spontaneously, whatever it was.

After taking a routine history and details about my menstrual cycle and contraception, his clinic nurse took me through to the couch for examination. OPD was a real old shambles of a department, poky and overcrowded. I could hear the goings-on in the next cubicle, so I presumed they would be able to tune in on my script.

I think the clinic nurse was the consultant's regular assistant, probably been in OPD since the year dot and clung vociferously to doing the same sessions each week. Still it wasn't a bad thing to have continuity and it probably speeded the clinic up with her knowing the routine well.

She checked that I had recently emptied my bladder, with that splendid euphemism of 'spending a penny', which never gets decimalised or is ever subject to inflation.

Then her list of instructions tumbled into one another like a well worn phrase. 'Pants off and lie down. Legs up – heels together – knees apart.'

She held a blanket at the ready to cover my ungainly posture, while I deciphered the order of movements.

The doctor passed a cold, rigid speculum into my vagina, in order to examine the cervix. In her ritualistic fashion, the nurse aimed the angle-poise lamp at my private parts to give him a clear view, then she stood at the ready with the articles she knew he would next be requiring.

I could see how horrifyingly embarrassing it can be for women subjected to internal examinations. Such a bold intrusion on the sexual organs, not even equated in intercourse. Legs akimbo and being searched around by a strange operator; the patient not knowing where to look, where to put her hands or what to think about. I searched the ceiling for some adequate distraction and concentrated on the slats of the roof. The nurse might have done better by reassuring this patient but my immediate feelings were for those less used to such intimidating situations.

In all honesty I wasn't too bothered. Having seen it all from the other end of the couch, my personal assurance was that he was poking at lower ends all day and, although to me, mine was special, to him it was another faulty organ in need of repair. In my present revolting state, I was feeling more pity for him on the receiving end. But, by the same token, I knew he wouldn't take it personally either.

He foraged around inside and took several smears and swabs. None of this was painful, as the cervix is insensitive, I was only aware of movement deep in my pelvis.

After the examination, the gynae. man explained how he had detected an erosion, a rough patch, on the cervix, which could be simply cleared up by cauterisation. The thought of a seering hot instrument burning at my innards gave me an instant picture of being branded with an iron. He would also burn off the tiny warts which were sitting like tiny pin heads around my vulva.

I was pleased to be getting the problem seen to and, being a staff member, it was to be soon. It was sensible to keep the workers fit and healthy and back to gainful employment quickly. Minor problems for the general public are often put aside and overshadowed in favour of major illness and immediate casualties but, for the person involved, a nagging, irritating little trouble can become a tribulation if left for long.

All these years I'd been taking people down to theatre,

getting them prepared and telling them not to worry. Now it was my turn to see what it was like for myself. This was my first time under the knife.

I knew from working in gynae. theatre that patients have their legs put up in lithotomy stirrups, to enable the surgeon to get a clear view of the perineum, that whole area which sweeps between the legs. It is a position akin to lying on your back with your legs bent and feet up the wall. I remembered the large weighted speculum which stretched the vagina and let the surgeon get to his place of work. However, I didn't feel anxious about anything, I was content that the general anaesthetic would make me oblivious to any pain or embarrassment.

I was admitted to Harvey, into one of their side-rooms, which was something of a privilege as a member of staff. But I wasn't keen on being cooped up, away from the action, so I spent a lot of time out in the general ward and down in the day room with the other patients. As I had no one at home to keep an eye on me, the consultant had kindly suggested that I stay in for three days, longer than would normally be necessary.

Janet Morrison left me a shave tray and one of the new-fangled disposable razors.

'Snip away most of it with scissors, then shave as much as you can, I'll be back to check it,' she instructed.

I sought out the privacy of the bathroom to shave the hair from my pubis. I was like a contortionist, trying to see what I was doing, yet keeping my head clear to retain a good light on the area.

The finished result felt peculiar; cool, draughty and empty. In the long bathroom mirror, I looked like one of those Greek statues of nubile girls. It had been a long time since puberty, when I had last seen my naked crotch. The absent triangle of pubic hair seemed like a lost article of clothing. I'd shaved women before, but only when I looked down at myself, did the impact of the strangeness drive home.

Janet had turned me on my side with knees bent up, as she checked my handiwork, back on the bed.

'Our man is a real stickler for skin preps.,' she said,

speaking to my rear end! 'I've known him send down from theatre for a ward nurse, if he's been dissatisfied with a shave. I make sure it doesn't happen if I'm here, we know his funny little ways too well, but it's awkward when I'm on leave.'

I felt a tickling as she removed the last few stray hairs.

'There. Clean as a whistle. That should suit his Lordship.' And tapped me lightly on the bottom to let me know she had finished.

'It's lovely now, it's when they start to grow again, it feels horribly bristly. I had it with both my kids.'

Doreen popped in to see me on her way off-duty that evening to wish me good luck for tomorrow. She had a bunch of garden flowers that she'd brought from home.

'You're a bit premature, Doreen,' I said. although I was thrilled that she'd been so thoughtful.

'I do hate to see an empty side-room. It looks so depressing.'

One single blue delphinium stood out from an otherwise perfect bunch of red and white carnations.

'That was Burrows' idea,' Doreen said, as she noticed my inquiring look at the stray member. 'She insisted. Pinched it from a patient's vase. You musn't have red and white alone together, it's a bad omen, symbolises death, so she says. She's always mucking up the sprays of flowers, you know how superstitious she is. Then she says, if we have one death it goes in threes. Mind you, on that, she's usually right.'

Doreen and I naturally talked about Parker and she couldn't help giving me a progress report on pertinent patients.

'Are you going to have a DNC?' she asked, being a bit vague on gynae. matters.

'No,' I laughed, 'I'm not having a D 'nd C.' This was an interesting instance where even the abbreviations get distorted. Jargon is only good as long as the speaker and the listener understand the shortcuts.

'I sounds horrid but they are going to cauterise my cervix,' I explained.

'Nasty,' was her succinct comment.

Before leaving, Doreen collected a vase from the sluice and

arranged her carnations, leaving the solitary blue flower in their number. Even she wasn't taking any chances. And I was glad.

I watched TV in the day room and savoured my evening drink, knowing it would be the last I would be allowed until after the operation. The ladies for tomorrow's list gathered in a significant group to mull over their fate. They identified with one another, a kind of emotional joining of arms in the face of adversity.

As a nurse, I was given a lot of details of their conditions and was surprised at how little most of them knew about their own bodies. All the more reason why nurses should be painstaking in their explanations – and doctors too – but it was harder to convince them.

Two ladies were in for 'scrapes', both giving explicit accounts of their 'flooding'. They were set in competition for who'd lost the most blood, for how many days a month and who'd kept the sanitary towel industry in business. Listening to their boastful accounts, they should have been exsanguinated but looked in fine fettle to me.

Two others were down for hysterectomy. Mrs Peters was subdued. Hers was to be a Wertheim type of hysterectomy, radical and extensive excision of all the organs of reproduction and the supporting pelvic tissue. It was a necessary operation which would hopefully prevent the spread of the cancer in her cervix but she wasn't looking forward to this major operation. I didn't envy Mrs Peters.

The night nurses were very sweet and popped into my room for a chat. One was a regular Staff Nurse who did a couple of nights to supplement the family income, the other was a student. Both seemed to enjoy having a staff member as a patient.

I was pleased to see that they didn't assume that I had complied with the pre-op routine; they were particular to remind me to drink no more after midnight. A 'Nil By Mouth' notice was hung above my bed. Their thoroughness was reassuring.

They offered me night sedation but I thought it unnecessary, as I never had any difficulty sleeping in a strange bed. I'd been accustomed to so many different nurses' homes and flats; some in the country and those on the main road, always with the din of communal life around. On periods of night duty I'd always managed to sleep soundly during the day. In fact at Cottingham, it became quite a joke, as I was the only nurse never recorded late for night duty due to oversleeping in the daytime!

Put me on a clothes' line and I could sleep happily. Of course it was easy to see why patients often did have restless nights, disturbed by a general hubbub of activity in a ward of ill patients.

The night nurses woke me at the usually horrendous early hour to take the statutory morning temperature. I thought it a bit unnecessary to disturb me, especially as I wasn't allowed tea, being starved to ensure an empty stomach prior to the anaesthetic.

The tea trolley rattled by and I looked longingly. How I missed that early coffee that was my habit while getting washed and dressed. My mouth was refreshed after a teeth clean and I crept back to bed.

That morning Sister Morrison conducted the final check prior to my going to theatre. It is a customary courtesy for the most senior nurse on the ward to attend to any staff patients when possible.

She checked the namelet on my wrist against the details on my case-notes.

'Right, countdown. Any hairgrips, jewellery, rings, ear-rings?' I handed her my gold choker. I'd meant to leave it in the flat but it slipped my mind, as I never usually take it off. She put it in a labelled envelope to lock safely away.

'False teeth? No. Dental plate? No. False legs, wigs, eyes – any contact lenses? No. Nothing to eat or drink since last night? OK. P.U'd (passed urine). Oh, and nails.' She looked to see my nails were free of any coloured polish.

Patients often get dolled up expressly for their big visit to the theatre and are very disappointed when asked to remove nail varnish. The nail beds are an important indicator for the anaesthetist that the circulation is adequate.

'Yes. Fine. It's your first time for GA isn't it? Are you nervous?' she asked me.

'No, not at all. I'll be so pleased to get this mess cleared up. I'm dying to sample the Omnopon, I've given so many pre-meds and watched them all go glassy eyed and cosy,' I said as I put on my op. gown.

Janet Morrison tied the strings at the back of the unflattering garment and I felt all breezy and unprotected. I knew now why people tended to hold them self-consciously folded across behind. The action is instinctive. Those, that is, who put the gown on the right way round in the first place. There are always a few who would tie them at the front, leaving even more exposed and breezy! Mind you, that was the fault of the nurse for not making it clearly understood.

My pre-op portrait was completed by a voluminous paper mop-cap.

The jab in my buttock wasn't nice but it was a quick sting over in a trice.

'No more getting out of bed,' she reminded me. 'Here's the bell. You may not think that the drug is doing anything but, believe me, if you stood up you'd take a tumble.' She pulled down the blind and left me in peace.

I settled with a women's magazine, thinking this was a useful opportunity to catch up on some general reading. Before long my head was feeling light and muzzy, in contrast to my limbs which were heavy. The atropine was also taking effect, as my eyes couldn't focus and my mouth was exceedingly dry. I snuggled under the bedclothes, relaxed and comfortable, with no thought of the forthcoming ordeal.

The next thing I knew was Janet calling me. Was that an hour up already? Must be. I couldn't focus on her face but recognised her voice clearly. My hearing suffered no distortion, it is the last sense to go in unconsciousness and the first to return.

A trolley was alongside the bed and I was all set to climb on. My legs were like lead and my co-ordination was poor. Janet helped me over, while the porter steadied the trolley. She discreetly kept my bottom end covered.

For the first time, I was viewing Gartland Gen. from the supine position, lying flat on my back. Everything looked hazy but I knew the route. From the collection of noises, I picked out the voice of Nurse Budhram and remarked with a slurred voice that she was still on the ward. My voiced trailed off.

We turned into the corridor and it was a peculiar feeling to be passively guided by someone else's hands. The windows flashed by. The ceiling was high and slatted. It had long neon lights held by chains.

We made a noisy entrance through the heavy rubber doors which marked the demarcation of the theatre suite. They transferred me to a theatre trolley, which didn't get dirty from traipsing all over the hospital. I felt the poles being pushed into the pockets along the canvas and was asked to raise my arms out of the way.

Janet stayed with me. I knew she had that responsibility until the anaesthetist relieved her of the duty.

'Good morning. Helen Davies, is that right?' He made doubly certain that I was the correct patient. I gave a drowsy affirmative and heard Janet whisper that I was 'Sister Davies'.

He asked me where I worked, as he was doing his final check of the anaesthetic machine and drugs.

'Of course. I've seen you on Parker.' He peered closely at my face. A theatre cap, which covers all the hair, provides a perfect disguise.

The anaesthetic nurse took over from Janet, who wished me good luck and said, 'See you later.' I'm sure all nurses say exactly the same thing when they deliver all their patients for surgery.

The anaesthetist took my hand and patted the back of it a few times to encourage a suitable vein to rise. He gave adequate warning and I felt a slight tingle as the butterfly needle glided through the skin of my hand. This fine bore needle with side wings remains attached to the skin, in situ in the vein, to facilitate the introduction of any drugs or infusions which may be required during the operation.

He held a syringe of Pentothal, the anaesthetic agent, poised by my hand.

'Helen, you will be going off to sleep now, I'd like you to start counting,' he instructed.

I wanted to see if I could get nearer to ten than most patients I'd witnessed going under.

'One, two three . . . ugh, I've got a nasty taste of onions in my mou . . .'

'It's all over, wake up now, Helen. Take the tube out.' I heard Janet Morrison clearly and opened my eyes to see her leaning over me.

I tried to say, 'Are you sure I've been done,' but I gagged on the rubber airway down my throat.

'Take it out,' she repeated.

It is the safest policy to wait until a patient removes their own airway. Only then can you be sure they are fully conscious and able to obey instructions, and to know where they are and what they are doing, so no longer in need of the device to keep the throat patent.

Pushing with my tongue, I partially dislodged it, then pulled it out and handed it to Janet.

The anaesthetist came to see me and gave the OK for me to go back to the ward. I slumbered on the return journey, aware of the rattling of the trolley and the swaying movements as we went a little too speedily around the corners.

Two porters lifted me into bed on the canvas, made rigid between the two wooden poles. They pulled out the poles, then I was rolled over as they retrieved the canvas. I felt a pad at my vulva and automatically reached down to keep it pressed close.

After routine observations had been completed and Janet had looked at the perineal pad, I fell into a natural sleep. I was conscious of their subsequent checks but they were not sufficient to disturb me.

It was the afternoon before I woke again. And I was parched. It had been well over twelve hours since any fluid had passed my lips. I couldn't spit sixpence.

Janet came in to see me and started me on sips of water which I tolerated.

'Feel OK? Do you want to try the loo?' It is routine that every patient who has had a GA is accompanied on their first trip out of bed.

My legs felt floppy and slightly achy, especially around the hips and knees.

'That's being up in lith. It plays havoc with the joints in your legs and you discover muscles you never knew you had!' Janet explained.

She helped me on with a pair of pants, to keep the perineal pad in place. I guessed I'd have to be resigned to going back to the dreadful old-fashioned belt and loop sanitary towels for a while – 'jam-rags' as our horrible male adolescent contemporaries used to call them at school.

I steadied myself on Janet and was fine once I got firmly on my feet. My head was pounding away, probably a combination of starvation, anaesthetic and too much sleep. A couple of aspirin and tea and toast would put that right.

I sat on the toilet, taking note of the slight bloody-browny discharge on the pad, of which I knew they'd be inquiring later.

'Jees ... us!' I gasped as the acid urine flowed over my vulva, stinging the open wounds left by the cauterisation of the warts. My jaws clenched tight and my eyes were held firmly closed, waiting for the smarting to pass.

Janet commiserated with me. 'Sorry, I should have warned you. You will find weeing is agony until those sore patches heal over. Try having a couple of wetted tissues at the ready, to wipe yourself quickly afterwards. Sorry also that we haven't got a bidet. It is on order – high priority – you know the kind of thing, sometime, never. Administrators get secretaries while the patients wait and suffer, it's all wrong.'

When I was feeling stronger, I took a mirror to see the cause of the discomfort, a cluster of tiny reddy-white raw patches, like ulcers. It made me wince just to look at them.

The pain on micturition continued for sometime afterwards and the pad came in useful as a comfortable soft cushion for the area. Discharge from the cervix also carried on for a short spell, browny but inoffensive, thank heaven.

I felt an awful fraud but enjoyed my few restful days on Harvey, being on the receiving end of my profession. It amused me to see how particular were the students when doing some procedure for me. Things were really done 'by the Book', not one of them wanted to be caught out taking the short-cuts which we all inevitably use at some time.

Doreen kept popping across, as did Burrows on several

occasions. Bridie made one fleeting visit, at the end of her lunchbreak. She hurried in and didn't even bother to sit down and talk. I had the distinct impression that passing the time of day with pleasantries for visiting the sick was not her forté. She seemed profoundly uncomfortable and looked pleased when her duty call was over. We were neither of us very good away from the common ground on which we met in connection with our mutual work.

I also received a visit from the Senior Nursing Officer, quite an honour by all accounts from Janet. But I think it was probably a statutory courtesy for her to visit any staff who were hospitalised at Gartland.

She was a dry old stick, not the most exhilarating of visitors that one could wish for. It was quite an unnerving switch of roles, me in the chair and her inquiring politely after my health. Janet stood obediently beside the SNO, who then felt obliged to do a quick ward round and talk to the other patients, as she was in Harvey.

The SNO held roughly the same position as what had previously been that of Matron. The changed structure of the nursing hierarchy after the Salmon report killed off that supreme and revered figurehead. It was a pity that no one, neither staff nor patients, ever managed to treat the SNO with the same affection, if any at all.

It didn't have the same ring as Matron or the historical backing that made her the kingpin of any nursing set-up. Matron was identifiable, usually by the grandest uniform and the largest cap, recognised and accepted for her fortitude. Here was the crusty hard-baked exterior, wrapped around a kindly, compassionate, but hard to get at, centre, which leaked out only on heartbroken nurses or distraught patients. Somehow she was a comfortable figure, head of the hospital, head of the nurses, all knowing, all seeing, finger on the pulse. But the SNO, in mufti, was dismissed as a paper-pushing administrator, detached from the reality of ward work. Although she had been through nurse training and risen through the grades to the top of the tree, her immediate contact with the nurses was fairly limited, she expected her Nursing Officers to keep her informed. Certainly I'd only met her at interview.

Susy managed to get in to see me one afternoon in between clients. Like many visitors, she was more interested in everyone else on the ward, she already knew the details of my insides. I was old news. Mrs Peters wasn't.

'God she's all wired up,' Susy muttered as we passed her bed. 'Drip, catheter, bed cradle – she's pale too, what's she had?'

'You'd be pale too. She's had a Wertheim's and that's no joke, getting on all right though. She's in the right frame of mind to get better.'

'I know what you mean, for some it's just too much trouble to recover. I hope you won't be like that,' she said in her serious voice.

'Hardly! I've only had a piddling little operation. Although at the moment "piddling" is the greatest problem of all.' And I explained to her.

It is really necessary to be a patient on gynae. to sample the full impact of the *esprit de corps*. No one is left for too long without a word of encouragement from a neighbouring patient. Fruit, chocolates, tissues and toiletries assume an almost communal ownership, anyone can ask to borrow anything and the donor is always very happy to be in a position to lend. New patients admitted who have forgotten bits and pieces are taken unawares of what they might need but there is always someone willing to share; newspapers, mags, writing paper, a pen, money for the phone, biscuits, a spoonful of *proper* coffee. Gynae. is the fount of female benevolence.

Ladies at an early stage of ambulation staggered along at a steady pace, holding onto the ends of beds or the occasional arm offered to them. I christened it the 'Gynae. Creep'. With pain in their pinny, a pad in their perineum and totally unsuitable fashion slippers, they shuffled up and down the ward. Along the way they were encouraged by those besides their beds or by nurses racing past. These patients would stop to pass the time of day as they rested by the bedbound, who were longing even to be joining in with that limited activity. There was usually someone who would offer them congratulations on achieving their final destination of the loo at one end or the day room at the other. It is all inconsequential chit-chat, but in hospital, everyone gets their share of being noticed. Patients were monitoring their progress by comparing themselves with similar cases. It was acceptable if a contemporary had 'lost' (had bled) for a while or had had urinary problems, sickness or felt unduly tired. The staff were consulted first but they always made a double check with other patients, as a kind of insurance. I even did it myself as I couldn't believe I should be wanting to sleep so much. Oh, yes, they all confirmed that a GA takes it out of you. And I felt better for knowing I wasn't being plain lazy or that anyone else thought I was.

The two D & C ladies were up and about, nicely settled in the day room, to make the best of their short admission. With the flooding problem cleared up they were now vying for championship over the bowels. One was positively euphoric that she had 'been'. Both were sitting cosily, hogging the footstools which would have been better used for patients having had major abdominal surgery. No doubt Sister Morrison would sort things out if needs be, I had to remember I was a patient now.

When I came to leave, I surprised myself by leaving a box of chocolates like everyone else does. It is after all the easiest thing for the staff to share, unless one nurse is to be singled out.

The gynae. consultant told me that all had gone well and discharged me. I was to have an out-patient appointment to see him again and no sexual relations until then. That wasn't going to be difficult.

I said goodbye to Mrs Peters and mentioned that I'd come across to see her from over the way. I knew she didn't have many visitors and it's a long day without contact from the outside world. She was sitting out of bed looking better than ever and a lot easier now the drip had gone.

She had received a card from an old friend who had promised to come and visit. 'Take a look, Helen. Isn't it smashing?' She gave it to me.

It was the one which I had seen so many times as a nurse, one that cheered patients tremendously, it was such a personal and timely message.

'Good luck. Today is the first day of the rest of your life.'

ELEVEN: REJECTION

Margaret Donovan, *Miss* Margaret Donovan, made a poor adjustment to her period of hospitalisation. She was an intensely fastidious and pernickety woman, almost to the point of being obsessional in her behaviour.

I imagined her to be the kind of person who loathed to visit public lavatories, preferring to burst her bladder than be reviled by such an unsavoury experience. No doubt restaurants were also viewed as dubious places, because of the behind the scenes, clandestine preparations. Miss Donovan was a napkin-with-tea lady, bath each morning, two pairs of knickers a day girl and lights out sharp at ten. Her life was so fixed by her rigid routine that having to fit into a new pattern imposed by the host hospital was almost intolerable.

Miss Donovan had held the esteemed position as headmistress of Gartland Junior School for as long as anyone cared to remember. From the safe and familiar teaching world, in which she felt secure, she had been thrust into the alien institution of medicine. She was clearly taken aback by the strange jargon, the special routines and the disruption of her personal programmed existence.

Coming into hospital is a stressful experience for anyone and is compounded by anxiety over their illness and its outcome and possibly worries about family left at home. No one comes in from pure choice, all are eager to get well and go home, but most manage to make the best of the occasion or even enjoy their time in hospital. All patients suffer from some degree of 'culture shock' and are bemused by the strange new environment.

It is the responsibility of the nurses to help to ease them into the situation and make them feel comfortable as soon as possible. The greatest favour any nurse can do for her patient is to remember exactly how bewildered and anxious she felt on her very first day in the hospital. Then she may be able to appreciate how much worse it must be for the patient, whose health, fate or even life may depend on crossing the threshold. There is usually a rather special bond set up between the patient and the first nurse whom she encounters on admission, the one who will be relied upon to provide the guiding hand in the all important initial orientation.

Miss Donovan was the top dog in her own profession. Now she was reduced to joining the treadmill at the mercy of an unfamiliar profession. She knew the teacher role but was uncertain and ill-at-ease in the patient role.

In her own domain, Miss Donovan was self-assured, self-sufficient and proud, yet to us, in many ways, she was irritatingly irksome, precious and vulnerable.

She had etched out a successful place in society, and was fiercely adherent to her independence. Having lived alone for many years, undoubtedly in sublime orderliness, she found it iniquitous to be subjected to the demands of communal living which are inevitable in a general hospital ward.

It was difficult for her to sleep dormitory fashion, with the subdued lighting and the unremitting noise from sick patients and attentive nurses. She found it offensive to share cups and cutlery that had been handled by strangers, many of whom were infirm and thus degraded in their habits. Miss Donovan would inspect and wipe all cutlery before use.

She would make a point of scouring around the bath before using it. Never a complaint passed her lips, but her silent critical behaviour was a loud index of her discomfort and displeasure.

The toilets on Parker were old and had been subjected to a lot of use over the years. Maria, our diligent worker, strove to keep them clean and in good order but accidents were bound to occur amongst twenty-eight women of varying levels of continence. I feel sure Miss Donovan shuddered at having to use them and am certain she never let her bottom touch the seat. She wasn't however unique in taking tissues for wiping herself instead of using the non-absorbent, harsh government issue.

Meals were not to her liking. Admittedly they were nothing very special but most patients found something adequate in the choice of meals, considering the constraints of cooking *en masse* and transporting the food around the corridors. Usually she settled for the salad option. She would scoop off the reconstituted mashed potato, then set to work scrutinising and dissecting the rest. The finished plate rim was neatly arranged with an assortment of rejected bits.

The tea was too strong and the coffee had too many toxins to be good for her. So, Miss Donovan requested hot water and a spoon, to which she could add her camomile tea-bag. In general her finicky eating habits were a threat to our dietary machinery and her healthy eating habits hadn't yet filtered through to hospital mass catering.

Her self-alienation had centred on rejection of the very system that was trying to help her. I was concerned that we, the system, didn't reject her.

The staff were piqued by her tiresome traits, so I chose to discuss her reaction at one lunchtime handover. We examined the ways in which people are stripped of their identity on coming to hospital. Put in a nightie, put in a bed, washed, wiped, toileted, forced to regress to the stage of a two-year-old, devoid of responsibility, being told what to do and how to do it. No longer bank manager, teacher, mother, team leader, just another one of those patients who accepts the traditional patient role, which we staff find much easier to cope with than people who rock the boat. Patients need to accept an altered life-style temporarily and must go along with good grace, realising that some form of order is necessary for the benefit of all patients and the smooth running of the organisation.

Miss Donovan was making a brave stand to retain her individuality. I felt we ought to make some effort to understand her feelings and try to tolerate some of her idiosyncracies, although I had to admit they were excessive, yet harmless. Perhaps she'd meet us half way.

On reflection, it was an unholy mistake that Sandra Dix was the nurse allocated to admit Miss Donovan. Her silly, patronising chatter would irritate a saint and to find that any patient should think Sandra was representative of the staff was unbearable. Miss Dix was not the kind of nurse guaranteed to inspire hope and confidence into an already diffident patient.

Margaret Donovan clammed up. It was her way of coping with a stressful situation. She remained polite but distant, giving nothing of herself. Speaking only when spoken to, she purposefully lowered her glasses and gave brief, mostly monosyllabic replies.

In the day room, she took her transistor radio and the ever-present, never-finished book. She would select a corner seat, furthest from the TV viewing group, plug in her ear-piece and wrap her dark quilted dressing gown around her in a protective pose.

Whenever possible she would retreat to her bed, put on her earphones and concentrate on the book held fixed before her. Eyes, ears, body and mind were firmly detached from Parker ward and its inhabitants.

The curtains were drawn a little way on both sides to discourage any communication from her neighbours. Patients who did stop to speak were given a hasty, tired smile with minimal eye-contact and reading was spontaneously resumed. Soon the patients got the message and didn't bother to stop and avail themselves of a rebuff.

The defence barriers were up. She had no wish to be part of the idle, superficial talk that was the meat of hospital ward exchanges. She wanted none of the small talk and gossip that was proffered by the other patients. Involvement in other patients' problems didn't interest her and, more pertinently, she didn't want them discussing hers. The opener for any hospital conversation is likely to be, 'What are you in for?'

Hers was a bowel problem and Miss Donovan didn't find it easy to discuss her bowels and her bodily functions freely. Nurses and doctors are used to dabbling in secretions, excretions and discharges but have to be aware that patients are entering a sphere of social taboo.

On this subject, Sandra Dix made another blunder. Passing by the bed, I saw Sandra remove the thermometer from Miss Donovan's mouth. While reading off the temperature, she asked, 'Yes or no?' and stood with her biro poised, waiting for the answer.

'Yes or no what?' inquired the bewildered Miss Donovan, with irritation.

'Yes or no bowels.' Sandra was too thick-skinned to appreciate that the error was hers, 'Bowels open today, yes?' she reiterated.

I explained to the patient and tried to ease the already tense situation. 'Nurse is forgetting that you are new to our jargon,' I smiled but felt like wringing Sandra's neck. 'I'm afraid the correct question of, "Have you had your bowels open today?" eventually gets contracted to a simple "Yes or no?" or even "bowels?" Patients often get so used to the routine they even sometimes give the answer without being asked.'

'I see,' she replied curtly, and with an unmoved expression that signalled that I had done my duty and could go.

I wanted to yell at Sandra but realised I would only be displacing my feelings of frustration onto her.

I was never sure how prepared Miss Donovan had been for what was to come. The medics always hedge their bets before confirming a diagnosis, until they are fairly certain of the trouble.

Miss Donovan had found blood in her motions and had been having bouts of diarrhoea which eventually led her to consult her GP. There was some doubt at first that the blood had originated from the bowel. Confusion had been caused because of the irregular vaginal bleeding that had been occurring as part of the menstrual upset at the menopause. The delay caused by this indecision may have let the disease take a greater hold than if she'd sought help at an earlier stage.

She didn't know she had cancer. Or did she? Was this powerful silence all part of shutting out the awful truth? The mind is very capable of playing tricks to convince its owner that all is well and to protect it from anxiety.

Burrows had been with Miss Donovan when Mr Martin did his examination. There is no dignified way of passing a sigmoidoscope. She was asked to lie on her side with her bare bottom towards the edge of the bed. The instrument was hard and uncomfortable. He gently pushed it into the rectum, to allow him to examine the wall of the rectum and snip a piece of tissue for biopsy.

Getting to know Miss Donovan as we did, or rather, not getting to know her, made me decide that she was probably the very worst person to be faced with the prospect of a colostomy. I couldn't imagine her coping easily with a false bowel opening, which issued faeces into a bag fixed to her abdomen.

It isn't an offer to be accepted lightly by anyone, but most people come to terms with the idea, especially when they realise that it is a life-saving measure.

Nevertheless, it still came as a surprise to us when Miss Donovan refused the operation. It is so rare for patients to contradict the advice given by the surgeon, even though they have the perfect right to do so.

'I'm sorry, Mr Martin, but I couldn't face that.' She resolutely stood her ground as the accompanying members of his round were stunned into silence.

'That's a most grave decision, Miss Donovan', he replied.

'I had a feeling it would come to this and I've made up my mind, I'll take my chances.'

This was not the time and these were not the circumstances for coercion over such a serious and delicate matter. He promised to return later, to see her on his own. The team withdrew, shuffling away from the patient after this embarrassing rejection. I left the curtains partially drawn and Miss Donovan motioned that she might sleep.

I don't think she had a lot of faith in Mr Martin, he was too casual and jovial, hardly giving her the ideal impression of a consultant. Mr Simpson would have been nearer to her expectations.

Dr Ponampolam, his Sri Lankan houseman, hadn't been a whole lot better. He was very sweet, very willing, almost to the point of being effusive, but he wasn't the kind of doctor with whom Miss Donovan found it easy to discuss her intimate details.

Being new to the country, his grasp of idiomatic speech was limited and this made history-taking stilted. He needed a translation for 'waterworks', 'spending a penny', 'back passage' and 'motions'. She needed a translation for 'stools', meaning faeces, 'cystitis', urinary tract infection.

She blushed when he inadvertently asked the routine question, 'Any bleeding on intercourse?'

'No' was the answer to bleeding and 'no' was the answer to intercourse. He seemed oblivious of his *faux pas* and of her embarrassment; a history is a history is a history.

Mr Martin went to see her again.

'She's adamant, Sister, still refusing surgery. But it's early days yet, she's still reeling from the shock. I've told her there's a good chance I can clear the tumour before it gets invasive. I've told her all about a colostomy and she's well informed anyway, a bright lady. It's a hellish proposition but she needs time to get it into perspective. I'll leave her until the next round to mull it over. Perhaps you could have a try at convincing her and helping her out in this difficult period of decision.'

'Difficult period! Difficult person!' I was flabbergasted that he took it so calmly and he must have sensed my exasperation.

'I know. She isn't easy. She bristles with contempt and it's very threatening for the staff. Every now and again we get a patient who bucks the system and throws a spanner in the works. I'm only amazed that it doesn't happen more often. Still that's what makes working with people so much more interesting than working with paper – isn't it?' Mr Martin replied.

I had to agree. And smiled at his optimism.

Miss Donovan really did sleep after the round. On waking, all her defence barriers were set up again and she was as unapproachable as ever.

I needed to get away from the ward and took my tea-break in the canteen, meandering along the corridor to the staff quarters.

A lot of privilege was still attached to how you took your meals. The bigger room, used for lunches and suppers, was carefully segregated to provide tables for designated ranks of staff. The large round tables at the sunny end had water jugs and glasses and waitresses to remove the china and cutlery.

The élite of the hospital; sisters, doctors and administrators, received this superior service. The other end of the room was for all other grades of nursing staff, paramedicals and office staff coping with self-service and self-clearing.

Smoking was prohibited in the dining-room, so the many nurse addicts bolted their meal in order to fit in a quick smoke in their allotted meal break, across in the fog-filled sitting-room.

Tea and coffee times were a more casual affair. In the neutral territory of the snack bar, there was a natural mingling of all staff and passing of the weed.

I had to admit, I could have welcomed one myself that afternoon. I sat alone thinking how best to approach Miss Donovan. I was irritated and frustrated at not being able to get to her.

The midwives on the next table were besides themselves with excitment. They had had an unexpected delivery of twin boys, a rare event on the midder (midwifery) unit. And, moreover, the mother was intending to breastfeed both of them! Momentarily, I envied their being involved in happy work, although in reality, this was not truly always the case, they had their share of tragedies.

God, it seemed so awful to let someone slip through the surgical net when help was so close at hand. As it was we were all feeling rotten watching Ruth Abbott die, when nothing else could be done for her. I was sure she would have grabbed at an opportunity to live, would that she had been given the chance.

'Penny for them. Can I join you?' a voice asked.

I looked up to see a young doctor, holding a cup of tea. He looked vaguely familiar but I couldn't say from where.

'Yes do. Sorry, I'm miles away.' I pulled out a chair for him. 'I've seen you somewhere before but can't for the devil of me place you.'

He set down his tea and grasped the salt and pepper pots firmly. He straddled the table and pretended to apply them to the chest of an imaginary patient. With head bent intently down, elbows raised high, he looked under his arm. 'Recognise me now?'

'Of course. The arrest on Parker. You were the one with the defibrillator. I remember now.'

'Put two paddles in my hand and you'd know me anywhere,' he mimicked the violence of the shock.

'How did she get on? A Mrs Green, wasn't it?' I felt so awful having to struggle to recall her name, so many patients had passed through the ward since.

It was the same when meeting an ex-patient in the hospital, when they came to out-patients or visited the ward. They always glow at recognising 'their' nurse or 'their' Sister and it is often quite a job to fathom who they are, especially disguised in their day clothes!

'I always intended to follow her up, but you know how it is. Rather "out of sight, out of mind", there are always more pressing things to be done for the patients actually on the ward at the time,' I explained.

'That's right, pass your problems over to us,' he teased. 'Well, she got on fine, she'll probably be popping up back on your list before long.'

'Wish I could pass my present problem over.' I was hauled back to the reality of Miss Donovan.

'Oh, why?' he invited me to continue.

'A fastidious middle-aged lady, a school marm. Presents with a perfectly operable Ca. rectum. Is refusing a colostomy. And not the most amenable to discussion.' I gave him a quick resumé of the case.

'It's horrible. I feel so helpless, so impotent. We are giving her the chance and she won't take it. My hands are tied behind my back, yet I want to shake some sense into her.' I was livid.

'I know how you feel. It's all a bit of a kick in the crutch. A two fingers up to everything we are trying to do. And you wonder why she can't believe in it too.' He understood perfectly.

'Right.' I felt better for my explosion.

'Your feeling angry isn't going to help her. Honestly, that's the stage one of defeat. I'm sure she really does need time to think it through,' he reassured me.

'But I don't feel able to approach her. She keeps me at

arm's length, I feel inadequate, reduced to school-girl level; she saps my confidence.' She made me feel hopelessly young for the job and this was a crisis point in my career.

'She may be older and wiser and smart and worldly, but you have the knowledge, the expertise. You are the professional, with the experience,' he continued assertively, recognising my pain from defeat.

'That's just it. I'm afraid I don't. We used to have a stoma therapist at Cottingham on whom we relied to advise all the colostomy patients.' On reflection, it was silly to rely on the one person but it was, after all, her specialist function.

I told the doctor about Enid, our nurse with special training to help all ostomists, anyone with a false opening for elimination. She had an ileostomy herself and was a walking advertisement on how to cope. Enid was a marvellous person with a sunny outlook on life, who made light of her inconvenience, and imbued confidence in those about to embark on a stoma. She would see all prospective patients, advise them on appliances, diet and generally counsel them for their future life, especially giving support over the emotional trauma attached to this vast change. Her continued follow-up was equally exemplary and welcomed by the patients with whom she built a helpful relationship. Problems and queries often arose which could not have been anticipated or prepared for.

'Sounds great. We could certainly do with someone like her on medical block. We frequently get protracted cases of Crohn's disease and ulcerative colitis (chronic conditions of the small and large bowel) which end up needing removal and subsequent stomas.'

'Mind you,' he added thoughtfully, 'there *is* something in this theory that people respond to catastrophic major surgery if they have "earned" it. Unlike your lady who has been offered a colostomy from out of the blue, these patients have suffered miserably for so long with debilitating problems which disturb their normal existence. They literally welcome with open arms the relief offered by a stoma, as the end to their dismal life. It gives them a whole new perspective, and is the end of their troubles, not the beginning. Like I always say "it's a treatment, not a tragedy".'

His bleep went and the doctor was called away. 'See you again,' she waved. And I rather hoped I would.

As he reached the door, he turned to add an afterthought. 'Hey, you have to believe in yourself before you expect anyone else to.'

It was true. Perhaps I was being unreasonably vain and sensitive to feel that I should shoulder all the responsibility. But I saw it as a challenge, the watershed of my role, this terrible inability to communicate with my patient. It made me stop to think of how much of it was our fault or how much we had to accept individual human differences.

The following day I felt better and stronger, having given some thought to people and my boundaries of accountability in general.

Miss Donovan opened up slightly. She seemed unable to keep up the concentration, or was it the pretence, of reading a book. There was not one relative with whom she could discuss her dilemma. Equally, that made it more difficult between us, as there was no relative to whom we could turn as a mediator between us and her. Margaret Donovan was quite alone in the world with her pressing problem.

The situation affected us all as we tried to convince her to accept surgery. I was wary that too much verbal assault would make her feel attacked and there was a danger that she would once again retreat. Any approach was welcomed but I asked the nurses not to bombard her. I advised them to behave naturally, give her the encouragement and opportunity to bring up the subject herself and talk freely at her own pace.

A visit by the social worker was requested by Mr Martin. She had a long interview with Miss Donovan and left behind factual leaflets issued by stoma associations and appliance companies.

This gave me the legitimate opportunity to follow-on by showing her some of the disposal bags that we used. We discussed the handling of a colostomy to the limit of my knowledge, which in fact when tested, did seem considerable as I pulled on my cumulative experience.

I was talking optimistically about the ease of the stoma once it had settled down and how a careful diet could eliminate smells, loose motions and excess wind. I recollected the need to avoid onions and cabbage and fizzy drinks. We consulted the booklets to see which others were mentioned. In the end it would be experimentation which could prove what was right for her as an individual.

The colostomy bags were of modern materials, refined to prevent leakage and odour and were handily disposable. She could not expect to receive warning of its impending action as with normal rectal sensation, but the colostomy could be trained like a normal bowel to perform at a socially convenient time. As the stools were solid, once a routine habit of evacuation had been established, she may be able to dispense with the bags altogether. I somehow doubted that she would ever feel that secure.

She thanked me for taking the trouble to discuss all this but would commit herself no further. It was maddening. I maintained my calm, professional approach, although it wasn't easy. I left her with the young doctor's words, 'It is a treatment, not a tragedy'.

For the next two days, she gelled more in the ward, becoming more a part of the patient group, rather than resisting inclusion. It was obvious that she would be attracted to some more than others and she spoke at length to Ruth Abbott, full of diplomacy and of a similar age to Miss Donovan.

Mr Martin made his return visit to this patient – minus the team. He sat on her bed, as she was in the chair, and made himself comfortable, ready to spend some time in convincing her.

'I've made up my mind, thank you, Mr Martin,' she said abruptly.

'Oh?' he inquired.

'I'd like to go ahead with the operation, as you suggested,' she said with no hint that she was going to elucidate about her change of heart.

'Good.' He rose from the bed, not labouring the point any further.

'Could I get it over with as soon as possible?' she entreated of the surgeon.

'Certainly. I've reserved a place for you on the Monday

list,' he said without hesitating, having cunningly anticipated her decision. 'We'll get you prepared straight away, won't we, Sister?'

Mr Martin swaggered off down the corridor, looking very pleased. I accompanied him to the ward door and he recognised the relief on my face.

'Never underestimate the survival instinct, it's *very* strong,' he said, with a slightly sinister emphasis.

Having at last consented, Miss Donovan was then subjected to the invidious process of bowel preparation, up to and all over the weekend, five days in all. I involved Nurse Gordon in the total care of this patient, as she had expressed an interest in writing a nursing care study on the case. The nurse was a mature, amiable girl, to whom the patient responded well. I felt Miss Donovan would relate better to concentrated involvement with just one member of the team at the start.

The extensive preparation was to clear and cleanse the bowel, in an effort to minimise post-operative infection and complications. A low-residue diet was instituted immediately. So she was not allowed her favourite salads or fruit but was restricted to easily digestible foods like fish, potatoes, jellies and custards.

The intestines were sterilised as much as possible by giving drugs to eliminate the normal population of microbes which live in the bowel. The drugs carried the horrendous names of phthalylsulphathiazole and neomycin, needing to be taken with copious amounts of fluid to prevent them crystallising in the kidney.

In addition there was an ardous regime of daily enemas and rectal washouts, all necessary to thoroughly cleanse the bowel in readiness for surgery. The day prior to operation, clear fluids only were allowed.

After the normal routine preparation of shaving, bathing and overnight fasting as well, I think she was on the point of finding it a relief to be taken to theatre and get going with the surgical procedure.

Nurse Gordon watched the operation as part of her learning exercise and kept the rest of us enthralled as she reported on it. It had been fascinating watching two teams of surgeons work simultaneously. She now realised why it was called SCAPER, Synchronous Combined Abdomino-Perineal Excision of Rectum.

One team worked in the abdominal cavity, freeing the bowel, dissecting out the rectum with tumour, and fashioning a colostomy. The other doctors made their entrance at the perineum, between the legs, to close the anal opening, which would no longer be needed.

After two-and-a-half hours on the table, it was no wonder that Miss Donovan returned looking pale, shocked and shivering. There is considerable trauma from such extensive handling of organs during a long period of surgery. She was suffering phenomenal pain, which needed hefty and regular doses of a strong analgesic.

Slightly to our surprise, Miss Donovan proved to be a model patient, co-operative and diligent in obeying instructions to help her recovery. It was now that her strength of spirit and single-minded determination were paying off. Being a perfectionist, once she had come to terms with the operation, she acted to the utmost of her ability to make the best of her decision.

She coped amazingly well with all the impedimenta that this operation necessitated by gritting her teeth and getting on with it all.

A large wound ran vertically down her abdomen with a piece of corrugated rubber sticking out to drain the operation site of exudate. Another puncture wound lay at the left hand side, through which the cut end of the colon protruded. Yet another wound, in the most disagreeable site of the perineum, also had a drain with a sanitary towel acting as a dry dressing. This was held in place by a T-binder, up between the legs and tied around the waist.

The sum total must have caused profound discomfort to say the least, but she endured it with little complaint. We settled her half sitting and half on her side, to aid drainage from the wounds and relieve pressure from both operation sites. A cosy sheepskin was beneath her bottom to provide a soft surface on which to lie.

A urinary catheter collected urine from her bladder, to prevent soiling of the perineal wound area. It also obviated the need for struggling on and off bedpans and for that she was grateful.

The I.V. drip had originally replaced blood loss but after two pints the infusion fluid was changed to dextrose/saline, which had to remain up until the patient was able to take fluids by mouth.

After abdominal surgery, the bowel sometimes takes offence at all the interference and refuses to start working again. So another of her life-lines was the naso-gastric tube, aspirated hourly to remove juices produced by the gut that cannot be passed through the alimentary system while it rests.

She also had piped oxygen during the initial post-op period. Quite an array of medical hardware surrounding Miss Donovan. And Nurse Gordon had some task before her, documenting the on-going care of this patient.

Miss Donovan gradually shed her selection of piping as her recovery was assured. When doctor heard bowel sounds, the internal rumblings that indicate the muscular waves of peristaltic action have resumed, she drank. As this was tolerated and her oral intake increased, she could do without the drip. The wound drains had done their job and could be removed. Things were falling into place or, in this instance, falling 'out' of place and she was doing fine.

It did still sound a grotesque understatement when our telephone information about her was limited to 'making good progress and quite comfortable'. Never more uncomfortable, I should have thought. Still without resorting to greater detail, that was the gist of her degree of recovery. 'Comfortable' is a tired, over-used and ambitious euphemism after surgery, but what else?

The colostomy was covered by a transparent disposable bag but as yet it had collected nothing. Miss Donovan had been too preoccupied with all the other distractions to take much interest in the quiescent stoma.

On the third day it acted. Flatus (wind) was heard and

smelt, to the embarrassment and displeasure of Miss Donovan.

'Marvellous, it's working now!' I couldn't help but sound delighted at the positive movements of her bowel. I think she was comforted by my spontaneous and genuine approval and she was able to see that it was a sign of progress.

The wretched thing worked again before I could get to change the bag. Wind and liquid motions filled the bag and it blew off, spattering faeces over the sheets.

Damn and blast it, I thought to myself. I didn't want her put off before we started seriously to get aquainted with the colostomy.

'Teething troubles,' I tried to pass off the episode lightly as I cleared up the mess, 'it'll settle down in no time. All those washouts, starvation and liquids, there's no substance to the faeces.'

I cleaned around the colostomy, which was red, shiny and glistening, with the texture of tinned peaches in syrup. It looked like an inner tube turned back on itself, to expose the central stoma, meaning mouth. To us it looked a remarkably neat and tidy, healthy colostomy. But to her this was a totally new and strange sight, probably most closely resembling a piece of raw meat sewn to her stomach.

I invited her to look at it as a gentle introduction.

'Hm, it's rather smaller than I had expected,' she said simply.

'And it should get even smaller,' I added, spurred on by her optimism. 'It's a little oedematous, I mean swollen, at present, being so soon after surgery.' I was so glad that she hadn't been repelled by what she had seen.

This highly charged situation was diffused as Doreen appeared through the screens, shielded by a vast bouquet of flowers. When dismantled, it filled three large vases. It had been sent by colleagues from the school where Miss Donovan worked. Knowing that she had no relatives, they also organised a visiting rota and that enabled her to get happily back into talking shop; her shop and not ours. As far as the flowers were concerned, I had to take some credit. I had intervened when they asked my advice on their original suggestion that they send a 'useful' box of fruit. It would have been quite inappropriate for her at this time.

Margaret Donovan was clearly moved by this rallying around on the part of her staff. Perhaps this had been their first opportunity to get through a chink in her armour.

Parents sent cards, as did the children, often with small, handmade gifts enclosed. The little mite who had sent a bar of chocolate in his envelope might have been better advised to pick a cooler day! But the thought was no less appreciated.

Miss Donovan's next task was to learn how to cope with the colostomy, to clean and protect the skin and fix the appliances. Being fairly slim made the whole procedure much easier to accomplish. Daily she watched as the nurses attended to her colostomy. They knew how important it was to conduct the procedure in a matter-of-fact way, without suggesting any distaste with their task.

As quite a natural progression, she started to assist the nurses and the next step was to try to do it for herself. We later suggested she might find it easier to attend to her colostomy in the bathroom, where she could stand in front of the long mirror and remain uninterrupted.

She made exceptionally rapid progress to recovery and it was a joy to see her getting better day by day. Nurse Gordon monitored her exemplary dedication to the process of healing, which proved to hold the secret of her success.

Before she was due to go out, I arranged for a visitor from the Colostomy Welfare Association, a voluntary group interested in all aspects of welfare for a new patient with a colostomy. This contact would hopefully give continued support once Miss Donovan was back at home. It occurred to me that Miss Donovan herself might make an admirable advocate to the cause of the association herself, when fully recovered.

Almost three weeks after surgery, she left us to take a well deserved convalescence. She dressed for the journey and was pleased to note that the stoma had been carefully sited below her waist, so as not to rub on a belt line.

I gave her the TTOs (drugs To Take Out), a good stock of

colostomy bags and cream and cotton wool, plus an appointment to see Mr Martin in OPD.

We all wished her well and congratulated her on her smooth and speedy recovery, duly praising her efforts. She promised to come along and see us when she came back to the Out-patient Department.

Before she finally left, I couldn't resist asking her, to clear up in my own mind, why she had eventually changed her mind and decided to have the operation.

'Well initially I *was* totally repulsed by the idea, that is quite true. But my main concern was over my job. I naturally presumed that I would automatically lose my job, pensioned off unfit, especially as I work with children. I was miserable enough with the thought of the operation, what was the point of struggling to cope, if I then had nothing to do with my life?' she willingly explained.

So simple. So damn simple. I could have kicked myself for not thinking of it, for failing to recognise that area of misconception.

She continued, 'It wasn't until I spoke to the social worker that she put me right. I was asking about pensions and sick benefit and she assured me that there was definitely no reason for my job to be in jeopardy. She put my mind at rest. I'll be back at school next term. I'm not going to allow this colostomy to hinder me, my children need me.' She smiled and turned to Alma Gordon who, by way of seeing this case to the very end, was going to escort Miss Donovan down to the waiting ambulance.

Why had that never even crossed my mind? It is so easy to get wound up in the hospital situation that you forget that the patients come from, and go back to, the big wide world and all that it holds for them.

But I absorbed that little nugget of information. Never again did I fail to omit to discuss the vital question of future employment prospects if there was any possible doubt. It was a salutory lesson that served me, and my subsequent patients, well.

TWELVE: OPTION

'Damn bloody pirates!'

I looked up with astonishment from writing the Kardex. Mrs Witherden, a staff nurse from the 'old school' was a staid and correct lady, not given to swearing and especially not about the patients.

Whatever the nature of the problem, I knew she was referring to Mr Read, our private patient in the side-room. He'd been with us for two days and had managed to make himself pretty unpopular all round.

'Hey, what's he been up to now, Staff? It's not like you to come on so strong,' I enquired of Mrs Witherden.

'*Up* to. You've hit the nail right on the head. Poor Nurse Littleton, she's in the sluice in an awful state. Doesn't know where to put her face.'

'Why?' I was bewildered at all this free-floating anger.

'Well you might have asked one of the married girls to do it. You played right into his hands.' Now it was all coming my way.

Anne Littleton had been to prepare Mr Read for surgery, shaving his abdomen and pubic area. We had no male nurse and the other married girl, who was more senior, had been busy with a catheterisation. In all honesty I'd not given it much thought; she was available and it had to be done. A nurse is a nurse and she has to do a whole variety of jobs. It's not often we get to pick and choose.

'OK. She's new, she's young and she's shaved a man. For God's sake, it's hardly a complicated procedure, she's got to start somewhere and she'll see a lot worse things than that in her time. Good experience, I would have thought.' I was getting a bit irritated by the prissy, protective attitude.

'But not *him* of all people!'

'And *why* not, may I ask? He is a patient here, and that fact, perhaps, is getting ignored.' I looked straight at her but she clammed up.

It had obviously dawned on her that I wasn't 'one of the married girls' either.

'Right, so he had an erection. I daresay it would have been a physical impossibility for him to do otherwise in the circumstances, Staff.' That cleared the air.

A man choosing to be shaved, rather than attempt it himself, would usually politely cup his hand over his collection and choose to look the other way, thus providing a face-saving and dignified outlet for both him and the nurse.

'Yes, well rather than trying to conceal the fact, he kept on staring straight at her and grinning, taunting her all the time. Poor kid, her face was so red, you could have fried an egg on it. What a pig!'

It did seem a bit beyond the pale, I had to admit. I was caught in the midst of two loyalties and felt like a referee. The nurses had been upset by several jarring incidents with this man and he'd somehow started off on the wrong foot. I was aware of how their dislike of him was having a halo effect. The nurses were feeling exposed and threatened and finding him objectionable on all counts.

I had to be supportive to my staff but I was also the patient's advocate – a true devil in this case, it was becoming evident!

There was a powder-keg of hostility brewing and it was not going to be in his best interests, to make war with the nurses. He was bright and blasé today but I knew only too well how men crumple under pain, and he was due for a fair measure following surgery. Childlike regression is an understatement. He'd need all the support and kindness from the nurses tomorrow. This was in jeopardy. There was no danger of neglect but he might well be deprived of the human warmth and compassion which flows from a nurse on her own inclination. It can't be taught, it can't be bought, you just know when it's missing.

Far from getting the superlative care, to which he felt entitled, he'd end up with the necessities without the niceties.

I felt this to be a real danger and was going to have to try and pour oil on these troubled waters.

Anne Littleton came into the clinic room to clear her shaving tray. She looked sheepishly into the office. Probably by now she was more embarrassed that the incident had been reported than by the incident itself. My guess was that she'd gone to the sluice for a calm down in private. It was a popular hidy-hole for nurses in emotional states from any cause.

'I'll check the shave and complete the prep., thanks Nurse Littleton,' I called through the hatch. She looked relieved.

Thomas Read, 'Tommy to my friends, and naturally that includes you, Sister,' was admitted for a straightforward herniorrhaphy. An inguinal hernia is a common occurrence, particularly in men. The spermatic cord, which leads to the testicles, passes through the natural opening of the inguinal canal in the lower abdominal wall. Under substantial strain, the gut or bowel may protrude through this weakened area on the muscle wall, giving rise to a noticeable swelling in the groin.

Our Mr Read had sustained his rupture from some over-enthusiastic and over-ambitious weightlifting. This was just one of the symptoms of his middlescence crisis. Rising forty, a vasectomised divorcée – and making no secret of either fact – he was making a desperate effort to misspend some youth before it all passed him by. Casanova had nothing on him – except discretion.

Tommy was a self-made man, a local itinerant builder made good. Lady Luck had smiled on him and he'd done better than he could ever have imagined and had risen to dizzy heights in the building world. Unfortunately, he lacked the sophistication to shoulder his elevation to fame and fortune gracefully. He was equally as proud of his humble beginnings. His misfortune lay in believing that his new-found wealth could buy everything – and everyone. His attitude grated.

Mr Read had already received short shrift from Sister O'Connell on his arrival. His luggage comprised more booze than belongings.

'This is a hospital, Mr Read, not a cocktail lounge,' she clarified for him, in her own inimitable, efficient way. 'You would be well advised to do your liver a favour by keeping off alcohol. It will be fully occupied coping with drugs, without being plied with extra work.'

In Bridie, he recognised that he'd met his match.

'Purely for the visitors, Ma'am,' was his coy reply – he was lying through his teeth. He didn't seem to take too kindly to any restrictions, even those that were for the benefit of his health.

'I bet a day doesn't pass without he gets a skinful,' Bridie added, rather unjustly I thought, as later in the office she recounted their first meeting. 'A far bigger problem is his smoking. Mr Simpson told him firmly to cut down since the operation was first arranged. The anaesthetist will go spare at thirty a day and I doubt if Mr Read will enjoy a smoker's cough to aggravate his wound.' She dismissed him as a troublemaker from the outset.

Tommy Read had counted on me as a softer option and generally his assumption was correct. I liked to think I wasn't one for jumping in at the deep end at the slightest provocation. But barely before he'd got his bed warm, I was on the receiving end of a business phone call for our new patient and I guessed there were more to come. I couldn't let that situation continue, our telephone was too vital a communication link and my time too precious to act as messenger girl.

It was a shame that Tommy blotted his copybook from the start, although in this case it was no fault of his own.

'Yes, I told them where I'd be. I naturally assumed I'd have a phone in my room,' he said, without hesitation, when I broached the matter.

I apologised and explained that unfortunately we didn't have those kind of facilities. He'd have use of the telephone trolley but couldn't monopolise it, as it was to be shared with the rest of the patients in the ward. Besides you couldn't ring in to the hospital on it. In-coming calls on the ward telephone were to be restricted to matters concerning his health and his stay with us. That's all.

'I do hope you can appreciate this, Mr Read. There are twenty-seven other patients, all with anxious relatives wanting to phone in to make enquiries. Anyway you should be resting before your operation and leave your business worries at home,' I tried softening the reprimand.

'Fine bloody set up. I am private you know. I am paying. Surely I'm entitled to some privileges?' he retorted angrily.

It was obvious that he didn't quite grasp the implications of private care in an NHS hospital. I wanted to get the facts straight for him and nip any grievances in the bud. I had to pitch myself to be convincing yet stop at the plain rude, it was a delicate area to handle and I wanted to get in before any of the other nurses had their feathers ruffled and spoke out of turn. I was laying on the diplomacy with a trowel. No way did I want letters of complaint flying off to the Administrator, and I felt it to be a distinct possibility in this instance.

'Yes, Mr Read, you are a private patient. You are paying for the privilege of selecting the surgeon of your choice and having the operation at a time which is convenient to you.' Queue jumping is what it's called but I held fire on that one.

'This room is a versatile side-ward which is turned to for all manner of cases and patients. I'm afraid it is not equipped exclusively for PPs and neither is this hospital generally. Your money gives you privacy.' I nearly said 'isolation'. Being a people person, I had never been enamoured of solitary confinement but I could see the attraction it held for others.

'Your money also gives you a slightly better choice of menu than the other patients.' I clenched my jaw to prevent me adding, 'plus a tray cloth and an individual tea-pot.' That sounded too facetious, although nevertheless true. 'As you are on a female ward, one of the loos has been reserved especially for your use.' It was all I could offer and it didn't sound very ritzy.

'But surely I'll be getting special *treatment*, I mean *better* treatment?' he asked incredulously.

There it was. At last it was out. The usual misconception of private medicine. As if there were two ways of doing surgery, a superior one that money could buy, with a better cut, less pain, greater success, a tidier scar and a gold-signed guarantee of no complications.

I couldn't help getting rattled by this attitude. 'What do you think you might like? More stitches, more anaesthetic, instant healing? Mr Simpson does the same standard of technique for *all* his patients. He doesn't leave a patient to bleed because he isn't private, no more than he can give you extra stitches. Your bodies will react the same. And as for the nursing care,' I was anxious to defend my staff in case they were being passed off as second rate, 'we try our utmost to give the best of professional attention, across the board – to *every* patient.' I emphasised that point. 'There is no better than best, I can't say fairer than that.' I think I sounded cross and I was certainly aware of my hackles rising as I defended GGH. I hoped I also sounded convincing to him, as well as reassuring.

'I thought I might at least have had a pretty nurse at my bedside day and night, to hold my hand.' Tommy gave one of his Don Juan winks but it fell flat. However, those words gave me cause to suspect that some of his brashness might be reflecting a measure of anxiety. Could it be that under all this bravado he was plainly terrified of what was to come?

'If it is necessary, then you most certainly will,' I assured him, 'but after a straightforward herniorrhaphy, it is unlikely. Generally it is a luxury we are unable to offer, Mr Read. I have to deploy my limited number of staff as the situation demands and where the need is greatest. Our staffing levels are nowhere near as high as private hospitals, where they are able to offer higher salaries. My nurses don't get paid any extra for looking after PPs here.'

At this he raised his eyebrows in genuine surprise.

I wanted to probe further into his insecurity. If I knew about it, I could help him adjust to hospitalisation and the impending operation.

'You will have a bell to call us and, in any case, there will never be anyone far away. I can assure you that you are in safe hands and will get every attention you need. After all, Mr Simpson is satisfied to bring his privates here, so that should be recommendation enough.' I changed my tack. Feeling that I had won some of his confidence, I was sounding more amicable towards him.

'Honestly, don't be blinded by the frills. This is serious surgery not sexual adventure. Don't be beguiled by fancy hotel services, they are of least importance when we get down to the nitty-gritty. Have you ever been in hospital before, Tommy?'

'No, I've been lucky so far to keep out of the road of these people plumbers.' He smiled, looking more relaxed, and indicated tightly crossed fingers on both hands. 'I had the vasectomy but that was under a local anaesthetic – a lunchtime job.'

Our conversation was interrupted by the anaesthetist, who had come to give Mr Read his initial pre-op. check over.

'Excuse me then, the gas man cometh, I'll leave you to it.'

I left feeling that I'd broken the icy shell of Tommy Read and achieved some rapport with the inner man. The rest of the nurses were unconvinced, they were fraught by his grandiosity and liberty-taking.

Later that day Doreen had taken me aside. Mr Read had apparently been making enquiries into the ranks of the nurses – trying to decipher the shorthand of their different caps, dresses and belts. It is one of the more confusing and unnerving aspects of hospital life for the uninitiated.

He had been most upset to learn that Doreen was a mere auxiliary with no formal training. The laugh of it was that she had only taken a tray of tea into him.

'I suppose it's Sister or nothing for him. The cheek of it. The next he'll be bucking about is the coloured nurses or the learners. There won't be many left to choose from then!' she laughed. Doreen was too old, too wise and too familiar with the quirks of humanity to be put out by the likes of him.

'I explained that we work as a team, each doing what they can. The trained staff are busy with the operation patients and I'm going around with the teas.'

'Good for you.' I praised Doreen but it did occur to me that Mr Read may have resented her use of 'dear', her ubiquitous word with a patronising ring, which could take some time to get used to.

'Oh, he'll learn soon enough to value people for what they are and not for the qualifications they've got. No disrespect, Sister,' she added hurriedly. 'But why *is* he such a pain in the neck?' She asked out of genuine concern.

'He's new to this environment, it's strange to him and it's his way of coping. He's probably full of all sorts of ideas, faulty or otherwise, that are bandied around about hospitals. I suspect he's very insecure and frightened, just clutching at straws.'

'Well you could have fooled me,' Doreen replied.

'That's the idea. Shows how well it works then, doesn't it?' She got the point.

Nurse Littleton had already been shooed out of his room a couple of times while trying to get on with her allotted tasks.

'One minute he's busy on the phone. Next time he's got his entourage of visitors. He thinks I've got nothing else to do but wait around till *he* can fit *me* in.' I felt she wanted to say more but her deference to my seniority made her curb her tongue.

After the shaving incident, I think Anne was pleased when I said I'd complete his prep. It provided the chance that I had wanted to talk over the details surrounding the surgery.

But by now I was decidedly concerned about my divided and conflicting loyalties. My nurses had been upset by him and with this latest episode of distasteful behaviour, it was understandable that they were feeling pretty hostile.

On the other hand he was my patient, a rather difficult customer, but a patient nevertheless, and an anxious one at that. Somehow it was up to me to diffuse this tense, unpleasant atmosphere before it got out of hand and destructive. I battled on quite alone and experienced one of the true dilemmas of a Sister's role.

'All set for the big day now, I understand, Mr Read?' I couldn't prevent my own anxiety coming over in my voice. I was tense and prickly and angry with him for landing me in the mess.

'I'd like to check your shave, please.' I pulled the blind down over the window of the door, rather harder than I had intended, causing a rattling noise.

He obliged by slipping his pyjama bottoms down. I lifted up the bedclothes, and saw his naked genitals, clean as a whistle, denuded of curly hair. Rather an unattractive sight, especially in the male.

'Did she make a good job of it?' he asked, as I moved his penis to check the scrotum, which is difficult to shave thoroughly.

'Fine, but from what I hear, you are lucky she didn't whip the lot off. It's a dangerous job to do when your hand is shaking from nerves.' I replaced the covers smartly and gave him a stern, accusing look.

He hurriedly attended to the pyjama cord, looking like a lad who had been caught with his hand in the till, and had the grace to blush slightly.

'Ah come on, it was only a laugh,' he attempted to justify himself. 'You nurses see life, you can all take a joke.' He wasn't to know that his prank would become common knowledge.

'Some can, some can't. We are all different people. Individuals. We don't come out of "nurse" moulds like gingerbread men! That kid has only been a nurse for three months, this is her first ward. And she's straight up from the wilds of the country, transplanted to Sin City, still reeling from the shock. She's very junior, on her best behaviour, scared silly by any patient, let alone a man and a PP. Her corners haven't been knocked off yet like the rest of us and it is not in her nature to give as good as she gets.'

I was spent and he apologetic. I sat on the bed.

'Look,' I continued, trying hard to tame this cad, 'our professional ethic forbids us to exploit a situation or relationship with a patient for our own ends. Patients don't have defined ethics – but maybe in your case they should. Do you get my drift?'

'Go on.' The sod was enjoying every minute of my perspiring deliberations.

Something nearer his level was required.

'If you are on the receiving end of an intimate procedure;

something of a delicate nature, you wouldn't take kindly to her teasing you. You would expect her to observe your privacy and respect your finer feelings.' As I spoke, I wondered if he was the owner of too many of those. 'By the same token, if she has to perform that procedure, she doesn't expect the patient to take advantage of the situation as she goes about her business. It's a necessary job to be done as calmly and painlessly as possible for both parties.'

'OK, Sis, point taken. Maybe I was up to a bit of horse-play. Sorry about Nurse Littleton, I didn't realise she was an innocent.'

I was doubtful about his sincerity. 'She'll survive. Now what about you?'

I turned the conversation to his forthcoming operation. He confessed that he was nervous, not being very brave about pain. He was also concerned about having a GA (general anaesthetic). It was one of those irrational feelings but all too common. He appreciated that he was in good hands, although I felt sure that his opting for paid care was his emotional insurance policy. However, there is an underlying fear of being out of control, unconscious, unaware of your surroundings, 'drifting off to sleep – never to wake up again – going without even knowing it'. I had heard similar words before from so many other patients that I could accept it as a commonly-held terror.

I went over the plan of campaign for the next day, as I did routinely for those on the op. list. Nil by mouth after 12 midnight, no drinks, no sweets and no cigarettes, I emphasised. Early bath, op. gown on, empty the bladder, pre. medication at 8 a.m. and down to theatre at 9 a.m. I advised him to ask for the night sedation that had been prescribed, to ensure a restful night.

I gave him an enema as part of the preparation. Only a small one, a disposable pack enema to clear the bowel.

'Hold on to it as long as you can for the best effect, five or ten minutes at least,' were my instructions. 'Walk around and try to take your mind of it. And don't pull the chain, I'll want to check the result.'

'Is that *really* necessary?' he asked, turning up his nose.

'Don't worry, I don't mind, it's all in a day's work. Give me a call, then take a bath afterwards.'

The enema knocked him sideways for a while, they can tend to cause painful cramps and wind.

Mind you, he soon perked up when the physio came. He was incorrigible. Margo paid a late visit to go over his pre-op. breathing and leg exercises. She had spent a busy evening up on ICU and was in no mood for his antics.

'I've done Romeo, Helen.' She popped her head round the office door when she'd finished with him. 'Awful ropey chest. I'll have to rely on you girls to keep the coughing and deep breathing up with him in between my visits'.

I looked around at the faces of the nurses gathered in the office. I'd called them together to thrash out their feelings about Tommy Read and plenty had been aired. Better out than in, niggling away.

Staff Nurse Witherden spoke for them all.

'Don't worry, we'll keep at him,' she insisted, and gave a knowing grin.

I was sure they would do their best.

Susy sat eating her chicken and chips from the box while I told her of the day's events. She was highly amused.

'If that had been me, I'd have given it a smart flick to bring him to his senses.'

'And water to his eyes!' I added. 'Yes, we all think we know what we would do in theory but it isn't so easy at the time. Plus, she is just a beginner and he is private.'

'Didn't know you did privates there. You must *love* that!' Susy said sarcastically, as she licked her fingers.

She knew too well my views on private medicine and had heard me sally forth loud and clear on many occasions. It was a subject guaranteed to wind me up to explosion point and make me spring to the defence of the NHS. I was galled that in choosing private care as a first option, people would naturally presume that State care was second-rate and, by inference, less than adequate.

From what I had seen of PP care, I had concluded that it was one big con trick, designed to play on people's ignorance, and successful because it panders to vanity, conceit – and probably fear of the unknown.

My own experiences had been in some of the older private hospitals and in wings of London hospitals, long before the surge of purpose-built private accommodation took off.

Once I had passed my SRN, I was equipped to get Staff Nurse jobs through the nursing agency. It was so handy to use one period of annual leave for work, which would finance the next period for a holiday. It was a lucrative and interesting change from my training hospitals and also an eye-opener.

Armed with my professional expertise, I found myself on a continual round of puffing up pillows, filling water jugs and arranging enormous bouquets of flowers. I was like a glorified maid-come-companion and was irritated that my skills were minimally required.

It was a highlight of a day to do any real nursing procedures, like taking temperatures or testing urine. Giving suppositories was something to be savoured. Many of the surgeons brought their own 'nurse dressers' to do dressings, particularly for plastic surgery cases. Immediate post-op. patients always had a special nurse to stay with them. This was understandable as closed side-rooms are dangerous when confused or delirious patients are not visible.

I had four or five room-in patients under my specific care and acted as runner for any post-op. nurse in my rooms. Few of the patients were ill in any real on-going sense of the word. Most were in for booked, planned surgery.

It was demoralising to be asked to carry out tasks which were totally unnecessary and just being done for appearance's sake. We had to do superfluous care so the patients felt they were getting the utmost attention. It was quite ridiculous to rub bottoms when patients were up and about as if they were at home. Equally it was an exaggeration to continue taking four-hourly temperatures until discharge.

After what I had been used to, the whole situation was unreal. There was overstaffing to ridiculous levels. There was such an excessive waste of nurse-power, trained nurse power too, no students, pupils or auxiliaries to taint the elitist scene, that it seemed ludicrous to those of us who were used to busting a gut to get even the essential work completed. I couldn't come to terms with a place that was overrun with qualified staff, all under-occupied and rarely called upon to provide nursing as we understood it.

The jobs I was given were cushy in the extreme and the patients were generous with extravagant gifts when they left. It was easy money but it brought out a strain of professional dedication which I never knew I had before. I wanted my training and my work to be more meaningful.

This type of work suited some nurses but to me it was like being a student nurse and a lackey all rolled into one.

The regular PP nurses had spent so much time in their cosseted environment that they would probably keel over at the sight of a general ward. They insist that they are able to spend more time giving proper nursing care, which would have been true if any of the patients needed it. Where were the serious burns, the heart attacks, the overdoses, the head injuries, the terminal cancers, but in the NHS hospitals, not singled out for selective private treatment?

It struck me that it was a pity that there was such a great gulf in staffing. One side so understaffed that they were drained, yet the other so overstaffed that they'd almost lost recollection of the reality of the job.

The floor sisters were overlords to the staff nurses and true handmaidens of the doctors and patients. They had been there for so long, they had been sucked into the set-up. Obviously chosen for their tactful pandering to the whims of privates, they were absorbed by the delusion of their role, and professional nursing almost took second place. Most had perfected the art of kowtowing to the wealthy and spent their time answering complaints about the food and stepping two paces behind the consultants. They were there to gently tempt post-ops. with slivers of smoked salmon or pukey ladies with Perrier water.

In fairness, the patients represented the same varied cross-section as they did anywhere else. Some revelled in the luxury and treated the nurses like servants. Others recognised our skill and were grateful for the chance of a quiet rest and good care.

A few of the men got the idea that their payment included a grope with the nurse and, in the tantalising privacy of the individual room, might stick a hand up your dress.

One stroke patient had a regular line in trapping the nurse in his private bathroom. Considering his one-sided paralysis, he made quite an heroic attempt at seduction. Mind you, he was a gentleman with it; willing to stuff a fiver down your bra if he could get there. It was a bit of an impertinence and he was a trial to the nurses but we could sympathise with his boredom at being cooped up and captive all day. He was harmless and, in a way, it was one indication of his recovery.

In general the women were more demanding and finicky, and less likely to help themselves; a trait of female patients.

My classic anecdote retained always to clinch the futility of private care and the gullibility of patients rests with Mrs Pardoe, a delicate, spoilt old lady of noble birth, used to the best from every quarter.

I had been irritated beyond distraction by a morning of her frivolous, pernickety instructions. She dictated my every move, so I felt like a manipulated puppet and I couldn't escape from her clutches.

'Wash my back here – no, don't put soap on my *neck*!'

'Talcum powder next – the freesia today – to go with my blue nightie, not the sandalwood, that goes with the pink.'

Talc in every conceivable crevice. A selection of brushes and combs, used in a precise order. Skin cream, face cream, under cream, over cream, hand cream.

Sister had already been summoned in high dudgeon to sort out her battling goldfish, which had been delivered from Harrods the previous day. They were seemingly unaware of their grand surroundings and it was battle royal as the golden duo massacred the third. What pandemonium! What a waste of expert time! But to Sister ructions like this from eccentric inmates were an everyday event.

Panic was on. The 'specialist' was due.

Mrs Pardoe continued to fuss on about her flowers, the curtains, the bed linen. She tidied her locker and squirted Dior perfume as an air freshener.

The blue bedjacket matched the nightie but the ribbon was

slightly soiled, so she settled for the white one, begrudgingly. My patience was stretched so thin, I could have happily told her to 'stuff the lot'.

I didn't. Was this really me, Helen Davies, SRN? Had I done three years' consistent hard work to be sorting out lingerie for a pedantic old girl with anaemia?

'He's coming to give me an injection,' she gave an explanation for all the preparations.

Something intravenous or intra-articular, I assumed.

Floor Sister asked me to draw up 2 mls. Jectofer, a common intramuscular iron preparation. The specialist was coming to give it. Well I never. He was dropping in to give her a simple IM injection – and add an extra fee onto his bill. Here was I, fully qualified and able, probably even more recently in practise than he, standing by obediently, while the great man plunges the needle. I drew it up, I cleared the mess, he gave it, she paid through the nose – and happy to do so no doubt. It was a minor incident but disturbing, particularly as I felt the patient to be in the dark. She was jubilant at this marvellous treatment by her consultant and if she was satisfied, nothing was lost, except the continual and cumulative reflection on the State service as being under par.

I despised the set-up which perpetrated the idea that it was offering a superior kind of medicine. It was nothing of the sort. It was a superior kind of hotel service and highly trained maid-servants. I became a true advocate of the NHS and its egalitarian ideal.

The big fear was that our own system could become like the American one, where illness was based more on money than sense. The iniquitous situation where doctors advertised their wares, coaxing people to have surgery for the sake of it – 'Roll up, get your Californian hysterectomy, that's one less organ to go cancerous.'

Lawyers were forcing doctors into a corner, making them provide defensive medicine, and work continually under the threat of litigation. The insurance companies flourish but are selective on their cover.

Try going mad on insurance. You are supported for a

limited time, then it's over to State care, which leaves a lot to be desired.

Private care is fine for the glamorous part of medicine, the predictable, the planned, the resting up in a nursing home. But who clears up the road crashes, the knife wounds, the elderly, the handicapped? Who pays for GP service, community nurses, clinics and hostels? Even where services were sparse, a little was better than none at all. I always believed that in a serious emergency, in Britain you are in safe hands.

Lately I'd become less hostile and more philosophical. Let the private organisations cream off routine surgery and give breathing space to the waiting lists. But give our system credit where due. That was why Tommy Read had to have our best, to prove our worth to someone who represented the stereotyped thinking about private versus State care.

THIRTEEN: COMPLICATIONS

There was no earthly reason why a fit and otherwise healthy man like Tommy Read should have had anything but a smooth convalescence. But his recovery was fraught with setbacks and minor complications.

I had somehow anticipated difficulties with him. His attitude towards the operation wasn't right and he was unwilling to take advice. In common with many patients, he didn't realise that recovery was a positive thing, something to be worked at seriously, in co-ordination with the various members of staff.

Any fool could lie asleep while the surgeon did his needlework and consider it all over and done with. Wrong. That's when the patient's part begins. Coughing and breathing, moving and walking, waking and sleeping, turning and sitting up – not much of which is pleasant with a painful gash in the abdomen. He was rigid, immobile and, worst of all, wouldn't do as he was told.

His first mistake was to rush at the fluids.

We settled him on return from theatre and he was surprisingly alert. He wasn't happy to be sitting upright, he preferred to be curled up lying flat. I explained that sitting was necessary to help his breathing and, when he saw that I was insistent, he grumpily complied.

'OK, pax. Just let me have a drink. My mouth is like the bottom of a parrot's cage,' he pleaded.

I struck the bargain. 'Have a suck of this ice. It will freshen your mouth up.'

'Fine,' he said having done that, 'now a cup of tea, I'm *dying* for a cuppa.'

I sympathised. I knew how he felt but argued that it was too soon after the anaesthetic and might cause him to vomit. After ten minutes he was ringing the bell and insisting. I put him off for another ten minutes, then he rang again. Then I asked Doreen to prepare some tea – and to take her time about it!

I helped him with the first few sips.

'Oh, that *is* heavenly.' He sipped again. 'See, I'm fine.'

Miss Ashton was at the door, she had called to see me. She wished Mr Read a good morning and he replied by raising his cup in his inimitable cheeky fashion and giving her a wink.

While my back was turned, he threw caution to the wind and bolted down the rest of the cupful. He looked so pleased with his achievement.

'Any more?' he smiled and held out the cup.

Almost before the words had left his mouth, he grasped his other arm under his ribcage, heaved and started to vomit. I rushed to get the vomit bowl from the post-op tray on his locker and held it under his chin. He threw up the tea – and more. I guarded the wound site as he heaved and vomited repeatedly. His body was shaken by the waves of continuous retching, each single motion causing strain and agony to his recent operation site.

Eventually it subsided and he lay back on his pillow, exhausted, pale and tense with the pain.

'I shan't do that again in a hurry,' he admitted repentantly as he wiped his chin.

I felt like saying, 'serve you damn well right,' so irritated was I by his provocative behaviour. But his suffering had been a sufficient lesson.

I joined Bridie and the staff next morning for the night nurse's report. She had made sure Tommy had got a restful first post-op night by giving a dose of Pethidine, which I gather was much appreciated by him.

'He got stroppy when we took observations and plain abusive when I kept having to tell him to sit up and move his legs,' she reported. 'Still HNPU (Has Not Passed Urine) but he isn't complaining of any discomfort as yet.'

It is perfectly normal physiologically for the body to retain water as a reaction to the operation and anaesthetic. Because the patient has fasted prior to surgery and takes little fluids for a while afterwards, less urine is produced. With Tommy it was getting on for twenty hours post-op, a day and a night, and beginning to cause concern.

'Thanks, Staff, probably the Pethidine aggravated the retention. That's Andrew Jeffrey for you, he should have known better. Take the girls and go.' Bridie dismissed the night staff and organised the day team.

'Helen, would you mind taking Mr Simpson on his round and see to his private patient. He'll be here early today. I've got dysmen. something chronic,' Bridie said.

Burrows was in the clinic room, ordering the pharmacy, and I thought I saw her smile to herself.

Bridie shouted through to clinic, 'Oh, Burrows, pass me two Panadol while you are about it,' and added, 'Honestly, the combination of Mr Simpson, supercilious Dr Jeffrey, Mr Read and the galloping gutrot are more than flesh and blood could stand.'

Bridie took her analgesics and went to the kitchen for a glass of water.

I leant through and quietly asked Burrows, 'Why the smile, Mrs Burrows, doesn't Bridie like Mr Simpson's round or is it the PPs?'

'Both. She isn't fond of either. But what amuses me is the frequent references we get these days to her dysmen. It's almost as if she wants us to know that she still has periods. She's at a dangerous age.' Burrows put me in the picture.

Dysmenorrhoea is the medical mouthful meaning painful periods. Nurses are always talking glibbly about 'dysmen.'. It is also one of the stock excuses for the odd day off, to be crippled with period pains. Fine, except for one colleague at Cottingham, who got caught out in her lies by complaining of dysmen. twice in one month!

Mr Simpson reassured Tommy that the operation had been straightforward and that he should be up and about in no time.

'Drinking well, I see,' Mr Simpson checked with the fluid chart.

'Yes,' replied Tommy, looking at me out of the corner of his eye. He was doing fine now his system had been allowed to settle down.

'No stirrings in the waterworks, though. Let's have a looksee.' Mr Simpson stood back and waited while I ceremoniously drew back the bedclothes. He likes his round done in style and his sisters acting as handmaidens. I could see Andrew Jeffrey taking points.

'I feel that I'd like to go but it's so painful when I start to strain,' Tommy explained, as the consultant gently felt over his abdomen.

'Well you're too young for prostate trouble. It's not an uncommon problem to get urinary retention after hernia repair. You've got a moderately full bladder there, so we'll pull out all the stops to get you on the move. Andrew, can you write him up for Carbachol, if none of Sister's routine measures work. I hope it won't come to catheterisation.' He imparted his instructions to us minions and Tommy struggled to keep track of the conversation about his condition.

'Well done, old chap, we'll soon get you sorted out, never fear,' Mr Simpson said, placating Tommy and beaming an encouraging smile as he departed.

'It's all right for him, old chap, but it's me with the bladder rising up to my earholes. What's a catheterisation, anyway?' asked Tommy.

'It's a soft tube, a catheter, that is passed into the bladder to release the urine. Don't you worry, it's a last resort measure, only done when all else fails,' I explained.

He didn't like the sound of that. 'So what now, Sis?' At least it meant he was willing to co-operate and help himself.

'Take a drink while you try to pass water. A hot tea may do the trick.' I poured one from the breakfast tray.

He tried for all his worth but couldn't pass a drop. If only he could get started, it would be plain sailing.

'No good?' The answer was evident. 'We'll try you sitting out. A bit of movement. A bit of gravity.' That was next on my list of tried and tested methods to coax bladder function.

'Get up? You must be joking. I only had the op. yesterday.'

He looked astonished at my suggestion.

'We'd be getting you out anyway. It's routine mobilisation to sit out of bed the next day and keep all the systems on the move.' As I spoke Margo, the physiotherapist, came in.

'You're early,' I said to her, 'but just in time to give me a hand with our reluctant hero, Mr Read. He's got retention.'

'Jimmy Riddle problems,' Tommy added, joining in.

Margo and I lifted him forward on the bed, then swung his legs over the edge. We both felt the tension in his hunched-up shoulders and he groaned with every slight movement. Margo supported the wound but he was so anxious to reach the chair, that he slumped into it quickly, producing a sharp pain.

'Oh, Christ, it's agony. Should it be like this? Are you sure there's nothing wrong? Is everything all right?' he asked with concern.

'Everything is absolutely fine, just don't hold yourself so tensely. Your muscles are rock hard. Loosen up a bit. Relax. Nice deep breathing now.' Margo got him under control.

It was a vicious circle. He was tense, movements hurt, the pain created more tension and subsequent inactivity for fear of further pain.

We left him to settle down while we made the bed. It looked as if there was cigarette ash in the bed, I wondered where he'd managed to hide the dog-ends. A quick, crafty drag in the night, while the night nurses weren't looking, I presumed. He confessed and Margo and I were on at him again. He was resigned to his addiction. I was more concerned about the smoking in bed, the worst hospital fire hazard.

'Now back to James Riddell, Mr Read,' I said earnestly. 'Let's have you perched on the edge of the chair.'

He dangled his penis in the urinal bottle, while I ran the taps at full pelt to encourage him as he leant on the bed.

The taps didn't work for him but they did for me.

We helped Tommy back into bed and Margo did some breathing exercises with him. I went to find Dr Jeffrey to order the Carbachol, a drug used to relax the muscles of the bladder sphincters. I thought he might also have a mild aperient to keep his bowels on the move, we didn't want him straining for that as well.

These days we were constantly chasing Andrew for every little thing. He'd secured a registrar's job at another hospital and wasn't interested in his present post anymore, it had served its purpose for him and he was off. He had no loyalties or sense of responsibility.

He was after an easy ride to the end of his contract, with the barest minimum of work and nothing to rock his cosy boat.

As Andrew was writing the prescription, I mentioned the smoking and asked if he would like to speak with authority to the patient. I thought Tommy might take more notice of the doctor.

'I'm sure you girls can handle it. Use your womanly charms.' End of subject.

'Care to come and celebrate my promotion, Helen? I can't leave without buying you a drink at least.'

I refused the offer. I couldn't imagine passing a pleasant evening with Andrew Jeffrey and his greatest admirer – himself. He was the 'conquest' sort, one drink, into bed or send you home. His life, his work, his friends all revolved around ulterior motives, he was determined to make the top – at anyone's expense. I had grown to despise him and wouldn't be sorry when he went.

I gave Tommy the injection. Margo and I settled him on his side, cosily supported by pillows in his back, with the urine bottle placed strategically on the bed between his thighs.

'Relax now, have a rest and give it time to work,' I said as I tucked in the sheet.

By now he was feeling the discomfort of a full, tense and bloated bladder. He looked so woebegone.

'Poor guy, he doesn't know what's hit him,' Margo said as we left his room. 'He thought he could just lie back and enjoy it all. The truth is that you really have to be well to be ill.'

The next time he rang, Tommy paraded the bottle for us all to see, full of clear, dark urine. He was triumphant. There were no further problems in that region but his chest was another story altogether.

As Tommy began to feel better, his visitors poured in to

view the recumbent hero. He was wallowing in the attention and holding audience from his bed like some war-wounded general. Every day was party day in the side ward.

He was still reluctant to do his physio, making as short work of it as possible. Margo suggested that he walked down the ward a few times in the day, for gentle exercise. Yes, he was always going to, was just on his way, or in a minute, but something, or someone, else more inviting came along and, apart from the times when Margo took him, he never budged from his room.

On his fourth day post-op. a glamorous female came into the office to tell me that Mr Read wasn't feeling one hundred per cent. I caught the smell of her deliciously expensive perfume and envied her long vermilion talons, something to which I could never aspire whilst a practising nurse.

Tommy had not wanted to make a fuss but she had been concerned as he had actually asked her to go and leave him alone.

I went along to see him. Tommy had a pyrexia, which is a raised temperature, a rapid, bounding pulse, flushed cheeks and those glazed eyes, typical of a fever. He was harbouring an infection - somewhere.

Andrew wrote out the usual battery of path. forms to take samples to isolate the offending microbe.

'No indication of a wound infection. I've not disturbed the dressing. Probably his chest, it sounds bubbly. Get a sputum spec. and an MSU while you're about it. There may be a urinary infection following on after that spell of retention.'

He scribbled the forms, leaving me to add the details. Andrew knew full well that he was a frustrating bugger but his tactics worked. Ultimately it became easier to do the work than get exasperated arguing with him. And he knew it.

'Give him this Ampicillin cover until we see what the path. reports show. With luck it will kill every bug in sight.' Andrew left.

Tommy was feeling most sorry for himself by the time I went to collect the special urine specimen. I explained what had to be done but he really wasn't up to the rigmarole that surrounded an MSU, a Mid-stream Specimen of Urine. I offered to do it for him and repeated the instructions.

Pass a small amount of urine into the urine bottle and stop. Wipe the end of the penis with sterile water on a sterile swab, pass the next small amount into the sterile jug, then stop. Finish the last of the stream into the urine bottle again.

Between us we managed successfully. 'Good, that's the best we can do to ensure a clean specimen of urine directly from the bladder, without contamination from the skin,' I explained as I poured the sample into the sterile path. pot.

'Thanks for doing it. What a palaver, stopping and starting; bits here and there; sterile, unsterile, it's a lot to grasp for us non-medical bods.' He lay back on his pillow and did a weak 'ha ha' at his pun on 'grasp'. I was pleased to see he wasn't completely defeated by the bug. Some of the old Tommy shone through.

'I never realised that you girls had so much to do with the nether regions. Doesn't it put you off men – I mean sex – seeing it all the time?' he inquired with genuine interest.

Not wishing to commit myself on this very leading question, I said simply and truthfully, 'It's all in rather a different context.'

Changing the subject, well almost, I asked Tommy if he'd noticed that his scrotum was slightly swollen.

'Well, I had thought it looked a bit puffy. Oh, Christ! Not another ruddy problem.'

'No, nothing to worry about, a slight reaction from the operation, the soft tissue easily accumulates fluid. I'll mention it to Mr Simpson but it will most probably ease once you are up and about on your feet.' I didn't want him worried but I did want to encourage him to shift off his backside. Once the fever had died down he'd need to get on the move in a big way.

The door banged open and Tommy winced at the offensive loud noise.

'Tablet time.' Such was the coaxing invitation from Sandra Dix! She stood saucily dangling the medicine pot, waiting for the patient to turn over to where she remained. And then *he* had to ask *her* for a glass of water. Help was never readily forthcoming from that girl. She'd probably be best suited as a shopgirl, where, from my observations, an unhelpful attitude always seemed to me to be a prime pre-requisite. Cheeky little madam, I thought, as I helped Tommy turn over.

Just in time, I stopped him taking the red and black capsules, that I knew to be Ampicillin. This was the broad-spectrum antibiotic prescribed, which would attack a wide range of invading organisms, including hopefully the one at work in Tommy's infection. However, it was defeating the object to give it before all the raw specimens had been obtained. It would affect and mask the result of the C & S, culture and sensitivity, assessment of the sample.

I told Sandra to leave the capsules with me until I had obtained the sputum specimen. No sooner said than done. Tommy obliged with a very rattly, chesty cough and managed to shift some of the sticky, persistent sputum from his lungs.

'Hold that,' I said quickly, as I prized off the lid from the wax carton and held it out for him to spit into. The tenacious, thick green sputum stuck to the side of the pot and to his lips, causing him to give a further spit to get it clear.

'Boy, that beats a smoker's cough,' he said looking at the fruity expectoration.

'And plenty more where that came from. Lots of hard work to shift it too,' I added.

Of all the secretions with which nurses have to deal, I have always found sputum to be the most offensive. Watching a patient clear his lungs and move sputum is a satisfying result. Ever since I had had a bout of bronchitis, I knew how much easier it felt to be free of stubborn phlegm. But I was nauseated to the core by the sight of it. I was eternally grateful that I'd not been nursing in the days when sputum was collected and measured in stainless steel mugs, needing to be emptied and cleaned by the nurses. A job which no doubt was delegated to the most junior member on the ward.

It was an uphill climb to get Tommy's chest clear and we all had to work hard, not least of all him. The villainous micro-organism was responding well to the Ampicillin, which proved to be suitably effective. There was nothing especially powerful about the bug, we are surrounded by them all the time. In this instance it had just found a nice, warm and moist spot in Tommy's lung. Undisturbed by deep breathing or strenuous coughing or circulating clean air, it had settled and reproduced in the inviting conditions.

I used him as an example to discuss the commonly occurring post-op. complication of chest infection during one of my lunch-time teach-ins. It was by way of a cautionary tale. Hypostatic pneumonia rapidly develops when the opportunistic microbes readily take hold in static lung tissue. In smokers the chances are even greater as the hair-like cilia, which waft out debris from the respiratory tract, have been paralysed or killed by the action of the continually polluting smoke.

The teaching sessions were proving very popular and I was spurred on by my success. The nurses said how helpful and stimulating they found them. Mrs Burrows was particularly receptive and encouraged my efforts. I enjoyed the stimulus which kept me on my toes and abreast of modern trends.

Within a few days the fever died down and Tommy was feeling weak but perky again.

Margo gave him intensive physiotherapy twice a day, more if she was able. A couple of times I'd seen her come in on her way home to give him a last dose of back clapping, before the inevitable build up occurred overnight.

We ensured that he stayed upright in bed and were giving him copious quantities of fluid to fight the infection. The nurses did their best with physio. I'd tried to pick up tips from Margo but never got that confident, forceful touch which she had acquired over many years of working on reluctant chests and their owners.

Every four hours we gave him an inhalation, designed to loosen the secretions and ease the tightness in his chest. Tommy began to look forward to this treatment, which was soothing and extremely beneficial.

He'd sit in the armchair, poised on the edge, with the little table in front of him and a towel at the ready around his neck. I supervised as Nurse Littleton took in the tray with the inhaler. It contained hot water and the steaming Friar's Balsam, a very distinctive tarry-smelling aromatic medication.

'Going down,' joked Tommy, as he covered his head and

took deep breaths through the mouthpiece.

After a few strong inhalations, he would be stimulated to cough, as the secretions shifted and irritated his bronchial tubes – or 'bronical tubes' as Doreen would insist.

Tommy coughed and coughed, making slow but sure headway moving the phlegm. I watched Nurse Littleton, trying to encourage him, desperately wanting to help, almost wanting to do it for him. It looked so simple, just one more cough and that nagging sliver of phlegm would be out, it was almost possible to hear it moving on its journey upwards.

She strained forward, subconsciously cleared her own throat and held her own breath as he struggled to get it free. Anne was going through all the motions and getting puce in the face herself. She let out her breath forcefully as he spat. They both gave a great smile and sigh of relief as one more bit of gubbins landed in the carton.

After this session of hard work was over, he sang melodiously, 'The Sheikh of Araby' with the towel around his face, and whisked Anne around in a dance.

Anne Littleton enjoyed going in to Tommy now. He was no less of a rogue but she was well able to accept his playful jibes now. Relationships had levelled out, initial hostilities were forgotten and we were all less and less acutely aware of Tommy being a PP.

It was somewhat comforting to see him back to his old self, playing the wag; at least we knew he was on the mend.

Tommy was adamant about giving up smoking; it was getting to be an expensive habit anyway. At this stage we had every reason to respect the sincerity of his vow. But it was possible that when all this coughing and hacking and spitting and groaning became a thing of the distant past, the plan might not stick. A casual drink with the boys, passing a packet of cigarettes, 'Oh, just one to keep you company' and wham, resolutions out of the window and hooked again. Still, looking on the optimistic side, he would have spent a good few weeks away from the weed, which might be sufficient to break the habit. Many people find it repugnant after a rest from it; others find it delicious!

In the convalescent stage, Tommy was becoming claustrophobic in his side room and ventured increasingly into the day room to join the ladies.

That was mutually beneficial. He had a responsive audience for his showmanship and he fed from their enthusiasm. They were clamouring for the spicy stories and jokes that tumbled unceasingly from his mouth. For him, the laughter was the best form of natural physio available to help clear his lung fields.

The ladies enjoyed the engaging personality and tantalising encounter with a man of the world. It was something of a novel experience for the many housewives and mothers who rarely met such interesting males in the course of their daily suburban routine.

Before long, the women were drifting to see him in his room, taking in their chocolate boxes in exchange for a small tipple from the unofficial barman.

It was good for the ward to have light relief in the shape of Tommy, a character larger than life, who could cheer us all up. The ward was going through a cheerless and despondent patch. We would hit a low on occasion. We had a crop of heavy, bed-bound patients, needing plenty of concentrated basic nursing care. It was hard work, but not only that, they were a moany lot, disinclined to view any solitary thing with contentment.

We had also had a spate of deaths and the nurses were demoralised. Mrs Yates, with the secondary brain tumour, had eventually passed away without regaining consciousness. Burrows assisted Nurse Cathcart with her first laying out of a dead body. Another patient had died unexpectedly on the operating table and Ruth, a very lovable patient, was rapidly becoming the third of Burrow's trio of predicted corpses.

The nurses were disheartened and gloomy, so they latched on to the light relief offered by Mr Thomas Read and the band of lively ladies in the day room. You could see the nurses, one by one, taking a break from the pressures of the ward work to be revitalised by visiting the area nearest normality.

Tommy's ex-wife was not much in evidence, and indeed there was no reason why she should have been, but one day she did bring their son to see his father. They had very wisely waited until Tommy was well over his stormy recovery.

Young Tom Junior was a sturdy boy, very like his father in looks and mannerisms, although with insufficient experience to have developed the panache. He was at an age when children identify strongly with their same sex parent and it was apparent that he admired and idolised his successful father.

Young Tom was reticent at first when he entered the ward, shy, yet intrigued, by the unfamiliar surroundings. He was decidedly amused that Tom Senior should be on a female ward and I overheard some cavalier tale being spun to the gullible boy. Father and son sauntered down the ward, meeting other patients as they went. Visiting children always brought a bit of happiness and a breath of fresh air into the ward.

Bridie didn't approve of children on a general adult ward and she would usually insist they went down to the coffee shop whenever able patients were visited. But she wasn't on duty and his visit was up to my discretion. I turned a blind eye to the rules, while ensuring that Tommy steered his child clear of the more unseemly sights.

Tommy asked for another cup on his tea-tray and his son joined him for tea, demolishing every scrap available.

'He's a fine lad,' I commented, as I did the drug round later.

The two lady patients who were ensconced in his room agreed with an approving nod.

'He's the kind of child who you could eat when you see him lying there asleep,' he said so tenderly that the ladies 'ah-ed' melodiously in unison.

'And when he's awake you wish you had,' Tommy added quickly and we all roared with laughter.

But it is true of hospital life, that the happy, sparkling engaging patients are the well ones and these signs of return to his usual exuberance were indications that Tommy was fit to leave us soon. It was often difficult to say farewell to a patient whom we had got to know well and with a kind of intimacy, both emotional and physical, that is rarely encountered in anything other than a nursing or medical relationship. It isn't difficult to see why patients fall in love with their nurses or vice versa, but it has an unrealistic basis out of the professional context. Relatives are often jealous, and perhaps rightly so, of our intrusions into private feelings and behaviour which even they have never been included in.

Mr Simpson came to give Tommy Read his final checkover after I'd removed his sutures, leaving a fine scar. The surgeon warned Tommy against any heavy lifting or straining or sexual intercourse for at least the next two months.

I was pleased to hear the advice given on sexual activities after discharge. It is so often omitted and the patient goes home in ignorance about what is best for him - or her. Patients may be shy to ask the doctor or may not have given it serious consideration. During a stay in hospital, these basic needs often take a back seat and assume reduced proportions compared to the immediacy of surgery and recovery. Not until they return to the normal routine of life outside hospital do patients begin to think about the viability of sex, golf, shopping, lifting children and the million other things that have been suspended during a spell in the unique environment that is hospital.

'Can't think that I'll be romping around for a while anyway,' Tommy said after Mr Simpson had departed. 'Not in my state of *au naturel*.' He meant his shaved pubic hair which was beginning to grow through bristly. 'Rather like having it off with a hedgehog.'

There was no doubting that a randy male, or female, would be well able to achieve sexual satisfaction without needing to resort to physical gymnastics. If the need arose Tommy would surely find a way.

Thomas Read left with the same kind of fanfare with which he came. His going didn't pass unnoticed. The staff watched from the office, amused as he did a round of the ward, saying fond farewells and kissing hands.

He came to say goodbye to the staff and we were truly sorry when it was time for him to leave. It was certainly going to be quiet without him.

'Sorry that you had a bumpy ride but I hope you enjoyed your stay.' I must have been wreathed in a self-congratulatory smile, I was pleased that he'd settled in so well.

'I did. It was money well spent.' He produced half a dozen bottles of champagne. 'A little something for you girls to remember me by.'

I thought it would probably best be put aside in the Christmas cupboard – most of it anyway. We'd open one today to drink his health on his way, rationed to medicine-pot measures.

'Thanks, Sis, all the girls did a grand job. I enjoyed the personal touches – all of them.' He shook my hand firmly, held me uncompromisingly close and didn't release me until I had blushed to his satisfaction.

A rogue to the last but a personable one. He winked, kissed my hand and left.

FOURTEEN: TERMINATION

During all this time, Ruth had remained with us, slowly dying from the cancer which was rampaging through her body.

The operation was a palliative measure, one which would relieve distressing symptoms but could not in any way effect a cure. The malignant tumour had grown from the head of the pancreas and, because of its anatomical siting, soon caused obstruction of the common bile duct, which opens into the gut in the same area. It was this damming back of the bile which caused accumulation in the blood, thus jaundice, itching and nausea.

Mr Simpson had performed a simple operation to by-pass the mass. Any further heroic measures would have been futile and have added little to the quantity or quality of her remaining life. The tumour had infiltrated the surrounding tissues all over the abdomen. Metastases, secondary deposits, were certainly present in the liver. There was no way of telling how many other stray cells had migrated via the blood and lymph systems, to seed and grow in distant parts of the body, ready to cause havoc from their destructive processes.

The jaundice subsided immediately once the bile outflow had been restored and Ruth felt a lot better. Anyone else might have taken this dramatic improvement as an indication that all was well for a bright future. But she wasn't one to stick her head in the sands of false hopes, besides, she knew too much from working the other side of the bed. She wanted to know the precise nature of the problem, exact details of the operation and prognosis, or probable outcome - in fact how long she had to live.

Mr Simpson spent a good long time talking to her alone. It was his awesome responsibility, as surgeon in charge of the case, to divulge such news, whether it be good or bad. Ruth knew better than to ask any of the nurses and put them on the spot. Other patients often try to weedle out information from the staff, asking the same question from each nurse in turn, hoping perhaps for an optimistic view from one. It was very stressful for the nurses and in consequence they often, quite subconsciously, used avoidance tactics to prevent being interrogated. But Ruth knew *who* to ask and, without doubt, *what* to ask.

I was anxious to know what Mr Simpson had told her. It is imperative that all members of staff are aquainted with the policy decisions on such matters. Patients are not always told the full extent of their illness immediately and some do not really want to know.

In my new position as Sister, I was likely to be asked more searching questions by patients and I wanted to understand the way such news is imparted.

Peter Simpson explained his strategy and, following his enlightening explanation, I had been glad that I'd plucked up the courage to ask him. I saw Mr Simpson in a new light.

Patients would be told of their condition at a rate at which they could, or more importantly, on an emotional level, *would* accept it. No faster. It wasn't a question of not comprehending medical terms or jargon, this could be explained in easy terms. It was more an emotional readiness to accept the fact of dying. Some were prepared to know well in advance, others might only accept it at the very last. Certainly there was no earthly point in casting gloom and despondency or alarm on someone who might have many months or years of happy, useful life ahead. One thing Peter Simpson always said he avoided was to quote any time limit when patients would ask 'how long?'. He might make a wide, generalised and usually generously optimistic appraisal but he wasn't up to playing God and knew there were too many unknown factors involved that could affect the outcome: the unknown spread of the cancer, the fitness of the patient, other infective processes at work and definitely the mental attitude of the patient. If told they will die, patients may give up there and then and wait for the end. Those with great resilience can battle on and extend their sentence of death.

The secret was always to tell the truth, veiled perhaps, guarded maybe – a perceptive patient will challenge the detail. Never tell an outright lie, it is unethical and unkind. Patients will pick up cues if they are ready to know more.

For the condition affecting Ruth, he would start by saying that he had successfully relieved the blockage. If a biopsy was taken but no operation performed in a hopeless case, he would say some cells had been removed. Both are true.

What was the cause?

A growth. True.

Malignant?

Yes. Also true.

Had the operation removed all the cancer?

No.

Would it grow again and was there secondary involment?

Yes.

Could nothing be done to prevent the spread?

In this case, no.

Ruth pursued his strategic itemisation to its logical and painful conclusion. She felt happier being aware of the facts. Another patient might have been equally satisfied to know that the blockage had been removed and to feel well again. Unless they inquired further, they would be told no more, although the nearest relatives would be informed of the full extent of the truth. It is left to their discretion, knowing the patient as they do, whether to tell them of their fate.

It is an onerous and distressing task to carry such a secret about a loved one and to play out a happy and hopeful charade. Equally, for us, no nurse likes the burden of knowing a patient is in the terminal stages of a disease, when that person is blissfully unaware of the fact, being euphorically delighted with the success of their operation. I often wonder that they don't suspect through our curbed enthusiasm, or perhaps we really *do* develop the art of good acting. It must be a thousand times worse for the relatives who are forced to live this lie in the twenty-four hour company of a dying but unsuspecting loved one.

Certainly it made things easier for us and for Ruth and her family that she understood the truth and was able to talk openly about death. Mr Simpson had made no offer of cytotoxic drug therapy or deep X-ray treatment. In his considered opinion, the cancer was too widespread to respond effectively to any further therapies, especially taking into account their undesirable side-effects of nausea and hair loss. Ruth agreed with him, having no desire to enter protracted treatment and end her days in misery, even if it did mean providing a few more of them.

It wasn't usual for the surgical ward to have terminal cases. Our beds were too precious, always needed for acute surgery. Usually terminal patients recovered from surgery sufficiently to enable them to go home and, if need be when the time came, to be admitted to the medical side.

Ruth's abdominal wound was slow to heal, probably taking longer than normal owing to the presence of jaundice and cancer. A small and persistent sinus, a slim channel of infection, developed at the lower end of the wound where a stitch had been. This needed daily dressings.

Once this had healed she had further complications due to the cancerous involvement of the pancreas. This organ supplies enzymes to the gut to help digestion of food substances. It also supplies the hormone, insulin, directly into the blood stream to control the level of blood sugar. Deficiency of insulin causes disturbance of the sugar metabolism, called diabetes mellitus or sugar diabetes.

Almost simultaneously, Ruth had steatorrhoea – fatty undigested faeces – and diabetes. It was she who first noticed a marked increase in her appetite, and a craving for Mars bars, alongside a consistent loss of weight, which is characteristic of diabetes but complicated by her cancer. A routine urine test revealed the excess sugar in her urine, that was being excreted instead of being used by the body. Both problems were easily controlled but were a morbid sign of continuing deterioration in her general condition.

She kept up and about in the ward for as long as she possibly could, keeping contact with the patients who had become her friends. I noticed that she began to spend longer periods in bed. There were pains in her abdomen, radiating around and up her back, although characteristically for her she made light of her suffering. Andrew wrote her up for DF 118, a fairly stong analgesic, but she was one of the unlucky people who were made sick by this particular drug. She switched to Fortral but before long stronger medication was needed.

Ruth had hoped to go home but all she ever managed was a trial weekend, her last look at the home she loved, then back to Parker.

Her husband had a job that caused him to travel a lot, although his firm were being very generous about giving him leave at this particular time. They didn't want to lose a key worker and he didn't want to throw up his lifelong career. His wife knew how much his work meant to him and she was perceptive enough to know how much more it would mean to him when she had gone.

Professional staff are very glib at saying 'discharge home', 'back to the family', 'can be washed/lifted/toileted/ by the relatives', 'convalesce at home', 'die at home'. In reality it is rarely so easy with the tidy, tiny nuclear family, where roles are clearly defined and dependent invalids are a burden.

Ruth's only daughter was heavily pregnant and in no way able to care for her mother. It was a loving family, bonded even closer perhaps by these twin occasions, the ironic proximity of birth and death. Ruth was so near to becoming a grandmother, to seeing the third generation that would justify her own efforts at motherhood.

Ruth was still able to get out to the toilet, using the commode, a wheelchair with a seat that fits over the lavatory pan. It was the one thing that she hoped to do until the very last, to preserve her independence in this one area.

Her body was wasting away noticeably. The fat underlying her skin was gone, leaving it hanging in leathery folds, making her look prematurely aged. As she spent more time in bed her muscles atrophied from disuse.

The malignancy had penetrated all over her body, now consuming with ease and rapidity every part. Wherever the cancer had developed originally was of no importance. The condition was now called carcinomatosis, a generalised and widespread cancer. Cachexia is the term used to denote the accompanying wasting, emaciation and toxic results that occur in the final stages of the disease.

Oh, what madness is cancer. A few debauched cells stray from the orderly chain of nature and multiply with abandon. Multiplication beyond the needs of the body. Multiplication that must feed from the host, ravaging and eventually destroying it. The cells rage wanton destruction by their unbridled proliferation. But the ultimate engulfing death of the host body takes with it those impetuous cells and their many untimely, presumptious progeny. Oh, the folly of malignant cells.

Ruth was dying fast. Every day she looked worse, weaker and in greater pain. She was now virtually in need of constant nursing attention. Still, when she was free of pain, she would rally around to maintain an optimistic conversation.

It was getting on for a month or more since she'd had her hair washed and she asked if we might do it for her. It was the least we could do to make her feel more comfortable. I thought, with some sadness, that it would probably be the last time she would ever have it done.

Washing hair in bed was a procedure that I'd learnt about in my training but had never had occasion to put it into practice. Patients were up and out of bed so quickly these days in hospital.

Doreen and Staff Nurse Witherden set to and executed the task very efficiently. The mattress was pulled over the bottom end of the bed. This exposed an area of bed springs at the top, on which to rest the washing bowl. Supporting Ruth's head over the bowl, they were able to give a quick, clean wash in the comfort of the lying position, causing no strain or inconvenience to the patient.

Doreen completed the coiffure with the blow drier and some strategically placed hair pins to support Ruth's long mane. She lay propped up on the pillows. I noticed the demarcation line along her hair which indicated where she last had a tint. Her long blonde locks carried a crown of pepper and salt.

I became aware of all the little things that we, as women, do to keep up our appearance, even more as we get older. We take for granted being able to do them when fit and well but they are the first things to go by the board in illness. Controlling underarm hair, shaving legs, bleaching above the top lip, colouring and styling hair, plucking eyebrows, attention to nails, as well as the daily application of make-up, perfumes, deodorants and creams.

I particularly noticed Ruth's hands as I stopped to speak. Her wedding ring hung loosely on her slim, now bony, finger. Her nails were getting long, brittle and misshapen, with the patchy remnants of a browny orange nail polish that her daughter had put on for her. All we could offer would be for one of the nurses to trim her nails, although, on second thoughts, perhaps one of the convalescent patients might do her a manicure.

She agreed that she would be grateful for that. Then changed the subject.

'Please, Helen, could I please ask a favour?' she blurted out her request. 'Please don't put me in the side room!' She held my hand and unintentionally shook it as she repeated each 'please'.

'I'm so happy to be able to stay here, on Parker, with everyone I know. I feel I am amongst friends. I like hospitals. I like the activity, the liveliness. But I can't bear the thought of being shut away, left to die alone and in silence, with nothing to watch and no one to see me.' Ruth had tears in her eyes, she'd been building up to this earnest request. I'd never before seen her express herself so strongly over anything, she was always so placid. It meant a lot to her.

Obviously being aquainted with hospitals, she knew the routine of moving dying patients near the door, close to Sister's office where they could be closely observed and screened when the end was near, then easily despatched from the ward. A side room was an even better proposition from the ward's point of view, so that the harrowing sight of a dying patient could be concealed. Such is the concept of death in our present society and so often 'out of sight' does in reality become 'out of mind'. It means tidiness for the bureaucracy but isolation for the patient at a time when company is most welcomed.

Ruth knew this and it was the one thing that she feared, the loneliness that so often accompanies dying.

Death is something which the hospital institution and the staff within it find difficult to come to terms with. Medical and nursing care are so positively directed to healing patients that death can be seen as a failure of all that health care represents. When the intensely curative process of the medical machinery decides that nothing more can be done; that is, nothing to cure the sickness, then the patient may be left to die in an emotional and spiritual vacuum. In our minds we don't believe this is so and it is not a conscious decision to reject the dying patient but there will always be more 'important' work to be completed with the living.

I promised Ruth that I would try my utmost to comply with her request, although I wasn't so sure that Bridie would go along with the idea. I could only offer my best intentions.

At home, I had previously discussed with Susy the possibilities of hospice care, a home especially designed to cater for the needs of the dying. There was one within the district, with which Susy, as a social worker, had substantial contact.

Although run by Roman Catholic nuns, it was non-denominational as regards admission of patients. Susy spoke in glowing terms of this wonderful home, filled with an air of tranquility and pure love by the utter dedication of the nuns and their plethora of helpers. There was a high staff-patient ratio to allow extensive patient contact. They were committed to easing patients from this world with a mind and body at peace with the end. There was no preaching or religious indoctrination but there was an undoubted aura of spiritual uplifting, which gave a comfort to even the least religious person.

No one ever died alone. No one was ever allowed to die in pain, whereby the act of dying would be sweet, merciful relief. On the other hand no one was ever drugged to oblivion. The medication was carefully prescribed to alleviate miserable symptoms but not to push the patients to their end with a disorientated haze as their last confused view of life.

In the philosophy of the hospice movement, death is respected as an important part of life, not denigrated because it is the final part. Those who believe in an after life must be uplifted to think that earthly death is the birth of a spiritual life. Death is allowed to be lived through, as one tremendous emotional and, with the correct handling, no doubt a rewarding, maturing experience, a final coming to terms with one's existence.

It is unfortunate that in the hospital setting it is viewed as a negative experience; a failure; nature's final success over the battery of scientific offerings. We rarely accepted the fact with good grace, leaving the patient to lose out amidst our disappointment.

The hospice seemed the ideal solution for Ruth and it was both suggested and recommended by Mr Simpson. She dismissed the idea out of hand, preferring to stay, as she put it, 'in the land of the living.' He left her on Parker and must have anticipated that her end was precariously near. Mr Simpson always stopped to speak to Ruth on his rounds and she appreciated this. So often the hopeless 'case' gets overlooked and the person who is the 'case' gets ignored and passed over in the ongoing ward routine.

None of us could fail to admire the stoic acceptance by this patient of her forthcoming death. It was almost embarrassing for us that she faced it squarely, as we were also forced to look at it with her. That is unusual in our society and something which stirred up a lot of emotions with which we had to cope.

Often we would discuss Ruth during handover. It happened quite spontaneously but was an indication that we all needed to talk though our feelings. They were better out than bottled up.

The nurses expressed a lot of anger over the dying of this well-loved patient. The younger nurses tried to see some sense, some justification in this waste of a life. That was a hopeless view. Useless.

Ruth had been in her prime, sparkling and happy with life, kind to everyone. The world needed more like her, not less. What a waste, an atrocious waste of a meaningful, constructive life. Here we were busting a gut always to save it, and this patient was fading before us, beyond our control, all our expert control.

A second year student had just come from a spell in the

Accident Department, where fit, young people were brought in after suicidal or pseudo-suicidal bids. The successful ones, and there were many, even among those whose attempt may have seemed only an attention-seeking gambit that went wrong, threw away their long, healthy lives by choice. Life wasn't fair. It was easy to see how hostility was stirred up in nurses by the self-mutilators if they saw this action as a drain on their time, skill and resources.

The depressed, the old, the hopelessly crippled, they might welcome the sweet relief of death. Yet here lay Ruth and we were at a loss to save her. God wasn't fair.

It seemed that we, the staff, the nurses involved in caring for the dying patient, were working through the emotions of grief, denial, anger, bargaining and depression. Hopefully we would soon move to acceptance. It wasn't our province to moralise or criticise or offer judgement but that didn't stop us *feeling*. I'd hoped it was useful for those feelings to be brought to the surface and aired. It was good that as a team, we didn't all think we were alone in shouldering our anxiety and disappointment.

Nurse Littleton bravely expressed to the rest of us that her particular fear was of finding Ruth gone. That horrible moment of approaching a patient, not knowing if you are addressing or touching a corpse. Once you knew for sure, you felt OK, but the no-man's-land on the verge of life and death was eerie. Also she'd never seen a body and wasn't quite sure what to expect, either of it or her initial reaction.

Ruth Abbott had religion and it was a source of extreme comfort to her. Her belief in a better existence in the after life, a surety that she would see her family again, buoyed her along in a most commendable and comforting way. The chaplain visited the ward on his regular rounds and Ruth became one of his predictable stops. She took communion at an early hour when the night nurse would sit her propped up to join in the personalised ceremony and screen the bed to offer privacy.

She made her peace with God. She spent as much time as she could with her family. She wanted to see her friends, to say goodbye and put her affairs in order. Ruth made use of the time she had left and, for her, it was good that she knew her time was limited. Hers would be a tidy departure.

Ruth developed ascites, a collection of fluid in the peritoneal cavity, which made her abdomen swell up like a balloon. It was caused by back pressure, a damming up effect from the liver which was involved in the spreading cancer. It was an incongruous sight: her large, tense belly with prominent blue veins on the translucent skin. and her long skinny limbs poking out like a child's drawing of a matchstick man.

The sac of fluid was pressing on the diaphragm and encroaching on her breathing. Dr Jeffrey had to remove the fluid by passing a large bore needle into the peritoneal cavity and draining the fluid. I let two student nurses watch this paracentesis abdominis, as it is a procedure which only rarely needs to be performed. Nearly half a litre of yellow serous fluid was withdrawn, giving immediate relief to her embarrassed breathing.

She understood what was happening to her body and retained an unyielding and remarkable geniality. Ruth joked that she and her daughter would be racing towards D-Day, delivery day, with their vast spreading stomachs. It was the coming of this, her first grandchild, which gave Ruth a *raison d'être*, a will to live, when all else within her was crumbling away.

Ruth's appetite grew poor. This was not the place for rigorous medical intervention with naso-gastric or intravenous feeding. Whilst she was able and interested to take nourishment, we tried to please her taste and make it appealing. Solid food soon became difficult for her to manage and she tired easily with chewing. She liked the flavoured Complan drinks, occasional warm egg and milk and milky coffee, to which we could add a few spoonsfull of nourishing glucose.

Another of her favourites was yoghurt, tasty and refreshing, with a variety of flavours. This could be managed through a drinking cup with a spout or spooned into her mouth. Mr Abbott had watched the nurses feeding her and soon took it upon himself to take his turn. He would lift her head and give gentle support as he poured in small quantities of the liquid for her.

It was a tangible and practical activity that he could do for her. At visiting times, Mr Abbott would sit and talk quietly, almost as if pressurised to keep contact in these last few precious days. She seemed to welcome his visits but was getting too weak to reply very much. He always looked strained after a visit, each one that ended was a mixture of relief and sadness. There was a limit to how much of a lifetime you can cram into a short space of time and he was obviously realising this. He looked drained and exhausted, struggling to smile as the bottom gradually dropped out of his world.

Mr Abbott came daily with a supply of yoghurts but Ruth's appetite waned, so that just a taste would suffice. A backlog of yoghurts built up in the ward fridge and I had to tell him that we really had sufficient for the present.

He looked downcast as this last small way of helping Ruth was taken from him and my heart went out to him. It had been a small act to purchase yoghurts every day but, for him, the choosing, buying and fetching was a meaningful routine he could perform for his beloved wife.

'See if one of the other patients might like them, please Sister,' he said, as he handed me his latest, and probably his last plastic bag. 'They may help someone else.' His words barely audible, as he dug his hands in his pockets and left the ward.

Towards the end, Andrew Jeffrey wrote her up for heroin, the strongest analgesic and the final drug in the waning history of a cancerous patient.

He wrote the new prescription. 'It's quite predictable that there will be further build up of peritoneal fluid and she'll need another paracentesis,' he said calmly, but leaving out the unspoken words 'if she lasts that long'.

I checked the chart. 'You've forgotten the PRN,' I said, and offered it back to him.

Pro re nata (PRN) is the latin abbreviation for whenever necessary. He had prescribed heroin four hourly. As it stood, we were being instructed to give it every four hours, whether or not she needed it. Large and regular doses of heroin are addictive and lethal. Given when needed it is an effective pain reliever and euphoriant; excess will fuddle the brain and affect thought processes. The addition of PRN meant that we could give it no more frequently than every four hours but beyond that it was at the trained nurses discretion, depending on the patient's needs.

I presumed he'd mistakenly omitted the abbreviation. He bristled as he felt I was challenging his authority.

'No, that's correct as it stands. Those are my orders.' He stuck to his decision.

'Why? What's the point? There's no need to hurry the inevitable, her time will come soon enough,' I said to him.

'She's in pain, she's having complications. She's dying, there's no point in prolonging her agony.' His attitude was now one of haughty irritation as I challenged him.

I knew Ruth was fighting to live. The birth of her grandchild was imminent but the lazy blighter was already late.

'Well, I'm sorry, we aren't going to administer it like that. It's medicated murder.' I refused to condone such a barbaric method when it was so unnecessary. 'She'll get it when she needs it, not for your convenience.'

He was getting very cross and so was I.

'She is *dying*, look at her, it's criminal to let her suffer.' Andrew pointed to where she lay like a rag doll.

'Christ almighty, we're all dying,' I raised my voice to this arrogant upstart, 'we're all dying from the day we're born. It's a continuous process and I don't see who gives you such authority to end it.'

'Oh, very philosophical!' He mocked me then reverted to his aggressive stance. 'I'm not arguing with you. She's my patient, these are my instructions. Please make sure they are carried out.'

'No, I'm sorry. The days of nurses being the doctor's unthinking, unquestioning maidservant are over.' – although I doubted he'd heard or even been listening for that kind of news, – 'We are professionals in our own right, not blind and mindless followers. Ever heard of team-work, doctor?'

Stalemate. We glared at each other, adamant with our views.

Bridie came breezily into the office to start her late shift. 'What have we here, a lovers' tiff?' She was oblivious of the argument raging but aware of the tense atmosphere.

I'm sure Andrew wouldn't have been so forceful if it had been Bridie who confronted him. Maybe he was practising on novice Sisters like myself to wield power in his next job. Anyway now he was disinclined to lose face, having said his piece.

I explained our difference of opinion and my vehement remonstrations not to be part of his corrupt practice.

'Well, Sister Davies is quite within her rights to speak on behalf of the nurses. Such an instruction is preposterous. If you insist on this, you will have to give the injections yourself. I am quite happy to ask the night staff to wake you four hourly through the night,' Bridie said clearly. 'But first of all we had better check with the consultant; you see she is not *your* patient, Doctor Jeffrey, the final responsibility lies with Mr Simpson and I'd like to know what he thinks about his junior staff's decisions.'

She lifted the telephone as if to contact the consultant. I was totally convinced that she would go to any lengths to find him and expose this whole farce. So was Andrew.

He looked exasperated by her cool execution and correct procedural tactics. I was proud yet envious, wondering if I would ever be so strong and sure of myself.

Andrew added three large black letters 'PRN' and deliberately handed the board back to me.

'You,' he pointed the board at me and tensed his lips, 'are too bloody involved for your own good.'

I was on the verge of tears, particularly as I felt his words to be true. Were my feelings so transparently obvious? All of us were drained by this prolonged and laborious death. Was it unprofessional to be emotionally involved, did it interfere with my ability to think rationally? Nurses' emotions are usually tempered by all they experience but the dying of Ruth had penetrated our defences. Can we control it? Should we control it?

Bridie got the last word in with Andrew Jeffrey.

'And you are too detached for the patients' good. Helen is a good nurse, maintaining her professional standards. It is a pity that you have so few and a blessing that others are able to keep an eye on your scruples.'

He hadn't acted illegally. It is one of those grey areas of medical ethics, problems which have no definite right, no definite wrong, a borderline decision that some poor bugger is put on the spot to make. There'll always be someone, somewhere who can shout loudly to oppose it. It's the open debate that prevents corruption from gaining a foothold.

The Hippocratic oath, on which medical ethics is based, states, 'thou shall not kill,' also 'but shall not strive to keep officiously alive.' Modern medicine has invited modern dilemmas and it's often difficult to dictate when the striving has to cease.

Ruth slept a lot and lapsed into clouded consciousness now and again, slightly confused and unaware of the time or day. We made a point of telling her each time we attended to her, in an effort to keep her orientated to her surroundings. Nevertheless, she clung bravely to life and her struggle was the essence of self-possessed composure.

In all honesty, she looked ghastly: shrunken, emaciated, with a dull yellowey-grey taint to her dry skin. It was a conflict of interests, whether to do the best for one dying patient or to remove the offending sight from the rest of the other patients and visitors in the ward.

We had to move her up the ward, closer to the office. Luckily, the side ward was occupied by an infectious patient, so Ruth remained with us, as she had wished.

She needed total nursing care for all her bodily functions. Her frail, bony body was turned and repositioned every two hours in an effort to prevent the development of bedsores on the prominent parts. She was hardly able to help herself at all.

Her fluid intake was negligible and she barely even managed a few sips of fluid, despite our spooning it in. We moistened her mouth regularly and put vaseline on her lips. Even so, cracks were forming at the corner of her mouth.

Generally her eyes remained closed but occasionally she would struggle to raise her upper lids to peer through her dull, pink eyes.

She did so on the occasion when I imparted the news of the arrival of her new granddaughter. I was so happy to take the phone call and rushed to her, hoping against hope that she could take it in.

I whispered to her. 'Ruth, Ruth,' I nudged her awake. She lifted those heavy lids and with great effort focused on me.

'It's a girl,' I could hardly get the words out quickly enough, lest this important moment be lost forever. 'It's a girl,' I repeated, my voice now quaking with emotion.

'Your son-in-law has just this minute rung,' I imagined briefly the panic that there had been at their end in the maternity hospital. 'Can you hear me?' I checked.

She nodded slightly and mouthed a barely perceptible, 'Yes,' and wiggled her fingers.

I clasped her hand. 'A little girl, Jennifer Ruth they've called her, Jennifer Ruth.'

'Jenn ... ifer,' she whispered the name with her dry, salivaless mouth. A fleeting smile passed over her face, leaving a serene and happy look as she sank again onto her pillows.

'They're both fine,' I added, not knowing if she'd heard me. I wanted to say it all over again, to share that happy experience with her. But she had absorbed what she had wanted and that was all she could manage to concentrate on. I felt honoured to have been able to bring that longed-for news to Ruth.

It was as if she had clung on to life to welcome the latest tiny member of her family. People often seem to have some strange, inexplicable control over their own destiny, as if some strength of will can preserve them to unpredictable lengths.

Once the baby had arrived, Ruth let hold of life, unfortunately never even seeing her grandchild.

Later that evening her breathing changed to the ominous pattern of Cheyne-Stokes respiration, a common accompaniment of impending death. There was a period of rapid breathing, followed by apnoea, or cessation of breathing for a considerable period. Each period of silent apnoea could have been the last. Suddenly she would start up breathing again with an uncanny determination.

Mr Abbott sat with her but it was doubtful that she was aware of his presence, although we had no way of telling. Hearing is the last sense to be lost, so I encouraged him to speak freely as he wished in the hope that she might hear.

That unnerving pattern of breathing was repeated for several hours and the periods of apnoea seemed interminably long. We had to leave him alone, with the curtain drawn on one side, but he could see into the office.

As her gasping became full of effort, he sank into a silent vigil. No tears, he would not let her feel or hear his tears. It was his way and he would keep strong for her.

He concentrated on her face, as if trying to drink in the indelible memory of this his last look. He held her hand and twiddled with the wedding ring which hung loosely on her sinewy finger. I wondered what thoughts were passing through his mind at that time. The past? The future? How good it all was? How much better it might have been – if only. A funeral, a birth, a Christening, a life alone, an empty house. Who can tell, who could ever intrude or record the train of thought?

I was dreading that final moment and watched as he sat by the bedside, taking the pulse every so often as he'd learnt to do.

The breathing finally stopped, never to restart. Mr Abbott looked up, caught my eye and nodded. It was no false summons. Every system had stopped. Cancer had claimed another victim. After 8 p.m., just as visiting ended, Ruth died.

Mr Abbott looked as stunned at the passing of his wife as if he'd received news of her sudden death. No amount of preparation can ever alleviate that cruel, piercing moment of realisation that a person is with you no more and has gone for ever.

Andrew had to certify the death, then after a short rest period, the body was laid out. Kiki Sharma was pleased to complete this final honour, helped by Anne Littleton, who was doing her first laying out. Last rites was the task that most nurses dread, especially for the first time, simply because you don't know what to expect. I was glad for Anne that she knew the patient, that made it a much more pleasant task.

Mr Abbott had asked to see Ruth when she had been prepared before she finally left the ward. He'd had a drink from the evening trolley then walked around the grounds, no doubt making a few important phone calls.

It was my job to escort him behind the screens and remove the sheet, thus revealing the shrouded body of his departed wife. I stood respectfully beside her averting my eyes from him. He looked briefly at her, did and said nothing.

'Thank you, Sister,' he said with tears welling up in his eyes.

I made no reply. Oh, God, what was there to say? What words could help this man in his anguish? What words could escape over the huge lump that was filling my throat? I always felt so desperately sorry for the relatives who were left to suffer the pain of their loss.

I replaced the cover on Ruth and escorted Mr Abbott from the ward. He'd have to return to collect her belongings and for the death certificate. I watched as he walked down the corridor, slowly and silently, as if loathe to be separated from his loved one.

I met Kiki Sharma coming from the staff loo, her cheeks flushed and her eyes red and moist.

'Thanks Kiki, for taking Nurse Littleton. I'm sure she appreciated it.'

She smiled and patted the wet paper towel to cool her fiery cheeks before going into the ward. The patients would feel bad enough themselves, without having the nurses all dissolving into tears.

The ward stayed calmly reverent in the aftermath of Ruth's death. The patients gathered in the day room as the body was removed in the mortuary trolley.

My routine 'Goodnight ladies' was less strident than usual. Their reply was warm but sombre.

FIFTEEN: CONFRONTATION

For the month of August, Parker was mine. It was my first spell of *total* responsibility as Sister in sole charge of the ward.

During the first two weeks, Bridie was acting up for Miss Ashton, the NO, who was on holiday. Bridie hated having to do it but as the most senior ward sister, she was the one best equipped for the job. I thought she did it rather well, with her experience of Gartland and her direct and precise decision-making ability, plus extreme capability in a crisis.

It just wasn't her scene though, shuffling people about and having to be diplomatic when staff were in conflict. Bridie had been offered many opportunities for further promotion but she wasn't interested in the post of Nursing Officer. Or any other post. She wasn't career orientated, not like Kate Ashton, whose heart and soul were devoted to her work.

Bridie O'Connell was a diligent sister, who put her nose to the grind-stone and ran the ward well. To her it was a job that ended when she left the grounds of the hospital and resumed when she returned the next day. She had her own flat, outside friends, who were non-medical, and made a point always of telling me about the parties and the men who made passes.

I suspected that Parker had been a fill-in job until Mr Right came along to take her away from it all. He never did and there she remained. She stayed on Parker almost by default, a legacy of her non-progress in the world at large. Bridie O'Connell felt she was fast becoming an old maid who had missed the boat and I think she was very resentful of that fact.

During her period of acting up, she felt displaced by being positioned in the loneliness of the NOs office. So we used to see her a lot down on Parker and she'd make a point of making us her coffee stop. Nevertheless, I was in charge of Parker, and although there was always someone on whom to call for advice, the day to day running of the ward was my ultimate responsibility.

This continued for the following two weeks when Bridie took her annual leave. It had become her regular arrangement to have holiday at the same time as Mr Martin, who always used to be away in the latter part of August.

The ward wasn't particularly busy because his admissions were curtailed considerably during his absence and the theatre lists were much lighter compared to normal.

The staff were used to me by now, but the loss of a key member invariably causes some restlessness on the ward. It may have been that the staff sensed my disquiet and missed the security of the senior sister but we did experience a spate of staff problems at that time. I was of course keen to demonstrate that I was a perfectly adequate replacement for Bridie.

It was the peak of holiday time. The nurses with children naturally wanted to go away during the school holidays. Anyway it was certainly a popular month to ensure the best of the weather in England.

Doreen was on leave for a week, although she never ventured to go away. Frankly, I missed the support of my confidante and used to pop in for tea on my way home from work sometimes. She liked the company as she was always rather at a loss away from the routine of work.

Doreen used the excuse to come to the hospital to visit Mrs Witherden, who was on female orthopaedics with a slipped disc. That was one more absentee, my reliable staff nurse – a part-time – off sick with a PID, prolapsed intervertebral disc.

This is one of the commonest industrial injuries sustained by nurses, unnecessarily prevalent, caused by injudicious lifting which throws strain on the back. The injury seemed slight and they were trying to correct it by traction, a system of pulleys and weights which would stretch the back sufficiently to pull on the spine and allow the disc to slip back into place. Mrs Witherden had the characteristic sharp pain down one leg, due to pressure on the sciatic nerve, which Doreen insisted was her 'society' nerve.

Those original two first year nurses, Littleton and

Cathcart, had finished their allocation on Parker. I was proud that I had schooled them so that they were becoming useful members of the team and familiar with the ward and its routine. Then it was time for them to move on and put their knowledge and experience to use elsewhere in the hospital.

They were replaced by two other first years. A new girl fresh from introductory block was enthusiastic and willing but, owing to her inexperience, was decidedly limited in what she could be left to do alone. She required a lot of supervision and, although I enjoyed this, it was time-consuming, especially when we were short staffed and I had no other sister to relieve me. I felt that I missed a lot of the close contact that I had previously been able to have with the patients. I had to spend that much more time in the office doing administrative bits and pieces that Bridie normally took on.

The other new nurse had been on the medical ward for her first allocation before coming to us. I was amazed at how much she had learnt from just those few months in nursing, she was at ease with junior routine procedures. Generally I relied on Kiki Sharma to organise the nurses for work allocation. We tried to give individualised patient care, one nurse to a small group of patients but its success was very sporadic.

Andrew Jeffrey had finally left, such a blessed relief to us all. After the disgusting episode with Ruth, Bridie hadn't felt inclined to give him a rousing farewell, which I understood to be her normal practice. The charge nurse from our counterpart male ward, who also had the same doctors, volunteered to do it this time for a change. We made a short, polite attendance, a gesture towards his farewell, so he didn't quite fizzle out of our lives.

The new houseman was an Egyptian, widely experienced in surgery in his own country. This job was far too junior for his expertise but he had to take a drop in status while working under our different system. Mahmoud Salah was very courteous and conscientious but naturally needed guidance initially with our British methods, particularly in administration. I had extra work helping him to adjust to our paper work. It was time well spent as he picked it up quickly. His first few weeks must have been utterly bewildering and he was continually seeking the assistance of 'Sheeshta Darvees'.

The perennial problem from which there was no escape was Sandra Dix. What is more, she appeared to get worse with the absence of Bridie's strict and guiding manner. She was a girl who responded favourably to a disciplinarian and that wasn't my way. But on this occasion I suffered for my democratic style.

Sandra was an SEN who had trained at Gartland and was assigned to Parker just after I had joined the ward. A State Enrolled Nurse takes a shorter, less academic training than a registered nurse, and SRN. Their course concentrates on the practical aspects of nursing and they are groomed to remain as bedside nurses.

Sandra Dix was a poor nurse by anyone's standards, slipshod and lazy about her work, curt and tactless to the patients – and sublimely oblivious to all her faults. She wore the uniform. She was the cat's whiskers. She was ten feet tall with her achievements and all criticism fell on stony ground as she lacked accurate self-perception.

God alone knows how she ever managed to pass the State exam. Why we ended up with her was another question for the Almighty.

She had worked on Parker as a pupil in training and had requested to come back to us when she qualified. Bridie had taken her on willingly. 'Well, who can afford to be choosey with all these staff shortages?' she said. 'She is a pair of hands,' Bridie added unflatteringly.

'More like two left feet – and both in her mouth,' said Burrows hotly, as she couldn't abide the girl.

Sandra and Burrows were daggers drawn. Poor Burrows, she felt so strongly that Sandra Dix was a disgrace to the profession and worse, she was letting down the side of the SEN. Burrows, herself also a proud SEN, was adamant to uphold the worth of the role, feeling that it was always being denigrated as second rate compared to the SRN.

For Mrs Burrows the final exasperating moment came when Sandra hoitily criticised Doreen for taking temperatures. Doreen, who had been nursing on Parker since before Sandra had even been born! This was just too much to stomach and their working relationship remained very, very frosty.

Sandra was status-conscious in the extreme. She was respecting of Staff Nurses, Sisters and above and would carry out their instructions implicitly, to the point where she became dangerously inflexible.

So when I asked her to help a post-op patient out of bed and that lady felt faint and nauseated, Sandra insisted that the lady stay up because, 'Sister says you *have* to sit out.' In a situation where I could expect a nurse, especially an experienced one, to use her common sense in the light of individual patient care, Sandra was unwilling to bend any senior instructions and stuck to the letter of 'Sister's Law'.

In the pecking order, she was a trained nurse and therefore senior to the students, pupils and auxiliaries. An SEN could normally be relied upon to guide the learners but she was so irritatingly bossy to her juniors, they disliked her and saw through her inflated idea of her own importance. She was not averse to imparting incorrect information in an attempt to impress them with her scanty knowledge. A glib, unthinking response was given, no matter how unsure she was of the answer to an enquiry. Sandra could usually be relied upon to get two and two to make five by the use of some ambitious embellishments. She was often the cause of that common complaint by patients, 'But I keep getting told to do different things.'

It was a difficult situation for me and I couldn't be everywhere at once. Here, on paper, I had an SEN. In reality I didn't feel I could use her to capacity as a trained nurse as fully as I would have liked, or should have expected to. More often than not I felt the need to check her work and sometimes I felt she was being carried by the rest of the staff. When it boils down to the ward work, paper qualifications are little compared to the capabilities of the person at the job.

Sandra was a mixed blessing and, in all fairness, she did have many good points. She was always at work on time and never one to take days off willy-nilly with frail, spurious excuses. She was unfussy about off-duty and obligingly liked to work weekends. When she did make a rare request for a special day off, it was usually mid-week, to coincide with her only bosom friend, another SEN working on geris. In that respect, Sandra was most reliable and probably thought she was God's gift to the profession by her virtuous time-keeping. Unfortunately coming to work is only the half of it, what you do in the time is more important.

I was finally forced to have words with Nurse Dix over the indiscriminate tea drinking, which was getting out of hand. I was no Draconian Sister about unofficial tea-breaks and knew full well that nurses grabbed a quick cup from the patients' drinks trolley. They knew I did it myself often enough but it was done discreetly, without fanfare.

In strict terms it was against the rules, the thin end of the wedge of stealing hospital property. There was the occasional blitz from the top, usually following an episode where a senior member had found a nurse tucking into free food behind the kitchen door, taken from the ward rations. Picking at the odd irresistible juicy chip can soon develop into expecting full scale meals from what the patients leave. The logical argument being, why let the pigs have it? It is a very difficult line to draw. There was a fine line between concessions and expectations.

I was something of a tea and coffee mop myself, so was disinclined to come heavy-handed when the nurses followed the tea trolley into the kitchen to help themselves from the great pot. There was no conceivable harm in that but it suddenly started going further – and Sandra Dix was the instigator.

On the sweltering hot summer days when the ward was airless and our damp uniforms clung uncomfortably, it had become customary to make up a jug of squash and leave it in the kitchen for the nurses to take turns and help themselves.

But Sandra ruined the whole thing by not knowing where to stop. She lacked ability to set limits for herself, always needing someone else to set them for her. Sandra took it upon herself to make a regular afternoon pot of tea for the staff, setting out the cups and making it her business to go around telling them when it was their turn. The juniors weren't to know that this wasn't standard procedure, they were new to nursing and new to the hospital. They followed like lambs this senior nurse, who was supposed to be setting a good example.

Initially this happened when one of the Staff Nurses was left in charge, Doreen told me, then she boldly started doing it while I was on duty. The misdemeanour was compounded by opening packets of biscuits and cutting up cake sent for the patients. I had to call a halt to this cosy little set-up and had to speak to her severely to put an end to these tea-time antics.

I had been building myself up for a confrontation with this nurse whose work and attitude I found unsatisfactory in so many ways. But the look of bland astonishment which filled her face took the wind right out of my sails. She didn't fully comprehend what she had done wrong. It's true that you cannot sin in ignorance. There was no malice in her and that was one of the most infuriating things about her.

True to form, she accepted my correction with good grace and promised not to do it again. Was she perhaps bewildered that she was being chastised for kindness to her fellow colleagues?

The ward was a little less happy that day, this slight upset had spoilt the easy-going atmosphere for us all.

With good nurses thin on the ground, I found myself relying a lot on Alma Gordon, who was indeed one of the best students that I had ever come across.

She was a second-generation Jamaican girl, born in Glasgow, with a soft Scots accent. In London, people found this combination incongruous and many an eyebrow was raised in disbelief, not least my own on our initial meeting.

Into her third year of training, the heat was on for Alma to study hard and succeed in her final exams. She'd had a difficult and fairly disadvantaged upbringing, but now she was married to a fellow West Indian, and together they had managed to climb out of the pit of deprivation. They moved down South when her husband was offered promotion and brought with them her widowed mother. With her two children off to school and a built-in babysitter, Alma took the opportunity to embark upon her life's dream to train as a nurse. She had already attained plenty of skills from a short period working as an auxiliary in an old people's home.

Never had I seen a girl to whom nursing came so naturally. She was marvellous at the bedside – where it counts. Her main asset was an intuitive understanding of the patients' finer needs. Not the highly technical details which hit the headlines but the little things that can make or mar a patient's hospital stay.

And they loved her, she was warm and responsive, gentle and understanding. Her total care was exemplary and she could be relied upon never to gloss over details. Alma Gordon was everything you could wish for in a nurse, standing by your bed, holding your hand, asking the right questions, giving the right answers, an open and natural honesty.

The senior staff found it hard to remember that she was a student when it came to delegating responsibility, her ability and conscientiousness far exceeded her level of training. I had heard from the sister in obstetrics how marvellous this student had been on the midwifery unit. Nurse Gordon's reputation preceded her and it was not unfounded, she had no difficulty living up to it. She took great interest in every aspect of her work.

It was unfortunate that she found the academic demands of nursing such a struggle. She was a born practical nurse but the theory didn't come easy, whereas for some of her colleagues the opposite was true. Information could drip off their tongues, textbook jargon would flow from their mouths, yet they couldn't hold a candle to Alma as regards patient care.

So keen was she to get that precious qualification, it meant so much to her, that she took every opportunity to increase her knowledge and study. I couldn't resist helping her, her willingness flattered the teacher in me. I would take her aside for teaching when time permitted, usually in the evenings and weekends, when the ward was quiet. We would discuss cases and procedures, diseases and treatments. Her grasp was good but her retention poor, so we plodded on to get the facts fixed.

She was remarkably industrious with her studies, with grit determination to succeed and she certainly deserved to. Even with the demands of a busy home life and young children to organise, she seemed to pack twice as much into her working day as the single girls.

I had never ceased to be amazed at how the married nurses, with children and husband to pack off for the day and a journey to the hospital, managed to get on duty on time, looking smart and attentive. Whereas the single girls, two minutes away in the nurses' home, dash on duty, invariably late, pinning on their caps en route.

Suddenly all this changed. Alma looked preoccupied, frowning, weighed down by thoughts, as if arguing inside herself and ruminating. The sparkle had gone from her warm eyes. Her glowing smile had vanished. Something was wrong. So deep was her troubled look, that even the patients began to notice. To avoid their questions and their penetrating glances, she stayed with them less, hurrying about her tasks, then away to the sanctuary of the utility rooms.

Basically she was a private person, keeping her family life and professional life apart. Alma wasn't interested in anyone else's gossip – for which hospitals are notorious – neither was she keen to start her own. On the whole, she didn't have a lot to do with the other nurses. Contact with her colleagues was on a superficial basis, it is often like that with the married girls. It is something of a struggle to fit in work and the domestic chores, as well as studying, without being bothered with boyfriends or parties in the nurses' home.

But with Alma, it seemed that her deep-seated trouble was more than just pressure of physical demands. I wanted to let her talk about it in her own time, if she felt the need to. I was concerned that perhaps her children were in difficulties or someone in the family ill; I knew her mother was in uncertain health. There were plenty of opportunities for her to off-load and I felt she was as likely to talk to me as to anyone. She never did. Her isolation grew worse and her mind was increasingly preoccupied.

Already I had noticed small discrepancies in her work, for which I had had to reprimand her; fluid charts not filled in, hot drinks left on the locker out of the reach of a helpless patient, forgetting the occasional blood pressure or bedbath.

These were important but minor omissions – ones that could be easily detected and corrected. She was very apologetic and embarrassed about these errors and I knew how these lapses worried her, because she was normally ultra-conscientious about her work.

'Sorry, Sister, it went clean out of my mind,' she said about a phone message she had not passed on.

I was wondering just what it was that was absorbing her thoughts. 'Anything wrong, Nurse Gordon?' I asked tentatively, hoping this would give her the outlet to confide in me. There was no response.

The turning point came when we were checking the Pethidine for a post-op. patient. It is a strong analgesic, a drug of addiction, so one of those controlled by the Controlled Drugs Act. Stringent legal rules are applied for the checking of drugs of addiction in all stages of handling from manufacturer to the final destination of the patient.

In hospital, always they must be kept behind two locked cupboards and the keys handled by a registered nurse. Every dose given must be checked and supervised, signed and recorded by two members of staff, one of whom must be a qualified nurse or a doctor.

Mrs Wainright was to have 50mgs. of Pethidine. We had 2ml ampoules containing 100mgs of drug. She would require 1ml in the syringe and the other 1ml was to be discarded as waste, for which we would sign.

Alma Gordon drew up the drug, 2 mls into the syringe, replaced the guard on the needle and put the loaded syringe into the receiver. She proceeded to fill in the Controlled Drugs book, copying from the prescription sheet, 'Mrs Wainright, 50 mgs Pethidine, date, time,' and signed it.

I watched and waited to see if she would realise her mistake.

She offered me the pen, indicating that I should sign, as the checking SRN.

'Are you quite sure that is correct, nurse?' I enquired, looking straight at her.

She shrugged and looked puzzled at my persistence, quite unaware of her gross error. Alma pointed to the prescription sheet, repeating every detail, as she'd been taught.

'Yes, Sister. It's Mrs Wainright. 50 mgs Pethidine. Four hourly – last given at 3 p.m. now it's 7 p.m.' she checked her fob watch, 'date correct, not expired, doctor's signature correct.'

'Well to start with, I don't sign the book until *after* the patient has received the drug. I am signing to say that I agree that the right drug has been given to the right patient at the right time. You ought to know that point of procedure by now, Nurse Gordon.'

She nodded and took up the receiver, preparing to leave the clinic room.

'And now look at your syringe and the ampoule,' I told her as she was still in the dark as to her error.

As she picked up the two, it suddenly dawned on her.

'Oh, my God,' she said more despondently than angrily. 'It's a 100 mg ampoule. I thought it was a 50 mgs one.'

'Thinking isn't enough. Looking and checking, making certain are what it's all about. Observation. Awareness.' My voice quickened.

'That's twice the dose, isn't it Sister?' She looked up and her eyes were brimmed full of tears. This serious near-miss had shattered her, this previously faultless nurse.

'Now you see the sense in all this double-checking, it's so easy to slip up with a slight lapse of concentration. And I am the registered nurse, I take the legal comeback from faulty practice. This kind of negligence is serious, Nurse Gordon. The trouble is that it comes at the end of a long linc of petty mishaps. Now you are becoming a positive danger,' I laid into her rather heavily but was pleased of the opportunity to shake her out of her apathy.

'Whatever is worrying you? You must share it with someone. Your work is definitely suffering and the patients, I'm afraid to say, are at risk. I can't condone this wall of silence anymore.'

Alma leaned on the bench top and hung her head, the tears falling freely onto the taught brown skin of her arm. We both felt relieved of tension.

I let her cry freely, while I discarded the other 50 mgs of Pethidine.

'Wipe your face.' I touched her on the shoulder. 'Come

with me, let's give this to Mrs Wainright, she's in considerable pain. We'll talk after.'

I gave the injection into Mrs Wainright's buttock and we settled her comfortably to sleep. Only then did I sign the poisons book and drug chart.

I asked Staff Nurse Sharma to take charge while Alma and I had a talk in the empty side room.

'You don't need me to tell you that your standard of work has dropped off lately. A standard which I might tell you has been exemplary to date. You are a prize nurse, the patients love you and the senior staff would welcome you with open arms on their ward. Maybe you do have to put more into the theoretical work than most but you'll get there.' She still wasn't keen to divulge her troubles.

'Look, I've watched this deterioration, in your contact with patients, your manner, your skills, until it comes to this today. You started so well and appeared to be enjoying your stay here.' I was wondering if something, or someone, on the ward had upset her.

'Oh, I do, I really like the work here,' she assured me.

'I shall have to write a report on your allocation here. Now, in no way is that a threat, the report is intended to help and guide you in areas of weakness. It is also a guide to your performance as a learner and as a prospective qualified nurse. Your training is at stake.' I hoped that truth might bring her to her senses. 'Whatever is worrying you, you must speak to someone, the Occupational Health Sister, the Nursing Officer, your tutor or me, before you become a walking disaster area.'

My final comment was hard on her but I wanted her to grasp the seriousness of herself as a liability, as she would surely become.

'I'd rather talk to you Sister, I know you better than the others.' Her voice was hesitant.

To encourage her, I said, 'I can assure you that anything you say will be strictly confidential and, if we can sort it out, then the matter need go no further.' I had to cover myself, as I wasn't sure what to expect.

'My husband is messing about.' She blurted it out.

I let the fact settle and my mind sorted through all the ramifications of marital disharmony. 'Are you sure?'

'Well, I wasn't at first. I've had my suspicions for a while now but a bit of investigation has confirmed it. The usual giveaways. Lipstick-stained cigarette butts in the car ashtray. Strange perfume. Lots of "nights out with the boys".' She'd been giving it plenty of her thoughts and anguish.

'Has it ever happened before?' I probed a bit deeper.

'Never. Vince is a great family man. He loves his own home and doing things with the kids. He likes a night out too and a jar occasionally, but women, that's a new turn.' Alma looked weary with the pressure of it all.

'Do you go out together much?' I pursued this point.

'We used to. There's a club we belong to with reggae dancing and West Indian food. I like it too but I need the time to study now. When I'm off early, I get the kids to bed, the dinner out of the way and put in a few hours study. It's the only opportunity I get of some peace and quiet. Two more finals dates, then it's my turn, only eight months to go to revise the whole syllabus.'

She was getting pretty agitated about her exams and I thought her husband might be feeling pushed out – of her mind and his house.

'I know the academic work worries you. Do you think it has taken over your life – and your husband's?' I asked.

'Well maybe it is foremost in my mind all the time,' she admitted.

I ventured to be even more personal, 'And sex?'

She turned her face away but did admit that sex had also taken a back seat lately.

I could imagine how hard it was for her to study after all the pressures of putting in a full day's work plus the demands of family life. The effect was obviously rubbing off on Vince too and he was retaliating to what he saw as her neglect of him.

'Certainly it becomes a vicious circle. If you have troubles at home, worrying about those will interfere with your ability to study and you will defeat your purpose. Why don't you give it a rest for a while? Relax and give your husband some of your time, you'll probably find it will pay dividends in the end. Maybe you could even get him involved in helping you study, asking questions, revising procedures.' It certainly seemed worth a try. 'Perhaps you could have a weekend away without the children to lavish more attention on your husband.'

'We've been meaning to visit my cousin in Wales. Maybe we could go there on my next weekend off.' She appeared keen on the idea.

'Don't get too panicky about your exams. I believe you have a revision block nearer the time and you will be able to put in some concentrated study along with your group,' I reminded her. I sympathised as I well remembered my own anxieties prior to the big day and felt sure my chances would be ruined by some ghastly virus or a broken right arm – at the very least.

Alma Gordon's work improved and she became a reliable, mature student once more. I don't know that it was a result of my intervention – but perhaps I had forced her to confront her problem directly rather than let it gnaw away at her and affect her work. But whatever the cause, I was delighted with the result. I continued to help her whenever I could and to widen her experience on the ward. She was more likely to retain information of a case or procedure if she had seen it rather than just read about it in a book.

By the end of my time in sole command, I was feeling strained and tired and plain fed up with the routine of work. Apart from a week off when I got to know the local area, I had not had a real holiday since I started at Gartland.

My mouth was painful from the presence of a crop of pin-head ulcers, a sure sign of being run-down. The best cure for these dratted aphthous ulcers was a change of environment.

Susy was also having a tough time in social work, so we both decided to get well away from home. We booked a last minute package tour to Greece and let our hair down in no uncertain terms.

I sent the mandatory post card back to my colleagues in Parker to let them know how much I was *not* missing them or work. It joined the years' collection on the office noticeboard.

SIXTEEN: COLLISION

There wasn't much of the showpiece about The Stable – not if it was streamlined modernisation you were looking for. The whole hospital was serviceable, providing an adequate service for the locality, but having done so for the best part of a century, it was somewhat ageing in parts.

With exception. Gartland did boast a splendid, modern, purpose-built Accident and Emergency department, recently opened. I had had the opportunity to look around during my first week at the hospital and was impressed. It was spacious, clean and airy, with cheery floral curtaining and a feel of efficiency. I doubt that the patients waited any less time than normal for treatment, but the wait would be at least be pleasant.

I had a soft spot for A & E work, it being one of my favourite allocations during my training. Compared to the department at Gartland, the one at Cottingham left a lot to be desired. It had been poorly planned, probably by some bureaucrat who had never worked in a hospital, and gave the impression of having been a corridor, converted to provide cubicles. Poky was the only way to describe it. We were continually tripping over one another and when the real emergencies happened it was pandemonium.

But here was one you could *call* an accident department: areas were designated for carrying out treatments, with shelves full to the brim with sterile packs from CSSD (Central Sterile Supply Department). A complete dressing set or stitch set was at a mere arm's length away. Stainless steel trolleys gleamed invitingly. The resus. room was fully equipped and geared to receive any major trauma, respiratory or cardiac arrest; suction, oxygen, anaesthetic trolley and an infusion set up for immediate use.

The couches, with their clean white linen, looked too good

to use. Even the reception area was reasonably tidy, without the usual plethora of waste Coke tins, used paper drink cups and cigarette butts to remind us of the protracted wait by the many tax-payers. The chairs and tables were a sight better than the old benches we had on offer at Cottingham. I used to think they were left so awful in an effort to dissuade the customers. If that was the idea, the message was wasted, it failed miserably, as we were never short of work.

The clientele of any A & E department is much the same and made interesting by the infinite variety in cases seen. Regional variations may mean that inner cities see more alcohol-induced catastrophes, junkies and vagrants. Those close to sea or airports have special problems, not least those relating to immigrants and the need for translation. Departments at seaside resorts increase their workload in the holiday months, dealing with the influx of visitors and the inevitable accidents on the beach and in the sea.

No doubt this Casualty saw the seasonal variations common to all. Bee stings and sunburn in the summertime. Hypothermia and grotty chests in the winter. A prevalence of falls occurs due to inclement weather, mainly the old people unsteady on their feet. A slip on ice or snow gives a nasty fracture to the femur, the bone in the thigh. Common also is the Colles fracture of the wrist, caused by trying to break a fall and thereby crashing down on the outstretched hand.

Trends in Casualty cases are constantly altering, reflecting changes in society. Some years ago it was common to see septic criminal abortions, now rare since the introduction of legalised abortion. Coal gas poisoning was a frequently sought method of suicide, now a thing of the past since the advent of non-toxic gas. Instead there are the newer problems of battered babies, glue-sniffing teenagers and the victims of the ever-increasing muggings, street violence, and football hooliganism. The persistent and unremitting flow continues from RTAs, Road Traffic Accidents, OVDs, Overdoses, burns and collapse.

Work in casualty is interesting, varied and unpredictable. Along with the drama and the trauma, the nurse working in A & E can expect a steady staple diet of dressings, stomach washouts, tetanus injections, putting stitches in and taking stitches out. Fractured bones, cuts and grazes, strains and sprains, beads up noses, tampons stuck up vaginas. And a fair sprinkling of weirdos, winos, drop-outs and the accident prone who treat it like a second home, with a Casualty card recording their trophies of war. A few just like hospital and would do anything to get admitted; we had a regular who swallowed open safety pins and had an abdomen scored by repeated laparotomy wounds. Others never quite made it, the corpses who were rushed in but DOA, dead on arrival.

Sister Cas. gave me a whistle stop tour of her department during my orientation programme. Her name was Miss Barlow but everyone knew her affectionately as Cas. by the way she always answered the phone, 'Hellow, Sister, Cas.' She was in rather a hurry as she was about to accompany doctor with the list in the minor ops. theatre; small, speedy operations done under local anaesthetic that didn't require a stay in hospital but needed all the equipment and the expertise.

She spoke fondly of her department, 'It's still Casualty to me. I haven't moved on with the newer terminology, although I appreciate the sentiment,' she added, with conviction in her voice.

Accident and Emergency is a fairly new term for the old Casualty, designed to impress upon the public the exact nature of the work carried out in the department. Casualty staff think nothing of resuscitating the apparent dead, stitching up gashes or pumping out the stomachs of drug overdoses. But they do get maddened by people who wander in with what are GP problems, back pain they've had for six months, gynae problems of a chronic nature or a damn wart on the finger. It was sheer abuse of a twenty-four hour service and totally alien to the function of the department which is geared specifically to deal with accidents or dire emergencies.

In the course of my everyday work on Parker, I didn't have a great deal of contact with A & E. Our surgical men were called to see suspected surgical cases that turned up in the department and Cas. staff would ring to check if there was a bed for an admission.

It was one of those late summer weekends, when the English people rush away to the coast like lemmings in an effort to catch the last of the sun before it finally sets on the long winter.

The Sunday was a real scorcher and I had been sitting out in my lunchbreak, soaking up the sun in the tranquillity of the rose garden. This attractive area was close to the admin block, laid in an effort to lighten the dismal approach and allay fear for our earlier Victorian patients. It remained a well kept patch to delight modern patients and staff.

I leant my head back on the bench and felt the warm rays on my face. I was glad to be working, no way did I envy all those trippers who had before them the long haul back from the coast.

Boy, it was warm! I was cursing the long sleeves of my uniform, although I knew that before many more days had passed, I would be thankful for them.

Before I went off duty, I wanted to leave everything as organised as possible, because I was leaving Burrows in charge with just Doreen and a new student to cover for the evening. The new admissions had been booked in and preped for theatre, so it was an easy routine for them to manage.

I was looking forward to a decent, leisurely supper. Three of us were in the changing room when Miss Ashton burst in. She was on call for the whole hospital that weekend.

'There's been a large collision on the motorway. We're on Major Accident Alert. Could you all please report back to your wards, we need all the staff we can get. Sister Davies, could you take charge of Parker, you'll be one of the receiving wards.' She was rather out of breath, it being her job to round up any and all available staff and had probably been rushing to catch us before we left.

It never occurred to me that I might have refused this order, I daresay for some staff it would have been totally impossible, those particularly with dependants at home. Anyhow, I wasn't going to miss a piece of this action and I quickly rebuttoned my dress.

Burrows was in the office and naturally surprised to see me back, especially in uniform. She discreetely placed some observation charts in front of her cup of coffee.

'Make that two will you. I'm back to cover for a Major Alert,' I told her.

It was the first she'd heard of it. We foraged for the Major Accident Plan; often glanced over, never absorbed, dismissed with an 'it'll be all right on the night' syndrome. Panic! Tonight was *the* night!

All in all, our responsibilities were minimal, a mere extension of our normal job. We were to wait to receive patients who had been given primary treatment in A & E and patched up in theatre. It was hard to assess how many beds would eventually be needed or what types of cases to expect. We needed to make contingency plans to make empty beds available. The doctors were working flat out down in Cas., so it was left to the appointed senior nurses to decide who to recommend to the SHO, those patients who could be transferred to another less acute ward or be discharged home early. We made out a list in descending priorities and explained the situation to the patients, most of whom were gathered in the day room. They were all extremely understanding and helpful – thankfully.

Doreen and I shifted the empty beds up near the office. These had been allocated for proposed admissions tomorrow, whose entry was now in jeopardy. All patients booked for admission are told to ring in the morning before they come, to check that the bed is still available. We are never allowed to refuse an emergency admission because a bed is booked. It is obviously very disappointing and unsettling for someone who has planned to come into hospital but it is the luck of the draw.

We collected equipment in the clinic room, that I thought we might need to lay our hands on quickly; drip stands, suction machine, bedcradles and laid out packs of admission forms and the address book. I helped do the same on Harvey, who were also on standby for any general admissions into their empty beds.

Suppers were served and distributed by Doreen, with an auxiliary and student, who had been sent as extra help. Several patients also handed around the plates, cut up food and helped with feeding helpless patients. I'd never seen a meal served and cleared so quickly and efficiently before.

The team spirit was marvellous and the ward excitement was contagious.

I could feel the adrenaline pumping out and flowing in my veins, face flushed and muscles tense and tingling ready for the action.

The staff elected to take the shortest possible meal break, to get fuelled up while the place was quiet. I couldn't eat, I felt too alert and wound up, unable to relax or bother with food. Where were the patients?

When the visitors came, I had a chance to speak to some who might have to expect their relatives at home sooner than expected. Several were willing to return and collect their relative the moment the need arose. Obviously the first to go were the day's admissions for surgery tomorrow. So near, yet so far.

'Don't hesitate to ring me, Sister. I can get here within three minutes. Those poor people out there. It's the least we can do to help in the circumstances,' Mr Beaumont said. His wife had only earlier told me how relieved she was to be getting her haemorroids sorted out at last. Nothing like a tragedy to bring the British bulldog spirit to the fore, I thought.

Burrows returned from supper, fully expecting the mêlé, so was surprised to see the ward still tranquil.

'Give them a ring in Cas., Sister, see what's going on. The suspense is *killing* me,' she suggested.

'Better not ring. They'll have enough enquiries without us jamming the lines.' I said I'd go to A & E to take a discreet look and hope someone could put me in the picture.

What we had not allowed for was the time lapse. The Major Accident Alert is called when the incident occurs. It then takes time to mobilise the aid, get to the scene and start freeing the injured, before they even get to hospital. In A & E, the sorting out, assessment and primary treatment was another long job. Us on the wards were on the easy end.

It was a major pile-up on the motorway. One of those nonsensical accidents that should never happen, but so frequently do: cars too close and too fast, with drivers too tired, too irritable and too careless. Sun in the eyes, slippery road, poor judgement, who knows? But it was a nightmare end for some happy holiday makers, just a few seconds and lives were shattered.

I stayed in the background to observe the handling of this major incident, keeping well out of everyone's way. The last thing they wanted was an onlooker fouling up the works. No doubt the usual lascivious crowd of blood-thirsty sightseers had gathered by now at the scene of the accident. Still, was I any better? It's human nature to be curious – especially from a safe distance.

A soft buzz went round the department and I was quickly able to piece together the details of the crash, bearing in mind the distortions afforded from exaggeration, misinformation and heresay.

It appeared that a speed merchant in a white Mercedes collided with the rear end of a coachload of day tripping senior citizens, which, rightly or wrongly, had pulled out to overtake. A lorry shunted into the Mercedes and careered through the crash barrier, so involving traffic coming from the other direction. The collision was compounded by the build up of cars onto this blockage on both sides of the motorway. They crashed into one another like a pile of dominoes, until the whole road was jammed by the crumpled little boxes and their occupants.

Full emergency services were mobilised at the site; ambulance, police and fire, plus the speedy addition of one of the hospital's senior doctors. An incident control centre was set up, in contact with Gartland, as the major receiving hospital. The chief organisers had to formulate the casualty evacuation plan, and inform the hospital of the types and numbers of casualties to expect.

Police quickly took charge of other traffic and had to close off several sections of the motorway and keep intruders away. Some officers were trying to find clues to the cause of the accident, to assess road conditions and follow on to A & E to interview witnesses.

The fire service were on immediate standby to fight any

outbreaks of fire, likely from the spillage of petrol. They were busy hosing down the area as a precautionary measure. Another of their functions was to cut people free, to extricate those trapped in the mangled metal that was once called a vehicle.

Ambulances were kept busy ferrying the injured to Gartland and to our counterpart hospital, which was equipped to deal with all the burns cases direct.

One ambulance collected a mobile surgical accident team from Gartland and, sirens blaring and blue light flashing, delivered it quickly to the scene to give emergency first aid to those who could not be moved easily. The team comprised three senior and experienced Casualty nurses, an anaesthetist and the gynae. registrar. He was utilised as his speciality was not likely to figure prominently back at base but his surgical skills were needed out on the field of action. Each team member wore protective clothing with bibs, marked to identify their role, 'nurse', 'doctor', 'ambulance', 'police'. They also carried protective helmets and prepared packs of equipment to give drug injections, put up drips, operate, inflate chests and resuscitate on the spot.

Back at A & E, the results of this colossal RTA were the rich and tragic province for the general surgeon, the orthopaedic surgeon and the neurosurgeon – and the mortuary attendant.

A varied collection of injuries was brought in. According to the major accident plan, the surgical registrar had reported to A & E to sort the casualties into dead, critical, urgent or non-urgent. Sister Cas. was there helping him and they were taking a lot of details from the ambulance men, whose information could be vital in assessing the likely seriousness of the case: whether the patient had been concussed, if they had been trapped and manhandled to get free, choking, fitting, bleeding. Lots of blood and lots of hysterical screaming were not always signs of severe injury; a little seeping, spreading blood goes a long way. Often the quiet, comotosed ones are in more danger of dying quietly if not closely observed.

The Mercedes driver had been killed instantly, crumpled in an impact so violent that he received severe multiple injuries. His demise was repeated graphically. 'As they opened the door, he slumped out, like a bag of jelly. Every bone in his body broken, skull crushed like an eggshell and his chest caved in. There was no substance to his body, they couldn't lift him, had to roll him out onto a plastic sheet, in a blanket and straight off to the mortuary.'

For the most part, the old folk from the coach got off lightly, buffetted by its strong bodywork. However, all were shocked and distressed, none of which was helped by their advancing years. Some of the aged brittle bones had snapped under the impact, one woman I saw had the classical picture of a broken collarbone, or clavicle, protruding ungainly from her shoulder.

The waiting room of A & E was filling up with the 'walking wounded'. They were being supported and comforted by some of the extra junior nurses brought in, many of whom were unfamiliar with the work of the department. Blankets were brought from the major accident store cupboard to wrap and keep warm the shocked, pale and trembling customers. The six-bedded observation ward was serving well for those who needed to be lying down. Extra mattresses were available from the store if needed.

Several patients were nursing nasty bruises that seemed to be visibly swelling before me. Others had superficial cuts, covered with a temporary gauze dressing until they could be cleansed and stitched. The facial injuries tended to look worse than they really were. The soft tissue of the face swells inordinately to accommodate large amounts of fluid and the appearance is distorted. It is equally quick to settle down and a good area for speedy healing of wounds.

Flying glass, metal and debris and dirt were always an added problem to the major injuries in an urban environment. We were fortunate to have an ophthalmic specialist on the staff who could deal with any eye injuries.

I noticed another man sitting with his arm supported by a zip-up, transparent, inflatable plastic splint, probably harbouring a fractured humerus of the upper arm. Several children were also in the waiting area, clinging tightly to their parents. Some of the luckier ones had fallen asleep, out of conscious awareness of the surrounding trauma.

It would take time to decide if these casualties would be fit enough to go home or if they needed to be kept in for observation. I was amazed at how surprisingly uncomplaining were this group while awaiting their turn to be seen. They must have known they had a long wait ahead but probably fully realised how much better off they were than the people needing immediate care.

And, of course, the normal casualties continued to come in and join the queues in the order in which they would merit treatment.

I felt like a nosey, prying onlooker – which I was. I thought I looked conspicuous in my uniform, hovering about but not helping, although I doubt if I was noticed in the general commotion.

At that moment, I caught sight of the doctor who worked on the medical side.

Peter was down to lend a hand as a general helper, he wasn't one with a specific role in the major accident procedure. Still, at a time like that, any expert help was welcomed.

'Can I take cover and latch on to you?' I asked. 'I'm a fraud, sneaked down from my ward to be nosey and see what we can expect.'

'Sure thing. I only came to offer my help, such as it is. I'm a bit rusty on stitches and plaster of Paris but I think I can remember my embroidery lessons,' he said.

Peter was called over to get a drip started on a man who had been taken out of his car with a fractured femur. His bad leg had been splinted to his good leg, nevertheless the fracture was apparent. The leg was noticeably shorter than its partner and the foot turned uncomfortably outwards.

Blood loss from the large thigh bone was concealed, contained within the flesh, two pints was a likely amount. The patient showed all the signs of internal haemorrhage, with pallor and cold perspiration, a weak, thready pulse and agitation. His face was wracked with pain but it was hoped that the analgesia given by the mobile team would soon take effect. His lower leg carried a nasty gash which could be seen through the torn trouser leg. Congealed blood soaked the material and a gaping wound revealed the underlying fat, sitting like polystyrene bobbles.

Peter took blood for cross-matching and got the drip started, so I was pleased to have been able to give a hand. This patient would take his turn to join the theatre list and spend his first night of many up on male orthopaedics.

I asked Sister Cas. if I should be prepared to be expecting anyone soon. We at the receiving end were all ready. She and the surgical team were compiling the lists for theatre in order of emergency.

The surgeons were busy at present on a car driver who came in with a crushed chest and they were busy trying to stabilise his respiration. He'd be a likely candidate for a tracheostomy, a false opening in the windpipe, and would probably be on a ventilating machine and sent up to ICU.

A man with a ruptured spleen was next but he'd be going to male surgery upstairs. A female amputation resulting from a severe crush injury was heading for orthopaedics.

Just then the phone rang to inform A & E that one serious case would be on its way soon, once the truck driver had been cut free from his vehicle by the fire service. The steering wheel and column had been forced into his legs and pelvis and he was in a bad shape. He was in a pool of blood, unable to move himself, as he lay pinned to the seat. Fortunately one arm was free, so an immediate IV infusion had been started, through which was given a bolt of analgesic drug. Sister Cas. excused herself to get the emergency receiving room ready for this patient.

I gave a wave to Peter, who was putting in a couple of stitches in a head wound and knew this patient, as all the others, would require a course of tetanus injections.

The ambulances still continued to bring in a steady stream of mutilated cargo. All the patients were shaken by their sudden frightening experience. Some were openly crying, trembling uncontrollably and one I saw wandering around the department in a complete daze. Torn and dirty clothes, laddered tights, lost shoes and tear-stained faces were the hallmark of the injured. The final toll of serious casualties was in fact less than had been anticipated, although there were a lot of minor injuries. It is always difficult to estimate what facilities will be needed, so a major alert covers for all contingencies. Even if the chaos at the scene looks a lot, the damage to life and limb is variable.

As I left the A & E, the tea-bar was stirring into action. It was manned, or rather womanned, by volunteers from the WRVS, who would offer soothing sustenance to the shocked and bewildered casualties and the hard-worked staff.

I took the long way back to Parker, out through the Cas. entrance, where several of the porters were keeping the area clear of visiting cars to allow the ambulances and police cars to park.

I passed OPD which had been closed for the weekend but had been speedily organised into a control and press reception area. This was one of the jobs allocated to the hospital administrator and it was he who gave correct, precise, factual information to the clamouring press, without revealing personal details of the victims.

Police had the job of seeing relatives and informing them of injuries and fatalities to their nearest and dearest. The steady flow of relatives to the hospital were directed to the school of nursing, opened up for the occasion as a reception centre where nurses, police, social workers and clergy could see them.

Walking back, I became aware of all the many other departments who were having to get smartly organised to cope with the sudden burden of extra work; X-ray, medical records, porters, the telephone switchboard besieged by phone calls and the path. lab checking bloods. The regional blood transfusion service would probably be taxed to send emergency supplies, especially of group O negative, the universal donor which could be given to any other blood group without causing a fatal reaction.

Back at Parker, everyone was still awaiting the flood of admissions. And we waited. Our eventual number was not as high as we had expected.

ICU took the most severe cases, they were now full and had had to transfer two coronary care patients to one of the general medical wards. The orthopaedic department had the most admissions by number and neuro. received a few mes head injuries, one being the passenger of the Mercedes wh had luckily survived – although only God himself will evei know how. Several children were admitted for overnight stay on paeds., no one liked to take chances after a history of concussion.

Parker had three of the old girls from the coach in for observation with cuts, bruises and shock and the one with the broken collar bone. A young woman with a ruptured spleen had been to theatre for an emergency splenectomy and needed several pints of blood for transfusion. She needed close observation throughout the night, as did the two with fractured ribs and suspected concussion.

It was a hotch-potch of cases that came to us that day. Apart from myself, who'd been privileged to witness some of the management of the incident, no one else fully appreciated the fantastic organisation and co-ordination of the hospital and emergency services that came about to speed the despatch of the injured to a place of safety. I felt proud to be even a small part of the machinery that made it work so well.

On Parker, we received patients cleaned up, patched up, tidied up and sewn up – a neat surgical package delivered into clean beds. What a difference to the crumpled mess strewn across the motorway, that no amount of help could bring back.

to the bladder to enable a careful watch to be kept for any spect cancerous change in the growth and also to burn them f.

The hospital patient population can generally be reduced y one-third to a half over Christmas and New Year. Some ards are able to discharge patients home more easily than hers. Staff can take leave and it is, of course, a most popular ne for holidays. The wards still have to be manned to cater r all eventualities and do remain open to receive nergencies.

The festive season throws up its share of casualties; it is a rticularly high peak for black depressions and the erdoses that bring them to our doors. There are winter fogs produce bronchitis in the lungs, frost and ice to trip people to pavements and cause cars to slide out of control. The ld attacks the old and the very young, who are both doubly lnerable from the circulating bugs and influenza.

Hospital departments organise a rota for a skeleton staff to ovide cover for the essential services, like path. lab, X-ray, ysio, porters and catering. Where services close down, tra work is thrust onto the ward staff, taking bloods and CGs and sending the doctor to the pharmacy for a non-stock ug he prescribes. Luckily, I was reminded to stock up on ugs, surgical and domestic supplies and dry foods to suffice er the long holiday.

As a rule, over any bank holiday, hospital is plunged into nprecedented quiet; it is empty and peaceful compared to its rmal busy, crowded clatter. Fewer people, fewer trolleys, maintenance men, no OPD and precious little theatre ork.

Our ward was decorated within the previous week. This d to be kept within the rules of fire and safety, certainly per chains around any lights were forbidden. The ward had be satisfied with an imitation Christmas tree, which was npacked for its outing every twelve months and positioned own at the bottom end, far from any possible interference ith the general running of the ward.

Only at the central administrative area at the grand front ntrance did the hospital sport a magnificent tall, bushy *real* pine Christmas tree. It dropped its needles in proliferation over the nativity crib standing beneath but set a stately scene amidst the Victorian carved wooden seats and door panels and art deco windows.

On Parker, we turned the side-room into the Christmas 'staff room', where the majority of the cards and flamboyant decorations appeared. The bed was used as a convenient soft bench seat on which to rest and the drink and goodies were set out on a table covered with a hospital sheet. No one seemed in the slightest perturbed by its previous placements!

Towards Christmas, patients gave even more lavish gifts than usual, in anticipation of contributing to the staff celebrations. Vast quantities of chocolates and tins of biscuits came our way, as did the odd basket of fruit or bottle of sherry and Martini. Everyone turned a blind eye to the seasonal drink while on duty, provided it didn't get out of hand. Naturally staff were expected to consume in moderation and keep their wits about them to do the work. It was fun to visit each other's wards and offer refreshments, for once to mingle rather than be demarcated by allegience to 'my' ward.

The run up to the holiday period was pretty hectic and there was an element of pressure to get things completed before people and places packed up for the duration. I needed to get all the discharges arranged, with OPD appointments and drugs and to make sure that the GP or community services knew full well that their patients would be at home over the holiday. We also wanted to be free of administrative rigmarole for Christmas and make our work as uncomplicated as possible. General cleaning and tidying was completed and out of the way over the previous weekend.

I left Doreen in charge of decorations and she commandeered willing staff and patients to help. Doreen collected the box of assorted baubles and tags, all with remnants of sticky tape which indicated their repeated use on the many Christmases they had seen on Parker.

The patients loved helping to decorate the ward and some of those about to go home seemed almost disappointed at not sharing the actual celebration with us. I had to stop one enthusiastic lady who was keen to climb the ladder in order to help. Letting her take such a risk on hospital property was more than my job was worth.

It was agreed that we should follow the routine as in other years regarding presents. We all picked a paper with the name of a member of staff from a stainless steel bowl. Sandra thought a bedpan would be more appropriate but the jokey suggestion had a luke-warm reception. We each had to buy a suitable gift for that person, all spending the same pre-determined amount of money. Everyone would receive a present, no one would be left out and, that way, no favourites or unfavourites emerged. As it was, several patients had left individual packages for their special nurses and a nice pile was collecting on the tree platform.

Sandra Dix was galled by the disappearance of her personal little tree from her room; tatty tree though it was, she had to admit. After buying it cheaply down the open market, she had put it hurriedly into her waste-paper bin, with the intention of potting it and dressing it later in that same receptacle. The cleaner in the nurses' home had presumed it had been parked as waste and cleared it away with all the general rubbish. So much for Sandra's splash of extravagance!

The side-room looked super by Christmas Eve. The girls had made a good job of arranging the seasonal fare most invitingly, with poinsettia plants and table decorations of greenery. Candles weren't allowed. Holly trims set off the twists of crêpe paper that were pinned to the table cloth. Coloured tinsel framed the glass partitions and cards were stuck around the walls, as they had a dreadful habit of blowing everywhere. And of course, traditional mistletoe was displayed in a bunch, hung above the door lintel, to catch a kiss from unsuspecting visitors.

I guessed, rightly as it happened, that there was some unwritten competition between the wards, as to who could make theirs most attractive. Nothing was to be touched until the great day but it was only fair to leave out a selection of treats for the night staff.

I was so looking forward to Christmas morning, but it found me with a king-sized hangover. There was a party in the doctors' residence and I'd been invited by Peter, the medical houseman.

That party was something to remember, such abandoned fun. I was swept along with the atmosphere and the thrill of Peter's company. It was one of those marvellous times, so good that you wish it need never end. As much as I knew I should, I couldn't tear myself away. The more I stayed, the more I drank and the more I laughed. We had one hell of a time.

My head the next morning was another story. I had a humdinger of a headache, even though I was skipping along with elation. Three aspirins, two large coffees and I reckoned I'd survive until I got home that evening for an immediate collapse. It had been done before.

The nurses got to work by fair means or foul. Those without their own cars or lifts had hospital transport to meet them at pre-arranged pick-up points.

There was an immediate air of festivity about the place as the day shift took over and we all greeted the patients with a 'Merry Christmas, ladies'. The nurses bedecked themselves as far as they could within the confines of a uniform, using mistletoe and holly sellotaped to their caps, tinsel and rosettes pinned to their dresses.

All routine ward work on Parker was completed with amazing speed that Christmas morning. Admittedly, we had fewer patients but it was blissful not to have the interference of porters, postmen, papermen, pharmacy, phlebotomy or the demanding, insistent, constant telephone. It was all hands to the pump to finish the chores, so everyone would be free to enjoy the holiday.

The patients said how much they had enjoyed the display by the staff carol singers the night before. I hadn't participated that year, being busy with more selfish exploits. As a student, I had always been keen to join the band of peripatetic singers, circulating the wards to entertain the patients. We turned our capes inside out, to reveal the red lining and the traditional scene was set by the accompaniment of lanterns on poles held aloft. It was nice to see all the wards' decorations and to meet afterwards for coffee and mince pies.

Parker was impeccably neat and tidy by 9.30 a.m.; beds made, baths done, drugs and dressings all completed. We left the patients for a leisurely coffee, those who were able to enjoy it. Emily Pegg had found a fellow patient with a gorgeous tin of chocolate biscuits, which came out with unfailing regularity to accompany refreshments, much to Emily's delight.

Our whole day seemed to be spent nibbling at food of some description or another. Staff coffee and tea breaks were taken, by choice, on the ward and were our time for getting together. Doreen and Maria kept us supplied with a steaming pot of coffee and I had brought in a cassette player for background music.

Dr Salah came to do his routine ward round and I had a query for him over one of the patient's night sedation. The most junior nurse, goaded on by Sandra Dix, beckoned him in for coffee and took him completely by surprise by accosting him beneath the mistletoe. He was totally unfamiliar with our traditions surrounding the Christian festival, as he was a Muslim, but not a very strict one because he enjoyed the odd alcoholic beverage. The nurse needed to explain the English custom to him but she was quite bemused as to its precise origins.

Later on, the staff took turns to visit other wards as they wished. Sandra wanted to see her friend on geris, which was as full to the brim with patients as ever.

Being paediatric trained, I had a nostalgic yearning to see the kids' ward. It's the one place in hospital where all the stops are pulled out in an effort to make Christmas a super time for children who were forced by circumstance to be away from home at this special time. Great excitement was always generated when Father Christmas, alias one of the doctors, dished out presents to the children, purchased from hospital funds or donated by well-wishers in the area.

Doreen came down there with me, although she thought she might find it made her too emotional. I understood what she meant. That heartbreaking site of pathetic little mites, mustering all their energy to cling to life, at a time when children are expected to be lively and indulged to their heart's content.

The kids' ward was lavishly decorated with streamers, lanterns and huge cardboard cut-outs of popular cartoon characters. Each window bore a frosted stencil, expertly applied by some talented nurse. Every occupied cot and bed had been individually decorated. The ward looked a picture.

But it was unusually quiet for paeds. Every possible child had been sent home for the holiday, no doubt some wielding heavy plasters and huge dressings. The hush was forboding. As far as we were concerned, the criterion for recovery was judged in decibels!

A very small in-patient family remained, most with parents already in attendance at the side. A cheery little toddler in Gallow's traction to correct a fractured femur was lying on her back with her legs suspended by pulleys and her hips flexed at an angle of ninety degrees. She was surrounded by a sea of wrapping paper and newly opened presents, quite remarkably unhindered or bothered by the presence of the traction.

By Sister's office sat a lone mother who looked familiar with the ward, through months of intense visiting. The child lay motionless, deathly pale and flabby, with the moon shaped face typical of steroid therapy. She had a leukaemia that wasn't responding well to treatment. Her cot was festooned with Catholic symbols, pictures of Our Lady and a cross dangling by the child's head. The mother sat clutching her rosary and praying, as I guessed she had over the last few tormenting months. Surely today, of all days, the Lord would give compassion to spare this wee one. Oh, surely *just* this *little* one! If only it could be that easy. The mother's agonised mumbling was painful to our ears as we passed silently by the end of the cot.

On the way back to Parker we looked in on neuro. and the staff seemed pleased that we had bothered to give them a visit. Not much joy there, no let up on neuro, coma continues despite the revelry and decorations. The rows of unconscious people, some little more than vegetables as far as functioning brain power was concerned, remained to be washed, fed, turned and cleaned up on Christmas day as any other. Before the holiday was over, the staff could bank on getting their share of head injuries from careless drivers risking it in their cars after unrestrained drinking.

I went over to Harvey to check that the new staff nurse was all right. The atmosphere over there was fairly subdued, it was the place you'd choose to be at any other time but Christmas. This was the time when families needed their mums and mums needed their families.

One of the Harvey nurses had rung in with a genuine case of 'flu, so that left the ward rather short, but they were managing. I wondered if this was going to herald the start of a 'flu epidemic and the chaos that brings when staff go down like flies.

Christmas lunch was the annual highlight for us all. The able patients sat at the smartly prepared communal dining table in the ward and a box of crackers supplied each with a paper hat. Patients were allowed a small sherry, although Emily opted to stick with the medicinal Guinness which had been prescribed to her. All told, getting a full and hot lunch to each patient wasn't easy. It was a mammoth task to get all the bits and bobs – turkey and stuffing and sausage and bacon and sprouts and parsnips and potato and gravy, onto a hot place. The kitchen had done us proud and we sent a large thank you note back with the food trolley.

Doreen remembered the time when each ward had a turkey ceremoniously carved by a consultant, who then stayed to join in the staff lunch held on the ward. These days people were more inclined to put their family life first and treasure their off-duty. Those in the hospital made it as good a time as they could, coming in over a bank holiday.

We had the traditional lunch served in the canteen, which looked stark and bleak with few customers. I sent Sandra to early lunch as she was getting slightly sozzled from sampling little nips on an empty stomach. One glass of Tommy Read's champagne made her sillier than ever, so I despatched her to get some food to soak it up.

Duty times were relaxed, so that the usual long afternoon, created by overlap of the morning and afternoon shifts, was eroded. The evening shift girls came on late after lunch and the morning girls went off early, still ensuring the ward was left adequately covered.

Tea was served to the patients and, as a concession that only happened on these two days, to their visitors. I went round to speak to each individual family gathering. Emily Pegg and her newly-found friend, who had now progressed to a large box of chocolates, sat watching one of the many films on the day room TV.

All the staff, from both shifts, shared in an organised tea in the side-room, when we opened our gifts. There were mince pies and cakes brought in by the cooks amongst our number and they looked too tempting to be missed.

A timid knock on the side-room door came from Mr Alison, the batchelor brother of Miss Alison. Could we come and see his sister? She didn't seem 'quite right'. Where was Sandra? She was taking her turn on the ward. Getting an urgently required bedpan it seemed.

Things certainly weren't 'quite right'. I quickly assessed that she was in fact conscious although she looked vacant. Miss Alison was flushed, almost bloated about the face, her eyes open but vague and inattentive. Her mouth had fallen open, dribble fell unheaded from one corner. She wasn't able to speak but she could squeeze my hand in response to indicate that she could understand me.

Wouldn't it be during visiting? And on Christmas day too? Without creating any fuss, I drew the curtains, checked her mouth was clear and removed a couple of pillows to lay her back on the bed. I realised that Mr Alison was hovering behind, watching my every action. Sandra appeared through the curtains, so I asked her to escort the relative to the corridor and return with the suction machine, to keep at the ready.

I rang upstairs for Dr Salah, whom I knew was joining the men's ward for tea. The bewildered Mr Alison sat in the corridor with his raincoat folded neatly in his lap. All I could say was that doctor was on his way and would speak to him later. He was understandably worried and disappointed, as his sister had already had one major set-back after surgery with the paralytic ileus. I assured him the two were quite unconnected but I had already thought to myself it was a pretty unfair coincidence on one patient.

This time she had suffered a stroke. A spontaneous clot or

rupture in one of the blood vessels supplying the brain, causing interference with the function of selected nerves. Medically we talked about a CVA, a cerebro-vascular accident, to cover any type of cerebral catastrophe.

Once it had occurred there was little to be done, except to wait and see the extent of the damage. Close observation, making use of a head injury chart, was instituted. In Miss Alison's case, the stroke wasn't severe and it acted as a warning which enabled her to be treated to offset any further attacks.

When the shock had worn off, she emerged with a slight paralysis down one side, a hemiplegia, affecting her arm and leg and one side of her face. She made a steady improvement and her prognosis was good. For a few days her mouth and eye looked a little wonky and she had difficulty in speaking, and swallowing, rather like the sensation following dental anaesthesia. Physio to the weakened limbs maintained their tone and encouraged even minimal movement during the transient inactivity.

The incident brought the organised festivities to an early close and we were quickly back to the reality of our work. An acute appendix was admitted shortly afterwards and all told we had three appendixes in before Christmas day was over.

Life gets back quickly to the normal routine in hospital. We saw in the New Year, and the beginning of the real winter frosts and snow. On those freezing early mornings getting to work, how I wished that I lived in. The electricity bills in our damp old flat were catastrophic too. By comparison, the wards and the nurses' home were roasting hot and we all got spoiled by the luxury of it.

The decorations came down soon after. No one was quite sure whether the superstition was 'decorations down *before* twelfth night' or 'not *until* twelfth night', so we left the cards up in the office to cover ourselves from malevolent spirits.

Bridie was due back to the fray early on the Monday morning. It was throwing her in at the deep end but I knew she wouldn't mind. I had a dental appointment to keep, so needed to be off myself.

I was looking forward to seeing her back in harness, I really enjoyed working opposite somebody at the top.

The damn buses were delayed due to the fog, so I rushed straight into the ward bathroom to fix my hair and my cap. Doreen was beside me at another mirror, putting rollers in for a patient, masochistic enough to sleep with them in prior to visitors.

'God, what a rush!' I bleeted on about the traffic, getting more impatient with the grips that I was finding difficult to place with my cold hands. 'Did Bridie get back O.K.?' I asked.

'Certainly did. Yes ... she's back,' Doreen replied, but somewhat hesitantly.

'You don't sound too sure, is she all right?' I looked straight at Doreen, whilst blowing my fingers to warm them up.

'Oh, she's *fine*!' She emphasised the word in such a way to make me search her face.

'What do you mean?' I asked her.

Doreen continued fixing the rollers, took a grip from her mouth and simply said, 'You'll see.'

I was really too late now to stop and investigate Doreen's enigma. Quickly, I applied a brief splash of colour to my eyelids and lips and stuffed my belongings into my bag. I rushed to park it in the office cupboard and was waylaid by the inevitable telephone enquiry.

Bridie was coming up the ward and I gave her a wave. Yes, she did look fine, I thought, fit after a rest.

'Hi, had a good holiday?' I asked as she entered the office.

'Great. Just great,' she answered, full of her old-style enthusiasm.

'Couldn't be better.' She almost sang the words, as she raised her left hand to reveal a large and brilliant diamond engagement ring.

I was astonished, as I was sure would be every other member of staff in the hospital.

'My!' Was all I could manage while my mind ticked over the prospects of Bridie O'Connell, married lady.

'I'm getting wed to "the boy next door", an old flame rekindled,' she laughed.

Then it dawned on me. 'You mean next door in Ireland?'

'Right. It's goodbye to all this at long last.' She looked quite relieved and raised her eyes heaven ward.

'So it's over to you, Helen, and the *best* of luck!' she added.

'Huh?' I hadn't got that far in the reckoning. It could be that with less than one year in blue, approaching my first anniversary as Sister, I could have a ward of my very own. Would I feel ready to request that ultimate responsibility? Would the powers that be, be prepared to offer it to me?

I'd have to sleep on that one.